Edge of Hyperspace

By Scott Seldon

ARRANO-TALDEA GROUP
2012

Arrano-Taldea Group is a collective association of independent authors of genre fiction. Each author accepts full responsibility for the content of their own publications. Please contact the author directly to report any problems with this book. srseldon@gmail.com

All characters appearing in this work are fictitious. Any resemblance to real persons, living or dead, is purely coincidental.

EDGE OF HYPERSPACE
Copyright © 2012 by Scott Seldon
Cover Art by: Yotsuya

All rights reserved.
No part of this book may be reproduced, distributed, or transmitted in any form or by any means, including photocopying, recording, or other electronic or mechanical methods, without the prior written permission of the of the author, except where permitted by law.

Paperback Edition
Second Edition: May 21, 2014
ISBN: 978-1-4996-4117-2

Revision 4

For my father, Dallas
1944-1997
A rogue at heart

Also Available

Galactic Confederation Stories
Not Past Redemption

Zaran Journal Novels
Well of Dreams
Pirates of I'ab
Interlude of Pain
Dust Between Stars

Edge of Hyperspace
Tales of the Galactic Confederation

Contents

Introduction. 1
Running From Customs.. 5
Beautiful Trouble. 39
Where Legends Begin. 63
Test of Command. 101
Overture of Friendship. 129
Race On The Rim.. 151
Chased by Shadows.. 175
A Night At Nova Trango. 193
Seeking Justice.. 209
A Captain At War. 243
Index. 259
About the Author. 265

Introduction

For nearly five thousand years the Galactic Confederation has maintained the peace, upheld personal freedoms, and regulated trade throughout the galaxy. To most, the face of the Confederation is the Customs Corps as they police interstellar commerce. They are the bane of smugglers and pirates and the saviors to those in distress. Even so, they are eclipsed as the hero of choice in the entertainment vids by the independent traders.

In the many millennia before the Confederation was born, nearly all the species of the galaxy experienced wars and upheavals leaving great gaps, or dark ages, in their histories. But through it all has persisted the myths and legends of the independent traders and their hyperspace craft. From those tales come a lofty ideal of courage and valor.

It is not without merit. Hyperspace travel has always been dangerous, especially in the millennia before the Confederation. All gravitational bodies found in real space are echoed in hyperspace. Without precise charts, a hyperspace voyage could easily end in death. Even with the Customs Corps' highly detailed and frequently updated charts, ships still occasionally disappear without a trace.

In modern galactic trade, most goods are transported by the large commercial carriers, but they cannot handle every need. It still falls to the independent traders to move goods and people among the less visited reaches of the galaxy, for a price. It is a hard life that mixes fantastic adventure and boring routine on a regular basis. But in the background, it is the agents of the Customs Corps who make it all possible.

In light of the wild myths and legends, it is no wonder that the entertainment vid producers tend to focus on the modern independent trader for grand tales of adventure. But even through the veneer of the vids, there is always an underlying kernel of truth. Among traders there are quietly whispered names in incredible stories. Even the vids that echo these true stories have inspired countless generations of traders. But new traders quickly shed any romantic notions picked up from the vids and learn to deal with the dull routine runs dotted with the occasional spate of excitement.

It is not surprising, especially in light of the hard life compared to what the vids seem to promise, that many traders will turn to smuggling to make ends meet, get ahead, or just for adventure. Hauling illicit cargoes pits them against the Customs Corps in a long-standing duel, one thing the vids tend to get right. Even so, those who have lived this life or known real traders, know that the reality is far more gritty and incredible than the vid producers dare touch on.

On the other side are the rarely told stories of the agents of the Customs Corps who endeavor to keep the traders and travelers in line and the hyperspace lanes open and free. They usually feature as the adversary of choice in the vids, but in reality they are no less daring or brave than the traders, and their stories are no less interesting. They lay their lives on the line on a daily basis, neither expecting nor receiving much thanks. The strange truth is that most of the time customs agents and traders are on the same side. Pirates and crime syndicates don't stop to consider whether a trader's cargo is legal or not, but either way, the Customs Corps is there when they are needed.

Most tales of the heroic deeds of Customs agents and the fantastic exploits of traders come to us from witnesses to their actions. Customs agents are too tight-lipped and traders too secretive to be reliable sources. Instead, it is the passengers, port workers, family, friends, or others connected to their lives in some way who provide the true stories of what transpires. Without them we might not have any knowledge of the reality of these events and have to rely solely on the fictions of the vid producers. Yet these witnesses often have their own unique stories, not just of traders and Customs agents, but of their own lives.

In order to get a true sense of what life is like for these men and women, we have to go to the recorded logs, whispered rumors, and Corps scuttlebutt, but most of all, the eye witness accounts. Only then do we begin to have an idea of what life is like for traders, customs agents, and those around them. What we get is a different, yet strangely parallel, story from what the vids show us. From life and death struggles to the personal touches of daily life, these are the unvarnished tales of real people's lives. This is what life is truly like on the edge of hyperspace.

Galactic Library Research Division
Hissus Prime
4725 GCE*
(*Galactic Confederation Era)

Running From Customs
3625 GCE

Tramp was sitting in a quiet corner of the bar enjoying a rare quiet drink. No one really knew him on this planet, at least not by sight. He knew his quiet was over as soon as he saw Errubo and his goons walk in.

Errubo was a gangster, pure and simple. He made no effort to hide it. He controlled all the illicit drug trade in this sector and was someone that Tramp tried to avoid. Sitting in this corner with the short brim of his hat shading his face, Errubo shouldn't notice him.

Errubo surveyed the room and, as people noticed, a hush fell as all eyes were drawn to him.

"I have a job for an enterprising trader," he called out. No one missed the code that he expected someone to take it no matter the risks. His eyes surveyed the room again looking for a trader who might be able to pull it off. From the way he acted it was like he already knew who he wanted and was trying to flush him out.

"Come now. I am a fair man. I have a job and it will pay very well. There are some risks, but nothing an enterprising trader captain can't handle."

Tramp could feel the fear in the room. It was palpable like humidity in the air. He could only imagine what new torture Errubo had devised. He was a sadistic bastard who never did things the easy way. Tramp had the uncomfortable feeling his presence on this planet wasn't as unknown as he'd hoped.

Errubo motioned to his goons and in short order three terrified men were assembled in front of him. "When I come in here and offer someone a job, I expect to have my choice of volunteers," he said, his face never changing from the serene expression it always wore. "Now that I have three volunteers, which one of you will accept my offer? I have a cargo on the other side of the Arcanax Nursery that needs to be picked up and brought back here within fifty hours. And that would be from now, not from when you leave."

"It can't be done," one of the traders said, his incredulity at the mission overcoming his fear of Errubo.

Errubo moved in front of him and delivered a blow that sent him sprawling. "Since you are so sure that it cannot be done, perhaps you would care to try it?"

Hiding in the corner was doing nothing for Tramp's blood pressure. His years as a trader kept his external demeanor calm, but inside he was beginning to seethe. Errubo was baiting him. He had found out he was here on Prixnar IV and his spies had ferreted out what bar he had gone to for a quiet drink.

At least Errubo's timing was good in one respect, Tramp's urge to act had waited until he'd calmly finished his drink. He let out a sigh of satisfaction at the quality and potency of his drink. With the hush in the bar, there was no mistaking where that sigh had come from and no hiding any longer.

"Well, Errubo, you found me," Tramp said, still shrouded in shadows.

"What makes you think I was looking for you?"

"You are looking for the best and that would be me. None of these guys could make the run you are asking."

"It takes quite the egotist to make such a statement. There are many good captains here."

"Oh, I'm sure any number of these captains could do many things better than I do, but not a run like this." Tramp stood and walked over to Errubo. The eyes of the three traders were on him and he motioned for them to go back to their seats. He didn't much care that all eyes in the bar were on he and Errubo. As far as he was concerned it was just the two of them. "Now, why don't you tell me your terms and see if you can tempt me."

"But I already have you hooked."

"Humor me."

"What does a ship like yours cost these days, two or three million? I'm prepared to offer you four million credits."

"What happened to your regular courier?"

"His first mistake was getting caught. He is going to be rotting in Confederation prison for the next fifteen years. His second mistake was costing me my cargo. That will cost him his life so he has fifteen years to live."

"Someone at Customs caught on to you. Your price is more than generous, but I can only imagine the size of the cargo if you are prepared to pay that much."

"You are a wise man, Tramp. The cargo will be a full hold for you. Funny how the size of the shipment is so perfect for your ship."

"I'm not laughing, Errubo. Lay out the payment agreement so we can get on with this. My time is slipping away."

"I'll pay in full on delivery."

"I want your blood oath on that."

"Now, Tramp. There is no need for that."

"You forget, I know you. It's either a blood oath or no deal." Tramp thought he detected a crack in Errubo's perfectly schooled demeanor, but it quickly passed.

"Very well." He started to pull out his comm pad.

"Not so fast. We use mine." He pulled out his comm pad and brought up a standard contract and entered the amount, the time, and the destination. "Is this accurate?"

"It is," Errubo admitted.

Tramp activated the DNA scanning feature. While they called it a blood oath, it didn't technically require any blood, only an accurate DNA sample to lock everything in and make it more binding than law. The Confederation didn't honor it as more than a witnessed contract, but the local Prixnar government held the death penalty for breaking such a sealed contract. No matter how he might want to get out of it, Errubo was bound to honor the contract if Tramp returned by the specified time with the full cargo.

"It's been a pleasure doing business with you this time, Errubo. I'll see you in two days."

"I have a lot of people waiting on that cargo. You know what will happen if you let me down."

"I know, Errubo. Don't worry, I've never been late before."

"There is always a first time."

Tramp let out a loud laugh and shook his head. He tilted his hat up like he always did when he was on the job and left the bar, still chortling.

When he had a choice, Tramp preferred to land in an open docking bay. Prixnar IV didn't have that option. While it was large enough to have sufficient natural gravity, it was an airless rocky moon orbiting a gas giant. It was a well laid out port and had all the amenities, but it made Tramp nervous when he couldn't get a good look at his ship. Jester, his first mate, gave him a hard time that he was more interested in the curves of his ship than those of women, but it really was a security issue as far as Tramp was concerned.

As soon as he walked through the airlock, Jester took one look at him and swore. "You couldn't manage to avoid getting suckered into a job, could you."

"I didn't have much choice. Errubo was harassing three poor traders trying to draw me out. Besides, he's willing to pay four million."

"I'll believe that when I see it."

"I made him sign a blood oath."

"Oh, that's different. When do we leave?"

"When everyone's here. Where's Mutt?"

"Now, Tramp, you know he doesn't like it when you call him that."

"But it fits so well. Where is he?"

"He's in his bunk."

"Get him up and meet me on the bridge in five."

Tramp went forward to the bridge and took his customary seat and began to bring his girl to life. No one made freight runners like Kenosh Weskil. There were newer and fancier models out there, but for Tramp, they had never surpassed the genius that was their model 938A.

Keeping the old girl in top shape was an expensive task. She'd been a classic when he bought her, but he kept her looking new and spotless. Errubo had talked of enough for a new ship, but he would rather put it into keeping this one in tip top shape.

"I hear we have a job," Dergo Fesh said as he took the navigator's seat.

"Yup. I need your expertise on this one, Mutt."

Dergo gave Tramp a look. "Then you should watch what you call me."

"We've been over this before. Jester and I have nicknames so you should, too. I don't know why, but Mutt just seems to fit you."

"If you weren't a damn good captain, I wouldn't put up with this."

"I know. Now, we are headed to the other side of the Arcanax Nursery and we have less than 50 hours to get there and back."

Dergo looked at him in shock.

Tramp met his gaze and said, "Yes, I'm serious. Now get started plotting your courses. Please, Dergo. This is important." Then he smiled as he added, "Your share of four million is on the line."

"Four mill... I'll have us back here in forty hours"

"I don't doubt that. I haven't made this run in a while, but as I recall, the first stop from here would be Dezera Junction so I'll get us there, you figure out where we need to go from there."

"Got it."

"Did I hear you say we are going through the Arcanax Nursery?" Jester said from the door.

"Given the distance and time, there really isn't any other way."

"Not even counting the navigation hazards, Customs heavily patrols along that route."

"That's part of the challenge."

The Arcanax Nursery was a huge grouping of stars and gases that made passing through the galactic arm at this point very dangerous. The stars and proto stars were so thick it was hard to find a safe path through them. Tramp was confident that Mutt could do the job. That's why he'd hired him. He used to think that he and Jester could handle things themselves, but a couple of years ago they'd gotten into a sticky situation and only a bit of luck in his navigating had gotten them out. He could have always ungraded the computer systems to be able to handle those situations, but he'd decided to keep the original factory systems intact and just hire a good navigator. Mutt hadn't turned out to be just good, he had worked some magic that Tramp was sure even the best computer couldn't duplicate.

Jester took the jump seat as Tramp did all the flight checks and called for departure clearance. By the time clearance was granted, they were ready to leave. Tramp disengaged the docking clamps and held the old girl steady for a moment before he eased her out of the dock. The well-crafted controls made precision maneuvering easy, but Tramp's skill make it look effortless. He always liked to handle departures himself.

As they cleared the moon's gravity, the great blue and lavender gas giant filled the port. Fortunately their course lay in a different direction or they would have to spend a couple hours going around it. Tramp throttled the old girl up to full, making the entire ship vibrate, and laid on the speed. Plotting the simple course to Dezera Junction had taken little effort so as soon as they reached the beacon, Tramp activated the jump engine and the space in front of the ship ripped apart and they were sailing on the hyperspace streams.

The route through the Arcanax Nursery was not well mapped. It was far too dangerous for a regular trade route and the Customs Corps tried to discourage smugglers from using it. Dergo spent the hours in hyperspace between Prixnar IV and Dezera Junction pouring over the star charts to find a safe route through that would also be fast. Too close to any of the stars or protostars in the Nursery and their trip would end in disaster. He also had to chart their gravity effects to be able to tell how they might be pulled of course. If he knew in advance he could compensate. He barely moved from the navigation terminal the entire flight.

"I'm worried about our boy in there," Jester shared with Tramp as they neared Dezera Junction.

"He'll manage, he always does."

"But this isn't your average hyperspace plot. This is a damn difficult maze you are taking us through. We've never done anything like this before."

"Have faith, Jester. He can do it. When I checked on him a while ago he had most of it done."

Jester shook his head. "I don't know where you get your faith in people."

"Ever known me to be wrong?" Tramp asked in a way that made it clear he was being serious.

"Well, no. But there is always a first time."

That set Tramp on a fit of laughter and even Jester had to smile at their situation. They either had to finish successfully and get paid or they were dead men. If they didn't laugh about it, they'd have to cry.

It wasn't too many more minutes until they heard a shout of success from the cockpit. They both hurried there to be sure.

Dergo was leaning back in the seat with a look of utter relief and exhaustion on his face. "It's done," he said when he saw them, but he didn't move a muscle. "Dezera Junction, through the Nursery, ending up at Azot-Siomar where we pick up our cargo, and back again."

"You plotted the return as well?" Tramp asked to verify that he'd heard correctly.

"Yup. I figured if I was going to all that work to find a good route, we probably could come back the same way. The points are a little different and we'll have to watch the gravity drift, but the segments were all identical."

"Good job," Jester said.

"Now if you guys don't mind, I need some sleep. It's all set for the first run. I'll be up by the time it's done."

"Go on, you've earned it," Tramp told him.

Normally when they came to a system like Dezera Junction, they would put in at the port, but with the hurry they were in, Tramp was bypassing that step. Mutt had planned for that and had left the starting point open. Tramp lined up the ship to their destination and entered their starting location and finalized the first leg of the course. "You ready for this," he asked Jester.

"No, but since we don't have a choice, we'd better get going anyway."

Tramp didn't waste a moment and activated the first jump.

Mutt was alert and awake before that leg was finished and he took over the navigation controls. He'd done a good job and the first legs of their course needed few corrections. As the hours and parsecs wore on, the legs became shorter and shorter and the corrections greater and more frequent.

Tramp took his turn getting some rest as they edged closer to the most dangerous part of the trip. They were sixteen hours out of Prixnar IV when they hit their first real snag.

"We're way off," Mutt said in a quiet, level voice. "This could take a few minutes."

Tramp knew better than to interrupt him and was grateful that Jester was getting some rest so he wouldn't pester Mutt. He might defend Mutt against Tramp, but he had a habit of commenting on almost everything. Normally it was a fun pastime, but right now that sort of thing could distract Mutt and that could lead to mistakes and death.

Tramp waited quietly for over half an hour before Mutt finally said, "Oh, there it is." Barely a minute later they were again in hyperspace.

As they drew deeper into the Nursery, the nature of hyperspace changed. Flitting among the stars, hyperspace was shot through with glowing streams that always seemed to parallel your course. If you approached too close to a star or large planet, there was a corresponding dark shape in hyperspace. But here where the stars grew closer and larger, the streams seem brighter and clumpy and the darkness of the stars loomed large and close. Tramp wouldn't ever admit it to anyone else, but it was a bit scary. They were at the mercy of Mutt's navigation talents.

There were a few more times when Mutt paused after a jump to recalculate based on their actual location, but not quite as long as that first time. They made it through the narrowest leg of the voyage with a better margin than Tramp would have dared hope for. Fortunately Jester didn't reappear until they were on the first sizable leg on the other side.

Tramp had spent most of the time while Mutt had been correcting their course, monitoring the scanners for anyone following them. He really hadn't expected anything, but there was no telling when a Custom's Commander might take it into their head that he was up to something. The course from Prixnar IV to Dezera Junction was a normal enough one that it shouldn't have drawn any attention and they had barely touched the outskirts of the system at Dezera Junction. The real danger of being followed would come when they left Azot-Siomar. It was a known source of the contraband that Errubo specialized in and he would be followed, he just had to lose them.

Two more jumps and they were on approach to Azot-Siomar. It was a big contrast from Prixnar IV. Azot-Siomar had an abundance of arable ground and produced enough natural food products to meet the needs of several sectors. Tramp, like most traders, subsisted off replicated food, but while it was nutritious enough, the taste put off a lot of people. There was a big demand for naturally grown food. It also made a haven for drug traffickers.

Replicators had their limitations, partly by design, Tramp suspected. They were great for simple items and foods, but for more complex chemical compounds found in nature, they were useless. Probably one reason why food usually tasted funny, until you got used to it. But it meant that Errubo's drugs had to be grown and processed planetside and then shipped to their destinations. The drug manufacturers on Azot-Siomar had been doing it so long and with such success that they operated with impunity on the surface but at the same time were hidden enough so that most people never knew they were there.

Errubo had given specific coordinates for the pickup. The location was far outside one of the smaller freight ports. Landing at the exact location would be like a beacon for the Customs enforcers to follow so he'd have to rent a ground transport and go out and get it. It would take time, but they were right at twenty-three hours out of the fifty allotted as they hit the atmosphere so they should have enough time. Tramp wanted to be finished and off the surface within an hour.

By Tramp's estimation, figuring that any interaction could lead to delays that would average out, they were still on schedule when they pulled up to the warehouse. Jester, who'd come along to help haul the cargo, was positive that they were running further and further behind. Tramp had initially found such complaints annoying, but as they had worked together year after year, he'd come realize that it did help keep him on track. This time was no exception. Jester had carried on a running dialog while they'd gone to get the transport and checked it out. Tramp made him drive it to the warehouse which kept him quiet and put him in control of any delays. When he checked his chron as the transport came to a stop, he saw they were still well ahead of where they needed to be.

"Let me do all the talking," Tramp told Jester. "Maybe you should wait here."

"I'll be ready to go as soon as we are loaded."

Tramp found the warehouse manager in the office. He was on the comm and didn't even look up for a minute. Tramp wasn't about to say anything, but he wasn't going to wait either. He grabbed a pad sitting on the counter and the stylus and scribbled down a quick note and showed it to the manager.

As the manager read it, he stopped paying attention to the person on the other end of the comm. "Yasha, I'll have to get back to you. I have an important customer here." He cut the comm and gave Tramp his full attention. "So you are here for Errubo's order?"

"I am. How fast can we get it loaded?"

"I'll get my people right on it."

Tramp very much liked the people the manager pulled to load the cargo. The lift loader operator was a very pretty young woman. He didn't have time to talk to her, but he certainly enjoyed looking.

He hadn't known exactly how much cargo there would be, but Errubo had hinted that it would fill his hold so they had rented a transport that was large enough to hold at least that volume. When the last of the cargo went in and Tramp saw how much there was, he wasn't so sure that it would all fit in the hold. That could cause a bit of a delay. He'd manage one way or the other.

"Here's your manifest, you're all set," the Manager said when they'd closed the transport up.

"Errubo is paying for it directly, isn't he?"

"He is. Now on the manifest it says this is a load of partially refined sugar, but it..."

"Don't say it," Tramp cut him off. "I don't need to know what it really is."

"You are leaving from here so everyone will know it is raw armon spice."

Tramp sighed and looked at the manager. "Did I or did I not say not to tell me?"

"What difference does it make?"

"It's courtesy. When someone asks something like that, especially in this business, you listen. Now, here is what we are going to do..." Tramp drew the manager in close and then punched the manager in the gut. "You are going to learn manners..." He drew the man up and punched him in the face. "And next time, if there is a next time..." He turned him around and kicked him to the ground. "Be sure you listen to your customers."

Several of his workers gathered at the door gaping in shock. Tramp flashed the girl a big smile and trotted to the transport.

"You'd better make tracks," he told Jester. "Their manager was rather rude."

"Oh no. Don't tell me you laid him out like that official on Tennarsus III?"

"Not quite."

"That's good."

"That official threw the first punch."

"What? I can't take you anywhere."

"Just drive."

They made it back to the port without incident and pulled the transport up to their berth to transfer the cargo. This was how Tramp liked to see his ship. Out is the sun, the golden stripes gleaming. He'd managed to land so the front cargo hatch was facing the cargo entrance and Jester backed the transport up so that there was only a few meters separating them. Tramp unstowed the loader and began transferring the cargo. He soon found that although she'd been pretty, that operator hadn't been too efficient. She'd left several gaps. Tramp was able to load the cargo far more efficiently on his ship.

He was just finishing when Mutt called down from the flight deck, "Hey, what did you guys do at the warehouse. I just got a call that we are being ordered to wait for the authorities."

"See what you did," Jester accused him. "Oh, we are in for it now."

"Relax. How bad could it be?" Tramp did know how bad it could be, but he said that just to see Jester's reaction. He wasn't disappointed. He let Jester rattle on while he secured the cargo and re-stowed the loader then sealed the cargo hatch. "I get it, now get on board so we can get out of here."

"You're not going to wait?"

"Who are you more afraid of, the authorities or Errubo?"

"When you put it that way, let's get Errubo his cargo."

Tramp raced up the gangway to the flight deck with Jester right behind him to secure the gangway and seal the hatch. He knew Jester would see to all the other preparations while he did the flight check. Since they hadn't planned on staying, most of the system were still active and their readouts showed blue. As he finished his check, the only indicator that glowed orange in warning was the flight clearance indicator. Well, they weren't going to get it so why bother.

"Mutt, Jester, strap yourselves in, this could get rough."

He'd timed it just right. As the ship began to lift, a local police transport arrived. The cargo transport blocked it from coming in the berth, but the officers inside quickly piled out. The comm beeped a moment later.

"*Thief of Hearts*, land and cut your engines immediately."

"No can do," Tramp replied over the comm. "I've got someplace I need to be."

"You leave us no choice but to force you down."

"You'll have to catch me first."

Now was when Tramps choice of ship and exacting maintenance schedule revealed his cunning. Once he cleared the port structures, he laid on the main engines and *Thief of Hearts* bounded for the stars with the ease her designers had intended. He had little fear that there would be any pursuit from the surface. They would have had to have something in the air already and the scanners didn't show anything.

He kept his eyes on the scanners and on his course. As he climbed to orbital altitude, he saw nothing so he turned his attention to what Custom's might do. Everything over a hundred kilometers from the surface was their domain.

Customs called as he expected. With his current haste and the nature of his cargo, he had no choice but to ignore it. It was worth the risk. Ignoring a customs search carried a hefty fine, but compared to the nature of his cargo, it was nothing. And if they caught him later with the cargo, this charge would still be insignificant. He would get in trouble and they might have their suspicions, but he couldn't afford to waste time conversing with them. Besides, they didn't have any ships in the area. He'd be at the beacon and gone before they would have anyone in position.

He was so concerned with weighing how to handle customs that he didn't notice the ship come up on him. When his comm started beeping incessantly, he checked the scanners and found a ship a couple hundred meters off his stern. From the strength of the signal, it was coming from that ship so Tramp answered it.

"How can I help you, friend?" he asked

"Do I have the honor of addressing Len Darvon, owner and captain of *Thief of Hearts*?" the voice asked politely. Maybe too politely.

"You do. And who do I have the pleasure of addressing?"

"You are being followed by Major G. L. Savvir of the Azot-Siomar Air Patrol."

"What brings you into space?"

"I've been sent to apprehend you for assault and illegal departure."

"Aren't you a bit out of your jurisdiction? Shouldn't Customs handle it now?" Tramp smiled at catching the Major in the wrong. His smile quickly faded at the Major's next words.

"My superiors informed Customs that I was close enough to initiate pursuit and I've been deputized to act on their behalf."

"Well, good luck to you," were Tramp's last words as he cut the connection. "Jester, Mutt, get up here," he yelled back into the common area.

"What's up?" Jester asked when he got there first.

"We've got company."

"What sort of company?" Mutt asked as he came in behind Jester.

"We've got a local Air Patrol Major on our tail and he says he is acting on behalf of Customs."

"They can't do that, can they?" Jester asked.

"Oh, they can, they just don't do it often."

"Then what do we do?"

"We don't have any choice, we run. We barely have enough time to get back as it is."

"What do you want us to do?" Mutt asked.

"Think of ways to evade him."

"If we are going to hyperspace, you should make a microjump in a different direction. If we do it right, he won't be able to follow us."

"You program it," Tramp told him. "I'll try to keep him off our back. Just tell me what beacon to head for."

Tramp checked the scanners and found that the Major's ship was slowly closing in. He didn't like the looks of that so he executed a deft evasive maneuver and watched in amazement as the Major made his ship do the same thing and stay right behind him. But his hadn't been a perfect imitation because he was now further behind. Tramp tried the same thing again with the same results.

The Major must have used a gravity slingshot effect to come up behind him and correcting course must have slowed him down, otherwise there was no way he could have gotten that close. He'd never seen such a skilled bit of piloting before. He wondered if it was the major or just one of his crew. He really didn't want to stay around and find out.

"I've got the micro jump plotted," Mutt announced.

"Good. Hit it on my mark," Tramp told him and then executed a different evasive maneuver that was more complicated. The major's ship managed to follow him most of the way through it, but couldn't come out of the last turn quite right and ended up a couple of kilometers off headed the wrong direction. As the Major's ship started to correct and come around, Tramp told Mutt to hit it and they were gone.

The trip through hyperspace lasted just a few seconds and Mutt was busy confirming their position sufficiently to make another jump. He had it in under a minute and initiated the next jump.

"That should lose him," Mutt announced.

"I certainly hope so," Tramp said.

"Don't be too certain," Jester said, "I have a bad feeling about this one. He's not the kind to just give up."

"He's a genius if he can follow us through that," Mutt stated.

"Let's hope he's not." Tramp said as he glared at Jester.

"What?" Jester said in his defense. "Not all the best pilots are on our side of the law."

Tramp let it go and went to his bunk to get a couple hours nap. In hyperspace there was little chance of encountering anyone. Incidents in hyperspace usually were confined to mechanical breakdowns. Tramp attributed most breakdowns to poor maintenance and had little worry of that with his exacting maintenance schedule.

The course that Mutt had laid out had taken them to a point off part of the great Nursery structure. A great glowing nebula stretched out and the star just off the tip provided a common marker in the area. Tramp's intention was to pass through as quickly as possible. The next leg did not have to be as precise as the ones that would follow. His hopes were dashed as they came out of hyperspace and picked up an emergency beacon.

"Just great," Jester said. "You're going to respond to that, aren't you?"

"I may operate on the fringes of society, but that doesn't mean I'm a barbarian," Tramp replied as he changed course to intercept the distress signal.

"It could be pirates." Jester continued.

"When was the last time a pirate sent out a distress signal?"

"I've never heard of it, but it could happen."

Tramp shook his head and checked their time estimates. It looked good so he told Mutt to re-calibrate their next course to leave from the source of the distress signal. They quickly closed the distance and it became obvious what the distress was. The ship was a small courier with twin stern engines and the port one had blown. The engine was cut in half and there was severe structural damage and the ship was leaking fuel into space. Tramp scratched his head for a moment when he realized that the best way to dock was at the cargo hatch, but they were so full up with cargo there was no way to get down there. It wouldn't be quite as fast, but their emergency dock could be deployed in under five minutes and it should do the job. It was a bonus feature because this class of ship had also been available to local systems for search and rescue. He'd never actually used it before, but he kept it up like everything else.

The ship was putting out a distress signal, but he couldn't raise them. He hoped they weren't too late. Less than fifteen minutes after first picking up the signal, the emergency dock signaled it had a good seal. Tramp wasn't one to be too foolish. He had donned a pressure suit while he waited for the emergency dock to connect.

He had a good clue why he hadn't been able to raise the ship when he found the hatch controls lifeless. It would make sense that the explosion that disabled the ship had taken out the power. He used the power cord from the emergency dock and plugged it into the hatch to power it open.

Inside the ship was a mess. The artificial gravity was down and everything that wasn't secured was floating around. It was a cramped little ship with far more cabins that he would have guessed from the outside. His suit scanner indicated the air was still good so he took off his helmet. "Anyone here," he called out.

"Who's there?" a female voice called from the cockpit.

"Captain Darvon. I'm answering your distress signal. And you are?"

"Mauri Frenit. Your timing is perfect," she said. He heard a small grunt and then she floated into the doorway. She looked as messy as her ship. "The emergency life support just died."

"How long have you been here?" he asked. Emergency life support should last for a month on a small courier like this.

"Two days. Some sort of debris shorted something back there. I couldn't get a suit out or get the airlock to function to check it out."

"Anyone else on board?"

"No, just me."

"Well, I can't offer much. My ship's a freight runner and I'm on my way to Prixnar IV. I can take you there, but if you want to go, we need to go now."

"Okay. I have everything ready."

Tramp was amused at how she struggled with zero-g and let her for a moment before his sense of time overcame his sense of humor and he gave her a hand to get out of there fast. She had one duffle stuffed and ready to go and he took it and her and went back out the airlock. It was pretty useless, but he sealed the hatch behind him and carried her over to the airlock.

He checked the chron as soon as he disconnected the emergency dock and the entire operation had taken twenty-three minutes. They were still ahead by almost forty minutes.

"Let's get going, Jester," he called as he escorted their guest to the common room.

"Roger," Jester called back from the cockpit.

"So, where can you drop me?" Mauri asked.

"Our next stop is Prixnar IV in about twenty hours."

"There's no way to get that far that fast," she said.

"There is if we are going through the Arcanax Nursery."

"That's suicide!"

"No. We just came from there a few hours ago and now we are headed back. Relax. I've got this covered."

Rather than listen to any more comments from her, he took off the pressure suit and stowed it and headed for the cockpit.

"What did you find over there?" Mutt asked.

"A girl."

"Only one?" Jester asked.

"Yes, and she is none too happy about our course. You go deal with her."

"Gladly," Jester said and hopped out of the pilot's seat.

Tramp waited until he was gone before he commented to Mutt, "I think I've found his match."

"Who do you think will win?"

"That's a tough call. I've known Jester for a long time, but just in the few short minutes I've talked to her I feel out talked."

They both chucked over the idea of Jester getting a bit of his own nonstop commentary. Mutt finalized his corrections and set them on their next hyperspace leg. It was a short jump to line them up with the first leg through the Nursery. But when Jester gave up arguing with their new passenger and set her on Tramp again, it turned into a very long trip.

"Tramp," Mutt tried to interrupt Mauri's almost nonstop tirade.

"What kind of name is Tramp?" she demanded, seemingly adding that to her list of complaints.

"It's a nickname. Friends call me that. Now if you will excuse me, my crew is calling."

"I don't care. I demand to be taken to a nearby planet. I don't want to end up dead."

"I'm thinking we should have left you on your ship."

That shut her up for a moment. "How can you say something like that?"

"Listen, Lady, I'm working a contract. I have a cargo I have to get to Prixnar IV by a set time. The only way to get there is back through the Nursery. If I don't get it there on time, it's my neck on the line. So if I take the time to drop you off somewhere, I'm a dead man and so are my men. It's not worth the oxygen you are using to say another word. Now go sit down, strap in and keep quiet." Tramp's raised voice drowned her out and his angry red face scared her into doing as he said. Tramp stormed off to the cockpit and tried to cool off after dealing with such an obstinate woman.

"That was not nice," Jester told him. "I don't know what you were thinking having me talk to her."

"I figured you could out talk her and keep her busy. I never dreamed she would get to you. You want to give it a try, Mutt?" Tramp asked.

"Nope. She's all yours."

Tramp sighed. "She's really getting on my nerves. I hope she makes it."

Jester let out a short dry laugh. He knew how well Tramp reacted to people arguing with him. More than one person had ended up dead, though usually they just got beaten up real bad.

Tramp hid in the cockpit as long as he could. When she started complaining vocally again, he turned the pilot's seat over to Jester and left his ship in their care to deal with his reluctant passenger.

"I don't like being ignored," she screamed at him as soon as he appeared.

"And I don't like being ordered around on my own ship. You do realize that on a ship, the captain is in complete command. We aren't in any system's jurisdiction, only mine."

"If you would be reasonable..."

"You are the one being unreasonable. I have a job to do and when we are done, we'll make sure you get passage to wherever you need to go. Until then, just sit tight and enjoy the flight."

"I can't, not knowing we could die at any second."

Tramp just looked at her for a long moment and looked through her outer anger and saw that she was terrified. There wasn't much he could do about it, their course was set.

"And I can't believe you don't know who I am."

"You're Mauri Frenit. You would have died if I hadn't picked you up and you are my guest. Did I miss something?"

She gave him a look that he took to mean that he really should have heard of her, but he hadn't. Her name didn't ring a bell. It was a big galaxy and he told her as much.

"You can't be serious. I was in four major galactic vids last year. That doesn't count all the interviews I gave or all the clips that I was in."

"Sorry, I don't pay any attention to that sort of thing. I listen to a few favorite singers when I want to relax, so if you aren't one of them, or someone I'd meet in my line of work, I'd have no idea who you are. And even if you were someone I knew was important, you'd still have to wait until we get to Prixnar IV. I run cargo for a living and this cargo literally means life or death to me. The guy I'm working for isn't a nice guy. I don't think he was born with a nice bone in his body. Now if you can't relax, I can give you something for it, but otherwise, you really do need to sit here quietly and not get in the way. Acting like you have is only going to make our jobs that much harder. Mutt's got the course all worked out, we came this same way, but he has to make adjustments so if you could stay out of his way, we'll get to our destination that much safer."

Mauri nodded. Tramp could see why someone would pick her to appear in a vid program. Underneath her tousled exterior, she was quite beautiful. Not that a famous star would give a freight runner the time of day in normal circumstances.

"Ever been on one of these fright runners?" he asked her.

"No, not a real one."

He gave her a brief rundown of the passenger area of the ship. The upper deck was comprised of the cockpit, the common room just aft of it, a narrow corridor with four cabins aft of the common room, and the engineering control room in the stern. During flight most things back there were automated and didn't need any attention. The common room had the food replicator, the airlock, the gangway, the toilet, and the comm center. It probably was the best place for Mauri to stay. He had a fourth cabin, but it was used most of the time as a storeroom and it would take too long to make it serviceable.

He ended up spending most of that leg of hyperspace keeping her distracted form their course and she seemed to calm down some. He was hoping she could stay that way when he felt them come out of hyperspace. She certainly talked a lot, which might just be nerves, but he didn't think so. He was just beginning to think it would be okay for him to go back to the cockpit when he heard Jester exclaim, "How did he get there. He's an idiot, but that is some flying," from the cockpit.

"What's wrong?" Mauri asked, her nerves fraying again.

"Nothing for you to worry about it. Wait here and I'll go see."

He actually felt bad about leaving her, she seemed so nervous.

"What is it, Jester?" he asked low enough that Mauri shouldn't be able to hear him.

"That local patrol ship from Azot-Siomar is sitting right in front of us. Mutt was just getting ready to lock in the course when he showed up."

"Has he seen us?"

"What do you think?" Jester said pointing to the muted comm showing and incoming signal.

"Well this just throws a wrench in the works. I'll take over."

"No, leave the piloting to me. You do the talking to that Major and that woman back there."

Tramp frowned, but Jester was right. He grabbed the little used headset and channeled the Major's call through it. "Hello, Major. What can I do for you?"

"Heave to and prepare to be boarded and arrested."

"Now you know I can't do that. Why don't you ask something reasonable?"

"As I told you before, I've been deputized by Customs to bring you in."

"Major, I've dealt with Customs from one end of this region to the other and never have I met someone so determined to catch a man as you."

"You are wanted for assault and judging who you assaulted, you are certainly smuggling contraband."

"You can't prove either of those allegations."

"The proof is on your ship."

"And to search it you'll have to catch me. I don't intend to let that happen."

"I am a highly skilled pilot and no one has gotten away from me before."

"That boasting might work on some, but I know you've never been up against me before so don't feel bad if you don't get what you came for." Tramp cut the signal and told Jester, "You'd better fly like you've never flown before. We've found ourselves some trouble."

"I leave the smooth talking to you, but you just leave the flying to me," Jester replied and set the ship on a wild course.

Tramp shook his head and went back to see to his passenger.

He caught her looking at the comm station and the look on her face was completely different from the angry visage he'd been dealing with. She actually seemed to be more frightened than angry. She saw him and the hardness returned.

"Why are we being chased?" she asked.

Tramp chuckled. "What do you have for ears? I didn't see you anywhere near the cockpit."

"My life's on the line here, same as yours. Why shouldn't I listen?"

"Well, to answer your question, when we picked up our cargo, I hit the manager because I asked him not to do something and he did it anyway. This crazy local patrol major claims he is acting for Customs and is convinced that I'm up to something illegal."

"Are you?"

Tramp just smiled. He wasn't about to answer that question. "Thing is, I've never heard of Customs letting a local do their dirty work for them. Usually if they think it is important enough, they'll do it themselves. I don't plan to stop."

"You didn't answer my question."

"No, I didn't. Now if you will please sit tight here, I need to make sure that Jester can handle this."

Jester was handling it just fine, but he and the Major were too evenly matched. Jester always was a little gentle with *Thief of Hearts* since she was Tramp's baby, not his. Tramp would have insisted on taking over except he saw that Mutt and Jester were working on a plan. Jester was going to put them in the right position and they would be gone to hyperspace. Headed into the Nursery, the Major would be crazy to follow, but then he'd been crazy enough to follow them this far.

Tramp watched as Jester performed another evasive action to get the Major off their tail, but this time he pushed the ship to the max and came out of the last turn in the clear. "Now," he barked and Mutt engaged the first of their courses through the Nursery.

"I was wondering why you were playing with him," Tramp said.

"I wanted him to get complacent and then not be able to see when we broke through. I told you I could do it."

"You did. I thought you were being gentle with this old girl."

"I was, but with cunning."

"I'm almost tempted to give you a bonus."

"Bonus?"

"Almost. Do you think he can follow us?" he asked Mutt.

"I don't see how. He didn't have a good shot of our entrance trajectory and he doesn't know the way through the Nursery."

"Not that we know of. Don't count on what he shouldn't be able to do. We aren't safe until that cargo is Errubo's hands."

"I will fly that way," Jester said. "How's our passenger?"

"Calmer. I think she's more scared than angry."

"It took you that long to come to that conclusion? You amaze me. You'd better get back out there and make sure she isn't getting into trouble."

"Since you can read her so well, why don't you?"

"We tried that, remember. Not a good idea to repeat it. Besides, aren't you the ladies' man on this ship?"

"I wouldn't go that far."

Tramp took a few minutes to check the ship over and make sure it was running properly before he went back to the common room again.

"I assume we are on our way to near certain death," Mauri said when he came in.

"I wouldn't put it that way, but yes, we are headed through the Nursery."

"Nursery! What a name for a place of death."

"It's not a place of death. It's where stars are born. The big ones don't tend to get far before they die, but almost all of the stars we life-forms live around were born in a place like this."

"That's fine for stars, but we aren't stars."

"As I told you before, we came through this way and we are going back on the same course." As he took a seat a thought occurred to Tramp and it wasn't too bad so he went ahead and said it. "You know, if you could see your way to cheer up a bit and you turn out to be a decent passenger, I'll take you wherever you want to go, no charge."

Mauri's eyes narrowed a bit. "Do you really mean that?"

"Yes I do. I'll draw up a contract if you want."

"Right after you drop off this cargo?"

"Right after. We'll head from Prixnar IV to wherever you want to go. Just tell Mutt and we will get you there by whatever route you want."

"Okay. You have a deal." She got up and headed to the cockpit.

"Where are you going?"

"To tell Mutt where I want to go."

"Not going to wait?"

"No, I know where I want to go. Why wait?"

Tramp shook his head and then bellowed, "Mutt, after we drop this cargo, we're going wherever the lady wants." He watched her shake her head and disappear into the cockpit. He didn't move. The common room was quiet. Kind of a rare thing and definitely something to appreciate. That stupid major would probably show up again to cause him trouble and he was sure that Mauri wasn't finished stirring things up, plus Jester never let anything rest. He just reveled in the quiet while it lasted.

Tramp traded places with Jester a few hours later so he could get some rest. Tramp had timed it so that he would be in the cockpit during the most dangerous part of the trip. It looked like there was nothing to worry about. Mutt was making all the jumps and quickly making the corrections until they came out after what Mutt freely admitted was the single most dangerous jump. Mutt let out a string of curses and Tramp felt his blood freeze. Not the sound you wanted your navigator to make. Tramp steadied himself mentally then asked, "What is it?"

Mutt didn't answer for a good minute. "We are way off course," he finally admitted.

"And how do we fix that?"

"I'll have to identify where we are exactly and re-plot."

"How fast can you do that?"

"How far ahead of schedule are we?"

"Forty-five minutes."

"Then that's how long I have. If we weren't in our present situation, I'd want a good two hours to get us out of this."

"Do you want any help from the second best navigator on board?"

Mutt accepted the help and they both worked furiously to identify where they were. In open space, it was easy to get the spectral signature of a couple of stars and figure it out. Most of these stars deep in the Nursery hadn't been properly cataloged and the dust, gas, and abundance of stars made checking further stars nearly impossible. Mutt quickly identified one star which told them they weren't completely lost. Tramp locked in the identity of a second one ten minutes later. It took Mutt another five minutes to identify a third star that let him zero in on where they were and he was able to make a more educated selection and moments later they had their exact location and Mutt went to work finding a way out. That wasn't something that Tramp could help him with. He just had to sit there and wait. He decided to check on Jester and Mauri and found them both fast asleep. He wasn't about to wake either of them. He returned to the cockpit and busied himself with several bookkeeping tasks that he was a bit behind on.

He wasn't prepared when Mutt suddenly activated the hyperspace jump. "You could have warned me."

"No time. To get us back on path in time I have to move and recalculate again."

When they came out of that very short jump, Tramp again helped him pinpoint their location, but this time it went much faster as they hadn't drifted much from their expected destination like the previous jump. Mutt was again lost in his charts and calculations. While the navigation computer did most of the actual calculating, there were far too many factors for it to handle everything in a timely manner. Mutt had to narrow down the range to limit the choices for the computer. He smiled and laid in a course, this time warning Tramp before he initiated the jump.

They came out in good shape. Not quite on their original course, but with the worst behind them, Mutt confided that he was confident that he could stay a leg or two ahead of where they needed to be. True to his word, when they came out after that second short jump, he had their location pinpointed and initiated the next course in under three minutes. They had to wait for two more minutes for the hyperdrive capacitor to charge.

"I was trying to avoid this system," Mutt said as they came out of one of the jumps. "It's too obvious a stop so keep your eyes peeled. If that Major called ahead who knows what we might find here."

Mutt's statement was oddly prophetic. As they were waiting for the capacitor to recharge, the comm beeped.

"It couldn't be," Tramp said, all the while knowing who it was.

"I would be amazed, but not surprised," Mutt said.

Tramp picked up the headset and activated the comm. "Captain Darvon speaking," was all he said.

"I told you it was useless to run," the Major said, unable to hold back the smugness in his voice. "The safe routes through the Nursery aren't public, but are well charted."

"Major, it's a pleasure to see you made it through safely. We didn't have the good fortune to have a precalculated course. If we had, you wouldn't have caught up to us. Now if you'd kindly move aside, we have a cargo to deliver."

"Not this time. You have a date with a Customs Court." The Major punctuated his statement with a volley from his energy weapons. Fortunately he was too far away to have an accurate bearing on them and missed widely.

"How fast can you get us out of here?" Tramp asked Mutt.

"About thirty seconds if we don't have to move. If you want to evade him, give me five minutes and be at this point," he said pointed to a set of coordinates on the navigation screen.

"You've got it."

Tramp sent his ship on a dizzying course that evaded the Majors next three attempts to get off a shot. He had to come back around so that he would be on the right course to hit the point Mutt asked for, and he nearly flew right into the Major's fourth shot.

"That was too close," Tramp admitted. "I think it's time we got out of here. Ready?"

"When you are."

Tramp executed his last evasive maneuver that ended with them flying in the opposite direction from the Major and dead on target.

As soon as Mutt saw they were headed for the target point, he locked in the coordinates and activated the jump the moment they were in position.

"Damn," Tramp said now that the hyperspace streams filled the viewport, "that man is a born tracker. How did he do that?"

"I told you that system was too obvious," Mutt said. "Their standard course through the Nursery probably ends up here on this side and starts in that system we were in on the other side. I think it was just bad luck that put us in this system. I was originally going to avoid it and just head straight for Dezera Junction, but that didn't work out."

"Did you figure out what happened?"

"We got pulled off course by a star that had moved. I found it when we were trying to pinpoint our location and it is way out of place. When I plugged it in with its present location, we ended up right where we should have. That's why the Nursery is so dangerous, they move so fast and the charts don't get updated often enough."

"We got lucky we didn't crash into a star."

"You're not kidding."

"I'm glad I wasn't awake for that," Jester said from the hatch.

"Finally up? What about our guest?"

"She slept through the whole thing."

"That's a mercy. I'll go check on her in a bit. We have a few more legs and then we'll be there. Looks like right on time."

"We lost our lead?"

"Yup. But at least we are still alive."

Mauri didn't stir until they were on the next leg of their trip. By then Tramp was ready to deal with her. He gave her some time to make herself presentable and get something to eat before he bothered her.

"How's our progress?" she asked when he took a seat at the comm station.

"Good. We did have a run-in with that Major again, but we are on course and on time."

"How did he find us?"

"This galaxy may seem like a big place, but those of us who fly around it are pretty lazy. We like places where we can quickly identify the stars to confirm our position. Mutt had wanted to come back a different route but we were forced to go back to a more standard route and he was going through the same system at the same time. It's really not that surprising. Not quite as surprising as a young woman such as yourself flying alone. Do you do that often?"

"Yes. I prefer to travel alone. Then I can't blame anyone else if I run late. My ship was equipped with a full autopilot and navigation system so I could get just about anywhere I needed to. I was supposed to be on Hafestbur Nuris for some location work at their ancient Jorar sect cathedral. I'll have to contact them and let them know what happened."

"When were you supposed to be there?"

"I've kind of lost track of time. I think I'd already missed it when you picked me up."

"Well, as soon as we land and connect into the station comm system, you call them and see if you can still show up and I'll get you there right away. And I did log picking you up with the time and location, but the hypercomm hasn't been able to connect. It should be date and location stamped so when it does go through, you can prove to your insurance company and your production company that you lost your ship."

"Thank you for that."

Tramp couldn't help notice that since he'd made that bargain with her and she had calmed down that she really was very pretty and really nice to talk to. She was evidently famous in some circles and he could see why she would be popular. She was much too classy for the sort of ladies he usually hung around with. Part of him regretted that their lives were so different. Now if she'd been a freight runner... well, things would have played out differently.

"What are you thinking about?" she asked when he was silent for too long.

He wasn't one for beating around the bush so he just stated what he'd been thinking, but in terms that weren't as graphic as his thoughts. She blushed slightly, but didn't seem to object too much to the idea.

"I still can't believe you haven't heard of me."

"Nope, never did. I even looked you up in the data files and read all about you and where you grew up and what vids you've appeared in and I don't recall seeing a single one of them. After getting to know you, I might have to rectify that."

"If you do, don't watch *Child of Daunish*. That one is the worst thing I've ever done."

"I'll keep that in mind."

They continued to talk about various subjects until the ship came out of hyperspace again. Tramp excused himself so he could make sure they were in good shape. When they were just about ready to jump, Mutt pointed out a ship on their long range scanners. It had to be the Major again, but he was too far away to worry with. He ordered Mutt to initiate the jump and they left without an encounter, but it had Tramp worried.

"He must have guessed where we are going," Mutt said.

"It's not that hard. With what we are carrying, Prixnar IV is the most obvious destination." Tramp hated being right about this. They would have to do something to beat him to landing or Customs would be all over them and he couldn't avoid them and still get Errubo his cargo. He had to admit it, at least to himself, that he was worried. That annoying Major could ruin everything.

"Mutt," Tramp began, "we need to rework these last jumps. I need us to dock at Prixnar IV before that Major gets into the system. Can you shave off two hours from our trip?"

"Not at this point." He did a quick calculation. "I can cut it down by an hour and ten, but no more."

"Then do it, that will have to be enough."

"Okay, but this is going to be a little crazy."

Tramp didn't like that sound of that and he didn't like what Mutt started doing any better. He hacked their current course and had it end in about ten minutes instead of a couple hours. Then he started plotting the new course, but he must have had it in mind already because it was done in no time. The hairs on the back of Tramp's neck stood up when he saw that he was ignoring the safety precautions. There was a small group of stars that they would normally go around in a couple of jumps, but Mutt was going to go through them and try to get them to Prixnar IV in one jump. To do that, he would be twice as close to the hyperspace gravity shadows of those stars as was considered safe. But it was either a daring move like that or getting caught by that Major.

He nervously watched as Mutt's course change went into effect and they dropped out of hyperspace. Mutt had their location and initiated his daring jump in five minutes.

Jester was as speechless as Tramp for a change. He'd been quiet the whole time. Tramp knew that meant that the Major was making him nervous too. He was all talk and fun when he could see the way out, but when he thought it was really serious he got quiet. They were in Mutt's hands.

He waited in the cockpit, forgetting about his pretty passenger, as the color of the hyperspace streams darkened as they drew close to the cluster. He wasn't one to listen to legends, but most legends had some grain of truth to them and he didn't like tempting a legend to show itself. He caught himself tightly gripping the seat-back of the navigator's station and didn't let up until he saw the streams visibly lighten again. Mutt had hit the cluster dead center and they had passed through. He couldn't be a hundred percent sure their course had held completely true, but it was true enough to get them to Prixnar IV. They could quickly make a micro-jump if they needed to.

It turned out his course was dead on. They arrived at the hyperspace beacon as planned and Tramp immediately went to the comm station. It connected perfectly and he put a call through to Errubo.

"Tramp, I see from the location stamp that you have made it back, with my cargo I hope."

"Everything is good except we picked up a pest. A local patrol Major will probably be here in an hour and if he shows up before you get your cargo... I'd hate to come this far and fail. I'm sure your customers wouldn't like that either."

"You do not play fair, Tramp. Let me see what I can offer you in the way of assistance."

"And you better not be planning on deducting anything from my fee."

Errubo grumbled and put him on hold. He came back a couple of minutes later. "We will have to be brief, the hypercomm relay is going down for maintenance any moment. You are cleared to dock at the same berth you left from. I'll see you there with a cargo team."

"And my money?"

"Yes, that..." Errubo was cut off as the connection died.

"Jester, I think I'd better handle this landing."

"If you are planning what I think you are planning, I wouldn't want to be the pilot if it doesn't work."

"It will work. You'd better go tell our passenger to strap in for a rough landing."

Tramp carefully plotted his course. He would have to apply the breaking thrusters at just the right time. As the ship approached the Customs patrol line, he didn't see any ships and didn't get a signal on the standard frequencies so he didn't slow down. With the hypercomm out, he was unable to properly declare an emergency. There really wasn't, but he was planning on using his passenger and her former state of distress as an excuse.

He brought the ship in hot. The purple gas giant lit the side of the moon they were landing on and cast strange shadows. Fortunately Tramp was relying on his instruments. He was on his final approach when the chron showed the time of the

Major's expected arrival. He didn't have time to worry about that. The breaking thrusters fired at the right time and the ship slowed. He brought it into the final turn and lined up on the berth Errubo had indicated.

He could sense Mutt's tension in the seat next to him and was glad Jester and Mauri were back in the common room, out of sight. He was in complete control and *Thief of Hearts*' forward momentum stopped and he lowered her into the berth. He activated the docking sequence and checked the chron when then panel showed them docked. Forty-eight hours and thirteen minutes from when they'd left. Forty-eight hours and thirty-nine minutes since the clock had started in the bar.

This berth was perfect for *Thief of Hearts*, it had a side dock and a forward cargo dock. Tramp exited the upper deck and went through the docking tunnels to the lower cargo hatch and opened it up just in time for Errubo's men. He recognized one of his lackeys. He stayed out of their way as they off-loaded the cargo into a maintenance tunnel where it would disappear from the official arrivals. They were very efficient and had the hold empty in less than fifteen minutes.

"Now that you have your cargo, I believe you owe me some money," Tramp said to Errubo.

"Two million I believe."

Tramp called up the blood contract on his pad and showed it to him. "That was four million."

"Even one of those is negotiable."

"Errubo, you've been trying to cheat me since we were kids. I've never let you get away with it before and I'm not about to start now."

"I'll never understand what my aunt saw in your father. She's a sweet lady, but you cause me nothing but trouble."

"But who else could have pulled this off."

"All too true. I'll give you that. Now take your money and let me try to forget we are cousins."

"Us being cousins is why I've never turned you in. And next time you need my help, don't torture the poor guys around here." Tramp processed the payment on his pad and smiled at his cousin when it went through. He didn't say another word and just stepped into the hold and sealed the hatch behind him. He was so glad he looked more like his father. No one had ever guessed he and Errubo were related.

The hold was clean enough so he took the gangway up to the common room. Mauri was at the comm station and it was evidently working. Convenient that it started working again as soon as Errubo had his cargo.

"Good, you're back," she said. "I made contact with the producer and checked with Mutt and if you can take me right there, everything will be good."

"Unless that Major makes our departure a royal pain, it won't be a problem."

"Speaking of the Major," Jester said from the hatch leading to the cockpit, "He's on the line for you."

"Wonderful."

"And so is the port controller."

"Double wonderful. Looks like I have some talking to do."

Tramp went to the cockpit and picked up the call from the port controller first. He was easy to soothe. He took the controller into his confidence and made it seem very secretive that he had a special passenger. When he dropped Mauri's name, the controller got very excited and asked for a favor. Tramp hoped she'd agree to it, but went ahead and made the promise anyway. The controller had been upset with the speed at which Tramp had entered the port and he could have cited him for that. Before dealing with the Major he checked with Mauri and she was more than happy to do a favor like that for a fan. All the controller had wanted was a pic with her, but she said she'd go one further and give him a short custom vid.

That settled, Tramp contacted the Major.

"What can I do for you Major Savvir?"

"Keeping me waiting is not going to delay my justice. I have contacted the local port about you. You are finished."

"I don't see how. My hold is empty and my passenger is someone the local controller would do anything for. I don't see how you could get me for anything that the local authorities would care to enforce."

Tramp half-wished he was using a vid connection so he could see the Major's face. The tone of his next words made Tramp believe he was about as angry as any human could be and not have an aneurism.

"You won't get away with this. I know what you were carrying and you will pay for your crimes."

"Major, I don't think you see the folly of your situation. My hold is empty. The station records show it was empty when I landed. You won't even be able get them to conduct a scan with that information."

Tramp knew he'd won when he heard the Major sputter in anger and then the connection went dead. At least that was over for now. Tramp had to give it to the guy, he'd been right there the whole way and correctly guessed where they were going. That wasn't so difficult as almost beating him here.

After he finished a system check, he wandered back to common room as the controller was taking his leave. It was clear he was enamored with Mauri and didn't want to leave, but he had a job to do and his assistant could only fill in so long before he would be missed.

"He was sweet," Mauri said after he left.

"Thanks for that. I probably could have talked my way out of it, but you doing that made it so much easier."

"My pleasure."

Tramp looked at her for a moment, sensing something different in her. They would be together for a little while longer so maybe he could find out if he was really picking up something or imagining it.

"Jester told me how much you were getting paid for that run. I suppose you don't really need a job."

"Not for a while anyway. After that one I just need to keep my head down and stay out of trouble."

"So you wouldn't be interested in another job?"

"That depends."

"Well," Mauri said with a devious smile as she moved closer to him, "my ship is destroyed but I still have places I need to get to. You could, at least until I find a new ship, fly me to a few places that I need to go."

"I see. And how long would this job last?"

"As long as you want it to."

"Aren't my ship and I a bit beneath your status?"

"Maybe the way people might perceive it, but I wasn't always famous. I'm still pretty simple at heart."

Tramp knew he wasn't imagining it. Between their conversations and the events that had transpired she had taken a liking to him. "I think I could use the sort of job you are offering. And since you've been such a good passenger, I won't even charge you for it." He pulled her close to seal the deal with a kiss. She accepted.

Beautiful Trouble
4312 GCE

The deafening noise in the transfer tube left Hazdon Brenker's ears ringing before he finally reached his destination and closed the door. The maintenance shop was empty, his contact had not yet arrived. He sat at the workbench and waited.

He'd cleared his schedule for this job and the guy had better be here or heads would roll. He had a schedule to keep and a crew to pay and was none too patient when it came to arranging jobs. Either this client wanted him to smuggle his cargo or he didn't. If he didn't show and there wasn't a good reason, Brenker would blacklist them and his word carried weight in this sector.

Pargila Vekris Station was not out of his way, but arranging this clandestine meeting had been a pain. The potential client didn't want anyone to know they were trying to smuggle anything and they had given directions to this maintenance shop just off the station's main internal transfer junction. Why they kept it pressurized on this station he had no idea, but it left his ears raw with the intense sound of starship engines echoing in the enclosed space.

This maintenance shop was long deserted and the few tools and parts scattered about were broken and useless. As a trader and smuggler, Brenker was used to waiting. He could sit unmoving at the controls of his ship for hour upon hour as they flew through hyperspace, but when it came to waiting for a client, his time was precious and his patience finite. In this case he was generous and gave them two hours of his time before he left.

He was more fortunate on the way out. There were no ships in the transfer tube at that moment and he made it to the egress hatch before the next ship could raise the din again. The station was in good repair and the operators kept it clean and nice, but in these disused back passages the station showed its age. Only the occasional light worked and the spotty circulation fans left patches of stale air. Still, nothing Brenker wasn't used to.

His frustration mounted when he reached the hatch that led back to the occupied portion of the station. It showed the hatch was unlatched, but it was jammed. He was tempted to take out his gun and blast it, but that likely wouldn't do any good. Instead he put all his muscles into pulling the hatch open once it finally signaled that it was unlatched. The door eventually gave, but not before his old shoulder injury popped and made him grunt in pain.

He cursed that healer on Valerapon and his inept use of the regenerator. He kept meaning to go back there and teach that idiot a thing or two, but he had too much on his plate for such small fry. It would take a good week and unless he was in the area, that was a waste of his precious time. Every moment that wasn't paid for in advance he used to find something that would pay. It kept his accounts nicely flush.

Once in the main corridors there was no need to sneak around so he headed back to his ship, periodically rubbing his shoulder. He contemplated stopping at the station's medical station, but decided against it. He knew what they would recommend and that would put hm out of commission for too long. His time was important and the shoulder wasn't anything he couldn't deal with.

As he neared the docks where his own ship was berthed, he began to get the feeling he was being followed. It had started when he had passed the main corridor that led to the station's administrative and residential section. He knew how to handle the obvious amateur trying to trail him. He'd spent more than enough time on this station to know all the ins and outs and places to hide and set an ambush. He knew just the spot and diverted to lay a trap for his shadow.

When he finally caught sight of who was following him, his curiosity got the better of him. The young girl was not the sort of person he usually had any contact with. She appeared to be in her mid-teens, petite with short brown hair. She looked very determined and intent, and as Brenker had planned, he caught her completely by surprise when he sprang his trap.

Her immediate reaction to being grabbed was fear, but as soon as she got a good look at him, she relaxed as if the trap had been her idea.

"What's the meaning following me?" he demanded of her.

"I've been looking for you, but you are a hard man to track down. Where have you been all day?"

He could not believe her reaction. He was a large man and the near half century he'd spent riding the streams had left its mark. He tended to intimidate anyone young or sheltered just by his looks, and here she was, not only young but looking like someone who had lived a sheltered life and she didn't seem to pay his rough appearance any heed.

"I've been working. It's something we traders have to do on a regular basis."

"Let's be up-front," she said as he held her against the wall, her feet dangling above the deck, "You are about as close to an honest trader as I am. You're a smuggler and I need a smuggler."

"You seem well informed."

"I hope so, I've been planning this for months. Everything is in place and I need to hire you right now."

"You... need to hire me...?

"Yes. You come highly recommended. Captain Berevazik said you would be perfect for this. He actually laughed and said you would jump at it when I told you the details."

"He did? Well why don't you tell me what you want to hire me for and let me be the judge. Berevazik may not know me as well as he thinks."

"Can we go someplace and talk? Like your ship."

"The last thing I need is for someone to accuse me of kidnapping a beautiful young girl, such as yourself."

"Someone would have to miss me for that to happen. I'm all alone now which is why I need to hire you."

"Oh?"

"Revenge, Captain Brenker. I get revenge for my family and you get a valuable cargo to fence."

"You are starting to talk my language, kid."

"My name is Chimra."

"Since you seem to know so much about me, I assume you know where my ship is berthed."

She nodded and he let her down.

"Lead the way," he said.

He'd realized she was tiny, but following her he revised his estimate. She could barely be a meter and a half tall and definitely carried less than fifty kilos. Definitely his smallest human client ever. He realized that even without hearing the rest of her plan she had already caught his interest. It sounded far more interesting than the cargo he'd planned on smuggling.

She definitely had been on the station for a while as she knew her way around. She led him back to the ship by a different route than he would have taken, but it avoided the most densely used portions of the station.

The berth entrance wasn't anything spectacular. The station was very utilitarian and there were no viewports to reveal the ship, only a simply labeled hatch that led to the gangway. A second hatch some distance away led to a second gangway for cargo handling. Brenker never hooked that one up except when he was actually moving cargo.

The girl, Chimra, surprised him by correctly keying the hatch and proceeding down the gangway to the ship. Her knowledge ended when they reached the ship's hatch. It was streaked with age, a hint of how weathered the rest of the ship was. Chimra deferred to him to open the hatch.

As soon as he keyed it and they stepped inside they were greeted by his large Ka'rhe'eran engineer, Rezav. Chimra gasped at the sight of him and Brenker couldn't blame her. At just over two meters and with features most humans more often associated with canines, his appearance took some getting used to. His silvery blonde fur and violet eyes sparkled at the girls fear, but he ruined the image when he spoke in his very gentle voice, "Who is this little thing?"

"Our new client."

"What about the one you had arranged?"

"He didn't show. I need to have a private word with Chimra here and then I'll fill you in on what we are doing."

"The ship is ready to go when you are."

Chimra was still breathing hard when they reached his quarters which doubled as his office. "Are you going to be okay?" he asked her.

"Yes. He startled me."

"Ka'rhe'eran take some getting used to. I've heard it is some primordial fear we humans have. They look too similar to a cross between a canine and a human."

"Or it could just be his size, the teeth and that fact that he startled me."

"That too. He's Rezav, my engineer. He keeps this bucket of bolts running, which is no small feat."

"I thought your ship was in good repair?"

"It is because of him. Without him I don't think it'd last a month. It's not new after all."

"True."

"Now take a seat and start talking. What is this mission you have for me that gets you revenge and me money?"

The laugh that came from her did not fit with her obvious youth and beauty. He would have expected such an evil sound to come from a jaded woman closer to his age. There was more to this girl than he had yet to see.

"I'll start with my motivation. I never knew my father and my mother was my only real family. A year ago she was arrested, tried, and sentenced for a crime she didn't commit. That's not to say she was entirely blameless, but she was framed for this particular crime and is serving a twenty-year sentence. If the real criminal would have been on trial, he would have been locked away for life on one of the remotest prison planets."

"And who is that?"

"Gadul Dakka."

Brenker knew the name and knew the man it belonged to. Not the nicest of people and not the sort of person he cared to interact with. "I know of him. A dangerous person to cross. What makes you think we should this time?"

"Because he has put everything into a gamble on this one cargo. He's counting on it to turn a huge profit. He's right, it will, but it only works for him if he gets the profit. We take the cargo and he'll have to answer to his bosses where the money went and we make the money he was supposed to."

"That is a risky plan. What makes you think we can pull it off?"

"I know every place that cargo is supposed to be. All we have to do is intercept it at the right place."

"Show me."

"No. Not unless you agree."

"It almost sounds like you don't trust me."

"You are a smuggler and I know you have worked with Dakka in the past."

"Do you know how it turned out?"

"No, but you aren't one of his stooges and you have a good reputation as a smuggler."

"Yes, I did work for him, about six years ago. I came away with a healthy respect for his power and quite a hatred of the man himself. There are a lot of risks in your plan and they all fall on my head."

"Not just yours. If he finds out I had anything to do with this, my mother won't be in prison, she'll be dead."

"So you do understand the risks. Now what is the cargo?"

"It is a shipment of Yuresh brandy."

"That stuff is as common as traders in hyperspace."

"Not when it is a shipment from Yuresh that has been sitting forgotten in a storage unit for well over five hundred years."

"Five hundred-year-old Yuresh brandy? It's hard enough to find a good fifty year old brandy, where did he find any that old?"

"In a warehouse they were tearing down. He's been trying to quietly move it and he's put so much time into it his other projects have fallen behind. Can you fence something like that?"

"I certainly can, but the trick is doing it without word getting back to them where it came from. I think I have a few contacts that would take it, but not for its full value."

"He's expecting to get about a hundred and fifty million credits for it from a collector."

"I'd be lucky to a fraction of that."

"Even a fraction of that is a lot of money. So will you do it?"

"And all you want out of it is revenge?"

"If I get anything else, it will make my mother a target. Me too, probably. I've already been gone for too long and it might be raising suspicions as it is."

"I seriously doubt that they would link you to this."

"You don't know. They keep track of me. They probably have noticed my absence already."

"It's not too late," he told her. "You can still go back. I'd even offer to take you since my business here is finished."

"No, I want to do this. I have all the information and I just need you to agree to it. You steal the cargo and then do whatever you want with it."

"It is far too good to pass up. I'll do it. Where do we have to be and when?"

"He's moving it in several stages. First he needs to smuggle it off of Menansel and then he needs to get it to Jedorfa where the courier will take it to his buyer. We have to get it before the courier picks it up."

"Show me what you have." She handed him her personal data pad and he looked over the copy of the shipping tracking manifest. It was impressive that she had laid her hands on this. Normally they were closely guarded secrets and he could only imagine how guarded Dakka would be with this manifest and schedule. He was partly curious as to how she had gotten it and partly scared to find out.

"I think we should leave right away and work on the plans in transit. My crew should be able to pull this off." It was just all too tempting. Getting Dakka like this and pulling some money out of it as well as helping this girl get her revenge all rolled together to made it the perfect job. Normally he would have turned the girl down, but this would be a challenge and the plus side of getting Dakka after how he'd jerked them around six years ago. He'd avoided getting his own revenge because it was too dangerous, but this was perfect.

When he opened his cabin door, his four crew members were waiting for him.

"Well?" Gelsulan, his burly Snagtharian cargo handler asked.

"We have a job."

"Is the kid that rich?" Kenzulat, the human lead pilot added.

"No. The kid has a cargo of five hundred-year-old Yuresh brandy for us to steal. She gets revenge and we get the cargo to fence."

"Such brandy is not for fencing, it is for drinking," hra'Sivana, the Stavian pilot said.

"If that is what you want to do with your share, we can certainly arrange it. We need to leave right away and then plan how we are going to do this."

His pilots headed to the bridge while Gelsulan headed for the hold to make sure it was in shape. Rezav remained looking down at the girl. "I hope the cargo proves to be everything we hope. It will get you your revenge and make us rich. At least until we spend it."

Chimra laughed at that, a much more appropriate laugh for a girl her age. Brenker showed her to one of his guest cabins and went to the bridge to oversee their departure.

His ship was from a different age. He had no idea how old it might be. He had found it derelict in a remote system, but nothing had come of it until he had found a good deal on another ship that had crashed, destroying the structure but leaving nearly all the systems intact. He and Rezav had salvaged this ship and used the parts from the crashed ship to rebuild it and create something truly fantastic and unique. The crashed ship had been larger so this ship was slightly overpowered. It was also armed, not something he advertised. No place was the age of the ship and difference between its current duty and what it had been designed for more apparent than in the bridge. The spacious command center occupied the forward half of the upper deck. It had originally had far more stations than the three that remained, but they had ripped them out and replaced them with blank panels. Brenker guessed it was a long antiquated customs design, but he had never been able to positively identify it. With the way things lasted in space, it could easily be thousands of years older than the Confederation.

He'd used Chimra's data to calculate a few likely places the cargo might move through and the best place for them to prepare and start the operation. Ekom-dorun turned out to be ideal. It offered easy access to both Menansel and Jedorfa, not to mention multiple ways to leave. He sat down to plug it into the auto-nav while Kenzulat took care of their departure.

One of the advantages of such a spacious bridge had been to include virtually all of the engineering controls. Rezav only had to go to the engine room if there was something mechanical that needed attention. He kept on top of the maintenance so that was rare. Usually he could handle any in-flight adjustments from the bridge. He was deep in his engineering panels and was oblivious to everything around him. He didn't seem to notice their departure or that Brenker was the one at the auto-nav.

Departing a station was a simple task. Once they had clearance, it was all a matter of undocking and maneuvering away from the berth, accomplished with very little thrust.

Kenzulat was skilled enough in throttling up slowly that none of them even noticed when he set course for the hyperspace beacon. The auto-nav had a good course through hyperspace laid out for them by that point. It was just a matter of approving the course and initiating the first jump.

Once they were safely in hyperspace, Brenker went to the guest cabin to work out some of the details with his new client. Unlike some traders who reveled in the beauty of the glowing hyperspace streams, Brenker found that they just gave him a headache. If he stayed on the bridge for any length of time, he put on a pair of shaded eye-protectors that muted the glow to a tolerable level. He would just black out the ports except both his pilots relied on the color of the streams to judge their progress. He was not one to get in the way of his crew so he usually left or put on the eye-protectors.

During the voyage he and Chimra went over the extensive data she'd gathered and identified all the weak points in Dakka's plan. Brenker was a cautious man and he didn't like putting all his effort into one plan so he carefully built contingencies into the plan to account for every permutation that he could think of. While planning was good, thinking on his feet usually ended up to be even more valuable. He often had to combine ideas on the fly to find his way to success. This mission was fraught with dangers and he had a feeling it would not be as simple as walking in and grabbing the cargo. Chimra, for all the excellent data she came with, had no idea what it meant or what to do with it.

"How did you come by this information?" he finally asked her.

"I have friends. There are many in his organization who may be scared to act, but aren't scared to help me act. Being a girl didn't hurt either."

"It is truly impressive. I just hope it proves to be accurate."

"I verified as much as I could. Everything checked out."

"But that was several days ago. We'll have to see if that still holds true. It won't be too long. We'll be at Ekom-dorun in just a few hours."

With the information that she'd provided, timing was crucial. The cargo wasn't going to remain in one place for very long. She'd been running out of time when she'd finally found him, but they had some leeway. If they hurried right now, they could get into a good position to pull this off without Dakka being the wiser.

As smooth as their departure had been, their landing at Ekom-dorun was rough. The world had a hostile atmosphere but the planetary leaders consistently refused to create a transfer station in orbit to help reduce the traffic through the atmosphere of those who needed to stop there. Brenker had made landings here with more than one ship and his *Sword of Lashus* handled it with more stability than any other craft its size. Even so, it was a rough landing.

Rough or not, his crew immediately went into motion. They had preparations to make and only a short time to do it in. He wanted to be ready to leave here on a moment's notice. His part of the preparations started with confirming Chimra's information. He had a few contacts on Ekom-dorun and within minutes of leaving the ship he was making his way to an obscure bar just outside the spaceport. The contact he was looking for frequented one of the back tables this time of day.

"Brenker, what brings you to this dive," Dazloth said in greeting when Brenker located his table.

"I have an unusual job and I need to make sure it is legit. I believe my client, but I'm not sure I trust the data she gave me."

"She? I see why you trust her. Let me see the data."

"Don't get any ideas. She's young enough to be my granddaughter."

"That's what you said about that girl on Petadaltora."

"That was fifteen years ago and I said daughter, not granddaughter." Brenker handed him the data chit.

"Well, if you must be so precise. Besides, I haven't known you to get excited over your opposite sex since that woman on Eknamatil broke your heart." He turned his attention to the data on the chit.

"Don't bring her up."

"My apologies." Dazloth went silent as the data took over. He was soon keying away on his portable device. It took a good twenty minutes of intense work before he slowed down and another fifteen minutes before he gave Brenker his attention.

"Remarkable. What a find. Truly, what a find. And every piece of data on here is legit and accurate as of right now. The cargo in question left Menansel on schedule. It should be passing through this sector in two to three days depending on the route."

"I'm correct that they can't take it directly to Jedorfa?" Brenker asked.

"Correct. But you have come to the one system that it will not go through. Landing on this hell hole would be too rough for such a delicate cargo."

"Coming here was deliberate. I can reach any of the others from here in just about the same amount of time."

"A wise move on the surface. But I think you need to move sooner than you are planning. From the data and my knowledge of the sector, I believe it will go through Iosep-Ebris. The beacon the ship used out of Menansel indicates that is their destination."

"That was the other thing I was going to ask you. So, the data's good and they are going through Iosep-Ebris. That means they should stop at Urasha-menda on their way to Jedorfa."

"It would seem logical, but don't count on it. If you plan for that, I predict a forty percent chance of failure. If you hurry to Iosep-Ebris and it turns out they haven't gone there for any reason, you still have time to correct. If you wait until Urasha-menda, you won't get a second chance."

Brenker understood the advice. He also knew that time was running short to follow it. His people were out gathering the supplies they might need and wouldn't rendezvous at the ship until it was practically time to leave. If any of them ran late, they could miss their chance. He hated playing things this tight, but he also hated to lose out on such a potential profit. He was surprised when Dazloth only asked for a small fee instead of a percentage. He really didn't think it was a sure thing and Brenker couldn't blame him.

He cut short his own preparations, only getting a couple items he really couldn't manage without, and went back to the ship. Rezav was still out gathering some spare parts. He and Gelsulan were probably together since the cargo master wanted to get some special supplies to help secure their expected cargo. He'd have to wait for them to get back before they could leave. He immediately informed his two pilots. Kenzulat had been up far too long and wisely decided to get some sleep and let hra'Sivana pilot this leg.

Chimra came out of her cabin to find out what was going on. "Why are we leaving already?"

"I had a contact I trust look this over an he caught something I missed. Iosep-Ebris is on their most likely route. If we leave now, we might catch them there. If we don't and they do go that way, we aren't going to be able to catch them before they reach Jedorfa."

"How did you miss that?"

"I think I miscalculated their route through there and I had it in my mind to come here first without double checking it. I am not infallible, but we have plenty of time to fix it, provided Rezav and Gelsulan get back pretty quick."

She didn't say anything more, but she was too nervous to return to her cabin and followed him to the bridge. He understood her concern so he didn't say anything.

As it turned out, they didn't have to wait as long as he had feared. Rezav hadn't found everything he was looking for and returned to the ship to use the ship's hypercomm to search for another source. Instead, he was quickly at work prepping the ship for departure. Gelsulan's excursion had been very successful and he was ready to stow the cargo when it arrived.

As soon as they had clearance, they lifted off. The ride up was as bumpy as the landing had been. But since they were in a hurry, hra'Sivana laid on the power as they gained altitude and they were quickly through the turbulent atmosphere and streaking through hyperspace to their new destination.

There wasn't a lot for any of to do during the trip, so it was a boring stretch of hours until they reached Iosep-Ebris. Brenker hadn't been to this planet that often, mainly because it had a large Customs inspection base and arriving ships tended to get searched more often than not. He wasn't surprised when they selected the *Sword of Lashus* for inspection. They had nothing to hide so they did as they were told.

It took Customs over an hour to dock and board and Brenker was soon very frustrated. Normally it took less than ten minutes. He carefully composed himself before the airlock opened so that the Customs Agent didn't sense his frustration at the delay.

"Manifest and ship's papers," the agent said with no preamble as he came through the airlock. Brenker had the documentation ready.

"No cargo?" the agent asked.

"No, just a passenger. She's looking for a relative so we have been planet hopping with an empty hold."

"I looked up your history. That really isn't like you."

"You can meet her if you'd like. She was left alone when her mother was convicted and she has just enough to pay me for my time after a cargo bailed on me. She can cover about a week before I start to lose money on the deal."

"Even so, I'll have to do a thorough scan of your ship. You've been known to carry some interesting contraband in the past."

"I've never been convicted of any offense."

"No, but we both know the type of thing you normally carry. I can't prove it, of course, but your record had entry after entry of suspicious run-ins and lots of notes from the responding agents."

"Search away. You won't find anything."

The agent nodded and had his guards start the scan. They seemed to take their time. Inwardly Brenker was seething. Outwardly, he didn't give any sign of impatience. If he had, they would have brought out the slower more powerful scanners that would go so far as to check the bolts and welds that held the ship together. He held his cool and before too long it was over.

"It looks like you were telling the truth this time," the agent said. "Keep it up and maybe you'll get off our watch list."

"I'll do my best." He knew he wasn't on any watch list. This particular agent may have his own personal criteria for harassing traders, but his usual haunts weren't so officious.

They descended to land at the main space port just outside the planetary capital. It was a fertile green world that not only abounded with its own ecology, it had adapted well to human colonization untold thousands of years ago. It was well settled with nearly five billion people scattered over the globe. It was a calculated risk landing at the main port. There were six other sizable ports that their cargo could come into, not to mention the many private landing pads that dotted the planet. To catch their quarry here, he would have to do a lot of work. He sent Rezav off to complete his errand. His engineer's contacts had told him the supplies he was looking for could be found here and Brenker hoped they were right. The last thing he wanted was to botch this cargo because of a mechanical breakdown.

Traders were a tight-knit group and Brenker was surprised that a seasoned gangster like Dakka seemed to forget that. Traders not only watched out for each other, but they kept tabs on each other. There were rivalries and hatreds and close ties of friendship like anywhere, but they kept it within their ranks. It was a huge crime against their traditions to take a problem outside their ranks. Even the traders who worked for the big corporations followed the same rules, even though they kept to themselves. Brenker was still surprised at how easy it was to track Dakka's ship. The official channels had nothing, but the trader circles had all the details.

The ship was the *Kekkal-Tarifa* captained by Jiggas Pottmis, a long time stooge of Dakka's, but not all his crew were so loyal to the gangster, nor were the traders they encountered. He had the full details of when they left and their destination and when they were supposed to arrive here on Iosep-Ebris and even which port they would land at. It was almost too easy, which worried him.

They had about half a day to prepare and they were ready to go when the *Kekkal-Tarifa* arrived. Kenzulat played the part of a port official while Rezav kept the real port official busy. He was on board the ship in minutes and signaled to the others. Rezav rejoined them and the three of them, dressed in port worker uniforms, boarded the ship.

Pottmis didn't have a very large crew and they certainly weren't expecting to be attacked by port workers. They were able to take them by surprise, but it wasn't an easy fight. Kenzulat had reported a crew of nine, including the captain and a couple of goons who looked like Dakka's men. Their first success was sealing off the bow of the ship from the cargo hold. Rezav worked his magic and had the ship's systems so convoluted that it would take hours for the three people, including the captain, in the cockpit to find their way out. Four on six were good odds for a crew that had been in more than its fair share of bar fights.

Brenker had wanted to avoid using weapons unless necessary. He found himself up against one of the gangsters and hard pressed to come out on top. The guy was little, but tough. He was so focused on taking him out that he didn't notice until after he'd dealt the knockout blow that he was the last one done. Rezav had taken care of three of them by himself. The cargo was all theirs.

They didn't really pause to look at it and loaded the three pallets onto a cargo carrier and hurried for their own ship. Rezav had some of the ship's systems automated so Kenzulat was able to call from his personal comm unit and the port controllers thought he was calling from the ship. It was useful for quick getaways like this. They had the cargo loaded and final clearance almost at the same time. Kenzulat had to take some extra time, with clearance in hand, to finalize the launch procedures before they could leave.

They were up and away before they really had a chance to examine their cargo and appreciate their success. Hra'Sivana was the first one to take a good look at what they had gotten and the others could tell by his expression that something was wrong.

"What is it?" Brenker demanded of him.

"Well, Captain, I don't think we have the right cargo. This is Yuresh brandy all right, but it is ten years old, not even fifty, much less five hundred."

"Are you sure? We should try it and be sure."

"We can do that, but I don't think it will make a difference. I know collectors and they would not allow anything be done to deface them for fear of diminishing their value. These bottles are all labeled 4302 GCE and the labels aren't fake or altered."

Brenker let out a string of swear words that his long dead father would have been proud of. "We've been taken for fools. I knew this was too easy."

Hra'Sivana double checked everything and handed Brenker a pad that had been attached to one of the pallets. When he activated the pad, it played a vid and Brenker immediately recognized Dakka's smug face.

"I can only imagine the sort of smuggler who would take this job," Dakka said in the vid. "You obviously aren't that intelligent or bright or you wouldn't have tried to go up against me. Face it, you have been outsmarted. You see, I knew the moment the leak happened, but I thought I'd allow it to seemingly go unnoticed to see if my young ward would actually dare to try and use it. If you are watching this that means she did. Please pass on my condolences to that little brat, Chimra, on the imminent death of her mother. I don't take betrayal lightly, but she may yet prove useful to me. Another strike and she will pay with her own life."

He hadn't seen the girl come into the hold, but the sob behind him told Brenker that she had heard what Dakka was saying on the vid.

"You can rest assured that this cargo has been tagged and even though the value is modest, you will never be able to unload it without leading me straight to you. I'd suggest you send Chimra back to me so she can be properly punished and then clear out of my sector before I find out who you are."

"What have I done?" Chimra cried as she collapsed in a heap on the deck.

Brenker could sympathize with her. It was a terrible thing to find out someone you cared about had been harmed by your actions. But once done, there really wasn't much that could be fixed. He'd found trying to make amends didn't really help. "We may not be able to help your mother, but we can still get Dakka for this. Hra'Sivana, we need to get to Jedorfa pronto."

"Yes, Captain."

"Chimra, I need you to go to your quarters. I need you ready to help when we get to Jedorfa. Can you do that?"

She numbly nodded and slowly got up. She didn't bother to wipe the tears that were streaming down her face and stumbled toward the gangway to the upper deck and her quarters. He didn't like to think about it, but he might be stuck with the kid now. He hoped he could find something better for her. This was not a life for someone her age who had yet to be completely ruined by the likes of Dakka.

Brenker spent his time on the hyperspace voyage plotting how to handle the situation at their destination. He would have to call in a few favors, but he had an idea. It was audacious, but it might work, especially with what they had in the hold. He enlisted hra'Sivana who agreed it might work and set him to the task.

As soon as they were out of hyperspace, Brenker was burning up the hypercomm trying to get the information he needed. The two hours as the closed on the planet and descended through the atmosphere were almost enough. Twenty minutes after they landed, he received the call that had the last of the pieces. He laughed at the thought of what he was about to do. Dakka would never recover if this worked.

He'd been able to track down the ship that Dakka had actually shipped the brandy on. It was due to exit hyperspace in just over an hour. The ship they were to meet was already here and waiting for their cargo. Brenker intended to make sure they had a cargo. The ten-year-old brandy had been carefully re-labeled and dirtied up to look like it had been moldering in a warehouse for five centuries, hopefully close to what the real brandy shipment would look like.

The protocol was the question and remained a sticking point. There was no way to be sure. Brenker would make the delivery solo with a hired cargo crew. Gelsulan was none too pleased about being left out of that part of the mission, but no one was going to argue with the captain.

Brenker rode with the disguised brandy that they had been tricked with and arrived at the waiting ship unannounced.

"What are you doing here?" a heavily armed guard asked.

"We just got in with your cargo. We had a communication malfunction and Mr. Dakka stressed that we were to deliver this as soon as we landed so I didn't take the time to find another way to contact you."

"Let me get the captain," the guard said.

Brenker hoped it wasn't anyone he knew. That could really spoil things. He was a bit nervous as he waited. He knew far too many traders and although there were millions of traders plying the hyperspace streams throughout the galaxy, he tended to run into the same people a lot.

He was relieved a few minutes later to see that this was not someone that he knew. He was equally glad his rough appearance gave credence to him being a gangster. The guard and the captain didn't seem to question that part of his story.

"You're early. I wasn't expecting you just yet."

"That must have been what the Captain meant," he said. "I think our navigator shaved off some time."

"He must be good. Do you have the manifest?"

Brenker handed over the manifest that had come with the cargo.

"Genius. Few customs inspectors would dream that the age of these bottles would make them worth so much more. I have to hand it to Dakka, he has really pulled it off this time. And we haven't even done anything illegal." The Captain motioned for the cargo handlers to move the pallets into the hold with assistance from his men on placement.

Brenker couldn't get out of there fast enough, but he had to look like he had all the time in the world. The Captain kept having one more thing to ask about. Brenker hoped he was giving the correct answers and tried to say as little as possible.

It seemed to take forever, though by his chron it was only a mere fifteen minutes from when he arrived. He turned the cargo handlers loose and rushed back to the ship. The favor he wanted to call in wouldn't work as long as the ship that had just taken delivery of the fake cargo was in port. There were lines that were hard to cross and diverting a communication from a legitimate ship was one. However, once that ship had lifted off, it was a simple matter to divert the local communication grid from a message that the ship had departed to his ship. So Brenker was glued to the command console on the bridge waiting for that ship to leave and hoping it did so before the ship with Dakka's real cargo arrived.

The timing turned out to be far too close. The ship with the real cargo was already descending through the atmosphere by the time the other ship lifted off. He immediately was in touch with his contact and before the real cargo had landed, the local comm signal had been rerouted. The next step was to wait to be contacted.

Dakka's men were not as eager as he would be under the same conditions. They waited nearly an hour before they called for directions to the ship. Hra'Sivana gave them clear instructions and they waited. The reason for the delay became clear when they finally arrived. They had paid for a premium transport service. Brenker conducted himself in a fair imitation of the other captain and conducted the cargo transfer in a precise and professional manner.

"You know, this ship looks a bit beat up for the type of customer you work for."

Brenker had heard many criticisms on his ship and had a ready answer. "My employer appreciates quality items of the past and this ship is no exception. He has helped me on any number of occasions to get the correct replacement parts for this old girl. She wears her age proudly. She is a unique model and if I fixed her up too much, she would lose a good deal of value. Besides she has a very soft ride for his valuable cargo."

That seemed to satisfy Dakka's man and they finalized the transaction. He had hra'Sivana check the cargo before signing off on it to confirm that it was the real thing. Hra'Sivana's eyes gleamed in anticipation of what the cargo might be worth. Unloading it was the least of his concerns right now, they just needed to get Dakka's men off the ship and seal the hatch and get off this world and then they would be safe.

The cargo was nearly loaded when Brenker started to get the feeling that Dakka's man was sensing something was wrong. He started talking more and asking some very pointed questions. Brenker finally stopped answering him and then things started to go downhill fast.

"For someone who supposedly deals regularly with rare cargo and valuables, you know very little about the process."

"I leave that to my boss. I concentrate on getting it from one place to the next in one piece. I'm a captain not a collector myself."

"So you just know ratty old ships."

"High performance antique ships."

"This ship looks like it could barely lift off the ground."

"Looks can be deceiving. You see a ship showing its age, I see a piece of history." Brenker was keeping track of the cargo and there was very little left. He just had to keep Dakka's man believing for a little bit longer and they would be in the clear.

"You have said all the right words, but for some reason I don't believe you."

"I am not responsible for making you believe anything. I'm just responsible for making sure this cargo gets to its destination. Do you really want to ruin the deal your boss and mine have worked out?"

"I'm here to make sure it happens like it is supposed to. I'm beginning to have my doubts."

Gelsulan signaled that the last of the cargo was secured in the hold and Brenker signaled back to seal the cargo hatch and a moment later the resounding clang of the cargo doors closing and locked reverberated through the berth.

"What's going on here?" Dakka's man said with a snarl.

"You are seeing problems where none exist. You are far too suspicious."

"Open that hatch."

"You have your orders, I have mine."

Dakka's man went to draw his weapons and in a flash Brenker had him on his knees screaming in pain and cradling his arm, bent between the elbow and the wrist at an unnatural angle. He grabbed the man and pulled him close and said, "The funny thing is that you are right, I am stealing the cargo," before slamming the butt of his own weapon on the man's head, knocking him out.

There was a minor scuffle as two men from the ship tried to interfere, but Gelsulan quickly persuaded them that their best option was to take their comrade and leave. Brenker rushed his crew on board and requested takeoff clearance. Long before Dakka's men could do anything they were airborne and on their way.

"Did we get it?"Chimra asked after they had cleared the atmosphere.

"Yes. hra'Sivana confirmed it," Brenker told her. "Now we need to lay low a while and see how it plays out. But I think to celebrate, we need to try this brandy and see if it is as good as everyone thinks. That is, unless you have someplace to be?"

"No, I don't have any place to go."

Brenker got her meaning. Perhaps there was something he could do about that. For now, she could travel with them, at least for a little while, at least until he unloaded the brandy and had some money.

He wasn't about to remain in that sector, but at the same time he didn't want to get too far away. Irbenrab was a good compromise. It was a desolate world, being little more than a refueling station. It had fallen on hard times in recent generations with the increases in fuel efficiency and increased hyperspace velocities. But like many places hit by hard times, it was becoming a haven for smugglers.

The berth at the port was cheap and they didn't rob him to hook up to the port power source, but at the same time, they didn't have a strong hypercomm signal. The one on his ship was better, even from the surface. It would be hard to keep up with the news, but if they got desperate, they could always go up to orbit and see if the signal improved enough for it to be useable.

The brandy had proven to be the best any of them had tasted and it was tempting to drink their cargo away. It would make about as much sense as what they probably would do with the money, but they all knew that the money would be more fun to spend. Hra'Sivana and Brenker both elected to take a case as part of their share. The bottle they split came from Brenker's case.

Chimra was not very happy. Being out of touch, there was no way to know if Dakka had carried out his threat against her mother. She was left to assume that he had. Brenker tried to find a way to find out, but even though they were just one sector over, but there were no direct trade routes in that direction so he had no luck.

He gave it two weeks before the need to unload this cargo and get back to work drove them up to orbit. He was sure Dazloth would have some useful information so he contacted him first.

"Where have you been?" Dazloth asked over the hypercomm signal. "You have missed some pretty exciting events."

"What's happened?"

"The nature of your cargo has gotten out. There are a lot of offers circulating. I'd be more than happy to help you arrange something."

"For a price, of course."

"Of course. But that is just for starters. Probably the best news is that Gadul Dakka turned up dead five days ago. That's when the news broke about the brandy and the deal falling apart. Everyone suspects that his bosses did him in, but the authorities aren't investigating."

"I tell you what, I'll let you broker a deal for the remaining cargo, preferably not in one chunk, if you can get me some information. My client's mother was in prison and Dakka had threatened to have her killed. Find out what happened to her. Her name is Aloca Veldagol."

"I'll get right on that. Do you want to come out of hiding and meet me?"

"As long as no one knows I was involved."

"They haven't heard it from me. Outside myself and anyone else you have told, no one knows who took the brandy, only that it a load of five hundred-year-old Yuresh brandy was taken right out from under Dakka's nose. Let's just say that Dakka is the butt of a lot of jokes and the recipient of precious little sympathy."

"We'll be back in a few days, just as soon as you find out about that woman."

"I'll let you know as soon as I know something."

Brenker found it safer to remain in orbit while they waited. There were no customs agents or local authorities to be annoyed by it. But they didn't have to wait long. Dazloth was back on the hypercomm in under two days. He was excited about sharing the news with Chimra, but first he ordered hra'Sivana to head back to Ekom-dorun.

Chimra had located a cache of old entertainment vids that a former crewman had saved in the ship's memory and had been keeping herself entertained with them. She rarely strayed from her cabin so Brenker was surprised when he didn't find her there. It turned out that she had been watching one of the wild dramas about fictional smugglers and had gone to ask Rezav some questions. He found them in the engine room talking about the realities of trader life.

"There you are," he said when he found her. "I've heard some news I thought you might like to hear."

"What is it?"

"Your mother is fine. Whatever Dakka may have intended, he never had a chance to carry out."

"Really!" she exclaimed as she jumped up and hugged him.

Brenker froze. He wasn't used to being thanked like this. It made him wonder momentarily what it would have been like to have a family. The thought was fleeting and did not come back. He carefully pulled Chimra off him.

She continued to be grateful all the way to Ekom-dorun. Brenker put up with much off it, but drew the line at her touching him. He didn't even like the ladies in his life to hang on him.

True to his word, Dazloth had arranged for three buyers for the cargo. The best thing was that they were ready to pick them up at the port, Brenker would be rid of the cargo in just a few hours. It wasn't the amount Dakka was supposed to get, but it was a lot more than he'd expected. He and his crew would be sitting pretty for quite a while.

When the cargo was taken care of and he had dispersed the money among his crew, it was time to find out what Chimra wanted to do. She was nowhere to be found. He checked her cabin and it had been cleaned out. As he searched, he started to get worried. There was no sign of what had happened to her. He checked the hypercomm records and found that she had been in communication someone. He pulled the security logs, a feature he was sure she had not been aware of. He was in shock as he listened to the messages.

She had played them. She had provided the buyers with the details of how to get the cargo and had gotten a cut. The amount was right there in the messages. Her cut was more than what he had taken as the captain's share. He sat there and laughed for a long time. He had thought he'd help her out and make sure she had a life, but she had been looking out for herself and had already taken care of it. Still, without her finding him and dragging him into this, he wouldn't have made anything.

He really should have known better. She was too pretty and pretty girls were always trouble. Not that he would claim to have learned any lesson. He probably would do the same thing again given the chance to do it over. Sometimes it really was worth helping people. Making some money at the same time certainly hadn't hurt.

Where Legends Begin

I

Out of the Forge
4585 GCE

"I'm sorry, Zaran," Captain Tursk said to the young man sitting on the other side of his desk, "You've got some bad habits and I just can't have that sort of thing on my ship."

"C'mon, Captain. I do my job and I'm here when you need me."

"Maybe in body, but you aren't all here. No, I've thought over this for the last couple of months. I warned you that if things didn't improve, you'd be out. I'm just following through with what I told you, if you remember."

Ven Zaran really didn't remember, but he had no doubt that the Captain was right. Still, he couldn't give up this position without at least trying. He started to explain to the captain what he'd done, but Captain Tursk cut him off. He had made up his mind and that was the end of it.

Ven went back to his cabin to gather his few possessions. The ship was in dock for maintenance and most of the crew had left the ship already to enjoy their shore leave, so there was no one to see him leave. Now he had to find another ship.

This had been Ven's first ship. He'd completed his apprenticeship and then stayed on as a junior pilot, but things had been going downhill for a while. Ven had felt this coming but couldn't fathom why. He did his job and no one that he knew of complained.

He could trace it back to when Jaf Darres had joined them about a year ago and he and Ven had become buddies. As he thought back his mind was hazy, but from everything he could remember, nothing had gone wrong. That other crewman had left of his own accord about two months back and Ven had continued with the activities they had spent their free time with.

He knew somewhere deep inside that his growing reliance on the drug Tint might have something to do with it, but he had no memories of anything serious happening. He never considered that things had happened that he couldn't remember. Tint affected the short term memory and once shown its effects, Ven had appreciated the escape it offered. He had his private ghosts and the Tint helped him keep those memories at a distance.

The one part about serving on Captain Tursk's ship that Ven had not enjoyed had been the first mate. She had taken a dislike to Ven had made his life miserable. An all too close reminder of his mother, among others. Things had gotten much worse when he'd become friends with Jaf.

This whole situation was driving his mind into the pit that was his childhood. Rather than give in to that, he headed from the ship to a Tint den where he shelled out the money for a two-day binge. He set a reminder of what he needed to do first when he woke up and let the attendant slide him into the sweet slumber of forgetfulness.

His old ship was long gone by the time Ven stopped recreating long enough to start looking for a new position. He didn't have any friends to speak of and the only thing he spent much money on was his Tint supply. He had been getting paid enough that he had a nice amount in his savings, but that wouldn't last too much longer. He needed another job.

At one of the port comm stations, he reviewed the ships in port to see if any were hiring or might take him on. Nothing stood out right away. First he filtered out any ships he wouldn't stand a chance with. They would check with Captain Tursk and send him on his way. He also filtered out a couple of ships he recognized as having really bad reputations. He sorted the rest into two lists. The first list included a few who were hiring, but most weren't, at least not that they advertised. Each one was a ship he would be willing to serve on. Their captains had good reputations, at least as far as he was concerned. The ships on the second list were hiring, but from the nature of the ships weren't his ideal fit. This was the list he could still be picky with.

Since he was awake and ready to do something, he sorted the ships on the first list by when they were leaving and started making his rounds. He didn't expect success right away and accepted the first couple of negative responses in stride. By the time he was done with this list, the ships would turn over and he'd make a new list.

His forth stop turned into a surprise. It was the *Clarion Spectre*, an ancient Kenosh Weskil medium freighter. One of the crew showed him into a waiting area. He took a seat, pushing the safety harness to one side. He didn't have to wait more than five minutes before a middle-aged man came out dressed as any ordinary crew member might. His neatly trimmed graying beard and the unmistakable air of command told Ven this was the captain, not just a crew member.

"Welcome aboard, young man. I'm Captain Karnock. I understand you are looking for a position."

"That's right."

"Let's go into my cabin where we can speak freely."

Ven took note of the ship as they went up one deck and forward near the cockpit. The ship mirrored the captain, well groomed, but not fancy. It was well cared for but at the same time it was a working ship and there was no mistake about what business Captain Karnock was in. He was a classic freight runner. There weren't too many of these left. It fit with the ship being a Kenosh Weskil. A classic ship for a classic type figure.

The captain's cabin just reinforced the image. It was plain, but warm and tidy. The very image of a freight runner from a century ago. Captain Karnock gestured for him to take a seat and then walked around to the other side of the narrow desk.

"You are in luck, young man. I recently had a position open up and I hadn't gotten around to posting it yet. So let's see if you have what I need."

He proceeded to get all of Ven's personal information, skills, and experience. When it came to the reason why he left his last position, Ven hesitated for a second. Captain Karnock noticed and said, "Young man, the why of your departure from Captain Tursk's employ doesn't concern me as much as your honesty. In our business, there are things we need to lie about to keep our hides, but there are also things you never lie about. I expect my crew to be honest with me. You know I'm going to check with him anyway, so just come out with it."

Ven still hesitated. In his mind he didn't have a problem, but on the other hand, it was that same activity that had cost him his position. "He didn't like how I spent my spare time and thought it impacted my work."

"That's pretty vague. What do you do in your spare time?"

Something in Ven snapped. What did he care what this captain thought of him. Chances are he wouldn't get the position anyway so he just blurted it out, "Tint."

Captain Karnock's face remained unreadable for several minutes then a slow smile spread across it. "I see. You don't think it is a problem but Captain Tursk did. Well, you do know that it affects your memory so you may have lost your memories of what it was that he thought was a problem. It is a dangerous drug and has ruined many good men. Are you going to be one of the ones it ruins?"

"I don't intend to let anything ruin me."

"Then you need to make some choices. I have a junior pilot position open that you would fit, from what I can tell. Your qualifications come up in the system and Captain Tursk didn't flag you as a risk. Still, this is a concern to any captain. Will you be with it when I need you or will you be lying in a Tint den somewhere, oblivious to the world? Will you be an asset to my ship or a detriment? How can we answer those questions?"

"I could stop taking Tint."

"We both know that isn't going to happen overnight. But are you willing to work on it? Don't answer now. Let me inquire and I'll get back to you. You already gave me your comm signal. I think that about wraps this up for now. Stay off Tint, at least until I call you back, Okay?"

"That much I can promise."

"Good. Do you need to me show you out?"

"No, I'm familiar with this model. I know where the hatch is."

"Now, I don't do business over the comm unless I have to, so I'll be calling you to come back here to tell you what I've decided. Don't be too far."

"I don't plan to leave the port."

Captain Karnock smiled as Ven left his cabin.

That had been a strange interview. Ven didn't know what to make of it so he just went on with his plan. He reached the end of his first list a few hours later. No other captain had given him an immediate interview. That left the second list, ships he really didn't want to serve on and he would be the one deciding if it was a good fit or not. He might get lucky and find a good match.

As he started on that list, he began to wonder how many ships on this list would migrate to the first list a month from now. How desperate would he have to be to sign on with some of these captains? It could happen.

Ven had goals in life and losing his position was a setback, but in the scheme of things it wasn't that bad. Captain Tursk had taught him the basics, but Ven had mastered everything he'd been willing to teach a year ago. He was ready for a captain who would train him so he could Captain his own ship someday. Captain Karnock's opening for a junior pilot didn't seem like it would take him where he wanted to go. He didn't want to be a junior pilot, that had been his position since completing his apprenticeship. He wasn't junior anything material anymore. He should have a real position.

He cursed his parents once again. They had held him back from his dream of becoming a freight runner. The vids may have glorified it a bit, but he'd seen through that to the excitement of traveling around the galaxy. His parents had wanted him to do something that they considered more useful and in more line with what they perceived as their status. Ven hadn't ever agreed with them on that. He'd set his sights on being an owner and captain when he was a young boy and hadn't let anything stand in the way so far, not even his parents and the hell they'd put him through.

He still smiled once again at what he had done. They had decided to send him away to school hoping a different setting might rid him of what they considered to be ridiculous dreams. They'd made the mistake of having him plan his own flight. Oh, he left on the right flight to get to the school, but at the first stop he'd changed flights and begun his adventure. The vids had over simplified what it took to change your identity, but he'd learned what it really took and vanished. The son of his parents had died that day and Vendarka Zaran had been born.

Not everything had gone as expected, but Ven had known that was likely to happen. It had taken him two months of trying before Captain Tursk had finally signed him on as an apprentice. He'd done his time and gotten certified and become one of the crew. Now he was in a similar position again, except this time it might be even harder and take longer. Most captains didn't look too favorably terminations.

A thought hovered at the edge of his consciousness warning that his use of Tint had gotten him here and would only make it harder to find another ship, but he pushed that through aside and concentrated on what he wanted next in life and his far off dreams of captaincy.

He was in the middle of a food break, eating a cheap cold sandwich from a kiosk replicator when his comm beeped. He hoped it might be Captain Karnock, but he almost choked when he saw it was Captain Tursk. He finished chewing the last bite he'd taken and tried to calmly answer.

"Captain Tursk, I didn't expect to hear from you."

"I feel some responsibility since you were one of my apprentices. I received a message from Captain Karnock. You aren't considering serving on his ship, are you?"

"I am. Is there any reason I shouldn't?"

"I've heard shady things about him. I don't think that would be a good ship to sign on with."

"I can't exactly be very picky. You sacked me. What's wrong with him anyway?"

"He's an old-timer and a bit rough around the edges. I've heard he does some occasional smuggling. If you get caught in a situation like that, even crew members can get sent to prison."

"I don't really see the problem. I hear you make more money that way."

"At what risk, Zaran? You're young and could have a long career ahead of you. Don't throw it away on a position like that. You can do better."

Echoes of is parents rang in Ven's head. Captain Tursk's words had the opposite of their intended effect. Ven decided right then that if Captain Karnock offered him a position, he'd take it. The glory of the vids crowded out his parents and Captain Tursk in his thoughts. "I'm sorry, Captain, your concern ended when you sacked me. Being familiar with your schedule, I know that you are in the middle of a busy run. Unless you wanted to come back and sign me on again, I don't see any reason to refuse any offer Captain Karnock might make."

"I'm sorry to hear that, Zaran. Good luck to you."

The connection went dead. Ven slowly finished his sandwich and let his thoughts adjust to the new line they'd taken. Smuggling had been a key activity in the vids, and not just the fiction. There had been plenty of documentaries of freight runners and how they skirted the law. In the last hundred years the term freight runner had gone from being a romantic moniker to an insult. Ven had never cared what he would get called, only that he wanted that life. Captain Tursk had always called himself a trader. Not that he really did any trading. He contracted cargoes to haul from one planet to the next just like any freight runner of old. Still, Ven had come to think of himself in that same way.

When he ran out of steam at the end of the day, he still hadn't heard from Captain Karnock and he hadn't found any other ships he would care to serve on. Mindful of the warning to avoid Tint, just in case he might yet call, Ven turned in.

He had neglected to check the schedule and was woken by his comm in the early hours of the morning.

"Ven Zaran," he said as he answered it.

"Zaran, this is Captain Karnock. If you're still interested in the junior pilot's job, get down here in ten minutes."

Ven jumped off the cot and told him he'd be right there. He didn't remember closing the comm. He quickly grabbed his belongings and stuffed them in his bag and ran for the ship. At a full run he made it there in nine minutes, out of breath.

"Glad you could make it, Zaran," Captain Karnock said in greeting. "I'm offering you the position. If you want it, just drop your things and get to the cockpit. I want to see what you can do."

Ven couldn't do more than nod and then did as instructed. When he entered the cockpit, the pilot got up and gestured for him to sit down. He quickly scanned the board and found the standard layout for this model. "Do we have clearance?" he asked the navigator in the neighboring seat on the right.

"Our departure window opens in fifteen minutes."

Ven let his hands fly over the controls as he commenced the pre-flight checks and the takeoff preparations. He kept an eye on the chron to make sure he would make it in time. Fifteen minutes was not a lot of time to do both the pre-flight and prepare for takeoff. Like his dash for the ship, he made it with seconds to spare. As soon as the port control confirmed they had clearance, he initiated the takeoff sequence and keyed the course to the port-assigned departure route. The ship lifted off smoothly and climbed with ease as the powerful engines carried them up out of the atmosphere.

Ven was busy with the ship and didn't have a chance to notice anything in the cockpit until they had cleared orbit. They were safely accelerating toward the hyperspace beacon when he noticed that Captain Karnock was standing in the hatch. As pilot on duty, he was responsible for the ship until they went into hyperspace so he continued to work and pretend he hadn't seen his new captain.

He hadn't been on the ship quite two hours when the navigator initiated the hyperspace engine and space seemed to rip open in front of them and the blackness of space was replaced by the glowing streams of hyperspace. Moments later Captain Karnock ordered the other pilot to relieve him and ushered Ven into his office.

"I see I chose well," Captain Karnock told him. "That was masterful handling of the controls of a ship I know you've never actually flown before. Tursk must have a good simulator program."

Ven didn't want to brag, but Captain Tursk didn't have a full simulator. Ven had picked that up on his own a couple of years ago near the end of his apprenticeship when they had a repair layover for a few weeks. He had a chance to tour a very similar ship. Even so, most ships had a similar layout, nothing that a decent pilot couldn't figure out in a few moments. "I pass, then?" was all he said.

"Absolutely. Now we need to get down to business. I like to have a contract with my crew members to cover the standards. It pays to know where you stand with everyone."

Ven just nodded. The captain slid a data pad across the table. Ven picked it up and started reading. It was pretty standard except that there was a clause on Tint usage. Ven felt his face start to show surprise at that and quickly schooled his expression.

"Yes, I did include that. Like Tursk, if you don't live up to my expectations because of Tint, you may be out of here. Unlike him, I'm not concerned if you use it, just when and how much. I expect you to be on time for every duty shift and on this ship when we depart any port. If you can't handle that then we will have to part company. You may also be wondering why I have hired you on knowing you have a drug problem."

Ven started to speak, but Karnock held up his hand to cut him off.

"Don't tell me you don't have a problem. Tint isn't something normal people do for recreation. It usually means you have a painful past you are running from. I don't need to know, I just need you to make the commitment to do what I need you to do. Can you do that?"

"Yes. It wasn't a problem before."

"To his credit, Tursk didn't rat on you. He said you were timely and didn't talk about why he sacked you, but we both know why. Tint addles the brain if you use too much. While you may technically be able to perform your duties, I need to you to have your full memory faculty when you are on duty. I run three shifts so you have eight hours on and sixteen off. Make sure that whatever you take has cleared your system before you go on duty. I'll give you the dosage data another crew member and I worked out a few years back. I understand you may have needs that exceed that, but I only ask that you chart our schedule and don't take any more unless we have some down time. I have that built in once a week. I follow one of the old religions and I believe in taking one day off a week so you'll find we always end up planetside on that day and you can do whatever you want so long as you are back on the ship and ready for your next shift."

"None of this sounds like a problem. Where do I sign?"

"You may not think it is a problem now, but you will realize how serious this is soon enough. You are messing with a dangerous drug and I can only help you as far as you are willing to ask for help."

"After you called him, Captain Tursk called me and warned me not to sign on with you. Why would he do that?"

"I'm an old-fashioned freight runner. I'm pretty rough around the edges and I do things a certain way. My crew is rough, too, and likes to play hard. We don't have a good reputation in ports. But," and Karnock jabbed a finger at the desk in emphasis, "we deliver our cargo without fail. We are always on time and early when we can. I take my job very seriously and when that is done, I take my down time seriously as does my crew. They are the best at what they do, just not the most polished. You may have more polish than most of the crew, but you have a more serious problem. Tursk doesn't like the type of people I hire, but he also doesn't know any of them. My men are the best and I think you have what it takes, especially after I talked with him."

"I don't have that big a problem," Ven said, defending himself.

Karnock just laughed. "My boy, I've been a trader for over fifty years and I've seen everything. You have a lot of potential. If we are lucky, I'll pull it out of you and make something of you. If nothing else, I'll give you a safe place to get through this phase. Those who serve with me usually go on to something better. There are twenty-six men out there right now captaining their own ships who once served on this ship. You could be another. I see it in you. Your Tint problem might even give you some edges if you can overcome it, but the first step is to admit that the way you use Tint is a problem. I won't force you into anything right now, but you keep that in mind. Are you still willing to sign on?"

Ven hesitated for a moment. While he didn't like what the Captain was saying about some things, he was giving him the chance at the career path he had dreamed of. His luck had been horrible up until now, but here was a man offering something almost beyond belief. If he worked at it, he could turn this turn of events into the fulfillment of his childhood dream. "Yes, just show me where," he finally said.

When the contract was properly filed, the Captain showed him to the crew quarters. "This is where my men bunk. The first mate has his own quarters just aft and the engineers bunk is just off the engine room."

It suddenly dawned on Ven that the Captain kept referring to his crew as male. "Are there any female crew members?"

"No. On this ship I cater to a particular type of crew and I won't subject a woman to that, no matter how she says she feels about it. Mind you, I have no issue with women in this profession, I even had a mixed crew when I first started, but this ship has become home to a very rough bunch and the two don't mix, at least not as far as I'm concerned. You'll notice everyone is human, too, for much the same reason. I have no prejudices, but I can't say that for everyone. Think about it this way, I take on the worst human males and I keep them in line."

"And how about yourself..."

"While I allow a certain familiarity, you aren't there yet, Zaran. You may address me as Captain, Captain Karnock, or just Karnock, but no personal questions until you earn it. Now settle in and report for duty in seventeen hours. And be careful of Bezzed, he can be violent before he fully wakes up."

Ven nodded and put his bag on the bunk Karnock had assigned him. The space wasn't much, pretty typical of most ships. If anything it was slightly better accommodations than he'd had before. It was a room just under two meters wide by just over two meters long. There was a bunk that took half the space with storage above and below. It could double as a table and there were some retractable seats. It opened on a common area where there were several tables and a food processor. Right now it was empty so Ven decided it was as good a time as any to eat.

The food was average, but the food processor was programable so he might be able to do something about it if he tired of the preprogrammed offerings. He ate in solitude and put the waste in the recycler when he was finished.

He didn't have many belongings to stow. He wasn't much for collecting personal things and what he did have he could just as easily be left behind and replaced, but there was something to be said for properly broken in clothes. They were just more comfortable. He had no personal mementos. He had loaded all of his belongings onto that liner those years ago and when he left to change his name, he left everything behind and started over. Since then he hadn't kept anything besides a few clothes and some useful items. He'd spent most of his time studying to get certified and since then he'd just kept studying to get better. Until recently when he'd begun using Tint. Since then he could never remember having any free time. He laughed to himself. Memory was the key point. Tint made him forget so he wouldn't really remember much of anything.

Ven truly didn't have any free time over the next few weeks. Karnock worked him hard. While Karnock took every seventh day off, he also liked to drag his crew out to socialize. That left no time for Ven to explore the ports they found themselves in. Ven observed that several of his crewmates had serious alcohol issues. They were barely able to function the next day and occasionally someone would have to take over their shift.

His chance for free time finally came at the expense of the ship. The lead pilot was at the control and Ven was waiting until they reached the hyperspace beacon so he could take over when there was a loud bang. Moments later one of the engineers was in the captain's cabin and Ven knew it was not good.

It turned out to be both better and worse than Ven initially feared. It was better in that it did not affect the rest of that flight and they were able to land safely. At the same time it was a very serious malfunction. Some engineer talk was over his head and all he could guess was that it affected the power systems, but it was serious enough that the ship was grounded for a week for repairs. Karnock was generous and paid his crew during the down time. Money plus free time and Ven was set to explore.

Unfortunately the port they ended up in had little to offer and Ven ran out of things to do before the first day was over. He'd found the Tint den, but at about the same time, a couple of his new crewmates dragged him into a nearby bar.

He tried to enjoy himself, but where he'd actually come to enjoy the days Karnock would drag them somewhere to socialize, he found this boring. Boredom led to thoughts he would prefer not to think. He soon excused himself and went straight to the Tint den. He paid for the maximum experience. He never stopped to consider the dangers or that he put his life completely in the hands of his hosts.

Ven struggled to wake up. He seemed to be in a fog and unable to escape. When he finally was able to open his eyes, he checked his chron, but stared at a date that meant nothing. 11.C.4585 could mean anything. He had no memory to connect with it. As his panic started to subside, he realized how thirsty he was and the panic rose again as he looked in vain for something to drink.

The man in the cot next to him was also waking up and offered him a flask. He took it and took a swig, thankful after the fact that it was water. He felt his barren mouth come back to life. He took a second swig and managed to choke out, "Thank you."

"You must come to these places better prepared," the man said in a thick accent.

"What do you mean?"

"Not all Tint dens are equal. This one isn't known for taking care of their clients as many are. Always keep a flask of water with you unless you know the place."

"How can I thank you?"

"Take better care of yourself. Not all strangers are as nice as I am. Finish the flask and get some rest."

"I'd rather get out of here. I just wish I knew how long I'd been here."

"And there is the paradox of Tint. It steals away our bad memories but leaves us wanting to remember. You will remember soon enough."

"What is your name?"

"Never ask questions in a Tint den."

Ven numbly nodded. He struggled to his feet and almost stumbled, but the man caught him. Ven managed to stand on his own and slowly headed for the door. He felt the man watching him and following him, but he made it out without further assistance.

The man sighed as Ven opened the door. "I will have to keep an eye out for you. I fear we will meet again, but likely you won't remember me."

Ven grunted his thanks and staggered off. Eventually he made his way to a transport tube. For a moment he didn't know which way to go, but the sign for the port lured him. He followed it and by the time the transport neared the port, he remembered that he had entered the Tint den on 7.C.4585, four days ago. When he reached the port, he checked the directory, wondering as he did how he knew to do it, and found what ship he was on. Again he wondered how he knew Ven Zaran was his name. Somehow it didn't seem to fit.

He found his way to the ship and one of his crewmates greeted him. He begged assistance and was guided to what must be his bunk. He changed into strange but familiar clothes and downed a liter of water and crashed on his bunk. He was out before he knew it.

He awoke with a start hours later. His head was clearer. His surrounding were still strange, but he knew his own name and what he did for a living.

He felt a strange anger stir and recognized it as an old friend. He'd done a four-day Tint binge in a seedy den and was paying for it.

He tried to stay in his bunk but hunger drove him out into the common room. Only one other person was there. He couldn't think of a name, but he knew it was one of the cargo handlers. He wasn't in the mood to be friendly so he used the processor to get some food and sat at an empty table. He was minding his own business when two other crewmates entered. Two of the pilots, he thought.

They had other ideas about him sitting on his own. He was grumpy enough he couldn't see they were trying to be friendly. Instead he pointedly ignored them.

"Hey, I'm trying to talk to you," the sandy haired one said. Ven responded by punching him in the face. Ven added a second punch to make his point and the other one tried to stop him and got a punch in the guts for his effort. The cargo handler stepped in and knocked Ven across the table. Ven was having none of it and slammed him into a bulkhead hard enough that he heard the sound of breaking ribs. The pilots tried to stop him and the sandy haired one received a sucker punch and was laid out on the deck. The other one managed to get in one good punch before Ven threw him over a table.

"What the hell is going on here," the Captain yelled from the hatch.

"I just want to be left alone," Ven yelled back.

Karnock looked hard at Ven and quietly ordered the men standing behind him to remove the injured. "You have your wish."

The door closed and Ven sighed. He was so glad to be alone he didn't realize he was locked in.

He finished his meal and went to his bunk. He sat there fuming at fleeting thoughts for several hours before sleep claimed him. The next morning he woke and ate something before he tried the door and found himself locked in. He could barely remember doing anything. He'd sat down to eat and three crewmates had attacked him.

Karnock came in a few hours later.

"Why am I locked up?" Ven demanded.

"After they were treated and could talk again, I found out you treated three of my crewmen with a sound beating for trying to be friendly."

"They attacked me."

"I keep all the common areas under surveillance. Do you want to watch the vid with me?"

Karnock phrased it as a question, but he didn't give Ven a choice. He played the vid and Ven sat in shock as he listened to the exchange and watched his own actions.

When it was finished, all Ven could think to say was, "I'll pack my things."

Karnock just laughed. Ven was sure there was something he wasn't getting, but he was also just as sure that his time on this ship was through.

"Zaran, if you think that is the worst fight that I've had on my ship, you don't know what a fight really is. You are far from through here."

"After that?"

"You haven't seen some of my men when they party hard. That was child's play. But in one way you are different. I see in you the makings of a captain. Are you willing to stick around and learn? It would mean you would need to work on your problem. But at the same time, your problem, if controlled, has lessons that can open up opportunities."

"How is that?"

"If you want to be an honest trader, you can make a decent living. If you are willing to skirt the law in trading like you are with Tint, you have the makings of a smuggler. Think of the vids, kid. They aren't that far off."

"You are serious, aren't you?"

"Indeed I am. I am an unconventional captain with an unconventional crew. What do you say?"

"I'm in."

"One last thing. You will have to deal with the crew. They aren't very happy about what you did or being locked out of the crew area."

"I think I can handle it. It won't be the first time."

"Then when you recover from what they have planned for you and the repairs are finished, you are up first on the schedule. Good luck."

Karnock left and the rest of the crew entered. Ven steeled himself. Three days later when he piloted the ship out of port he was still in pain.

II
Shaped on the Anvil
4594 GCE

Ven Zaran wasn't sure if he liked their new layover on Xinar Lamgun or not. In the nine years he had worked for Captain Karnock, there had been very few changes. Inexplicably, Karnock had rearranged his runs to take on a new customer leaving them on Xinar Lamgun for their one day a week break.

Karnock's crew was comprised of riffraff that few other captains would take on, and Ven was no exception. It had taken years to get to this point, but Ven could now admit he had a problem with the drug Tint. It blocked certain avenues of the memory and gave users a feeling like they didn't have any cares. Tint dens were not alike and this new location for their weekly layover left Ven with a quandary, especially since he'd never been here before.

The rest of the crew was meeting at a bar that one of the younger crew had recommended, but Ven's first priority was to check out the Tint den situation. He found the main one easily enough. It had a nice, nondescript entrance and was dimly lit inside. The host seemed knowledgeable, but it didn't have the feel that Ven liked. There were three others near the port so he checked each one out in turn and in the end didn't really like any of them. He'd have to find out their reputation, but for now he decided to meet his crewmates at the bar they were headed to. He took a small hit of Tint to keep his mind from wandering and followed the directions.

The place looked like a hole in the wall from the outside. The building was old and the windows were cloudy. Decorative lighting on the inside cast strange glows in the windows and the overall effect wasn't very inviting. When he looked closer, he saw that much of the age and seediness was for effect and the place was pretty new. The sign proclaiming it the Nova Trango

Bar was old fashioned, but bright and new. It couldn't be all bad so he went in.

The first thing he noticed about the place when he went in wasn't any of the sights, it was the smells and sounds of a real kitchen. The mix of smells was unusual and made his mouth water. He quickly spotted his shipmates and joined them. They immediately started raving about the food and Durkol told them, "Didn't I tell you the food was good?"

"I never expected a place like this would have real food. Usually it's only really high class places that have a real kitchen." Mezolik was a picky eater so if he was happy with the food, Ven knew it had to be good.

He looked around for the normal ordering system and didn't see anything. His shipmates chuckled and told him to turn around. He turned and saw a vision. She wasn't particularly tall and she must be nearing the end of her shift, but something about her stole Ven's heart.

"What would you like?" she said.

Ven was at a loss for the options so he said, "Whatever you recommend and something cold to drink."

She looked at him for a moment and then headed to the kitchen.

"Not only a real kitchen, but live people to take your order, and she wasn't even the prettiest," Durkol said.

Ven tended to keep his opinions to himself and this time was no exception. He thought she had been the mostly beautiful creature he'd ever seen. Such things weren't usually worth arguing about and when the crew did, it just caused problems. As senior pilot he tried to set an example.

One drawback to relying on a kitchen for food over a processing unit was the time it took to get the food. Ven was beginning to think he should have asked if they had a food processor when the young woman came to the table with his food and drink. He took one whiff of the food and knew that it would be worth the wait.

He was so engrossed in the food that he lost track of the woman who'd brought it until he was almost finished. When he looked around, she seemed to be gone. One of his shipmates was ordering a drink from someone else. As he looked around, he saw a couple other new faces. The sign outside said "always open" so they probably had shifts just like they did on the ship.

He went ahead and enjoyed the last of his food and joined his shipmates in their conversation.

When Ven consulted a few of his trusted contacts during the following week, he found out that he would have to get Tint elsewhere. None of the dens on Xinar Lamgun could be trusted. Both the Tint itself and the service they offered were very poor. That would pose a problem if they were here for more than the usual twenty-four to thirty-six hours, but it would usually work out. He made his plans accordingly as they traveled.

The week did not end well for Ven. When the seventh day arrived, Ven left the ship as quickly as possible and checked into a hotel just outside the port. He took a twelve-hour dose of Tint and a liter of water and crashed. As he tried to relax to let the Tint work faster, his biggest wish was that he could put his childhood behind him and just move on. The memories, when they broke through, were unbearable and impossible to push out of his mind without Tint.

He made it back to the ship in plenty of time. He was a touch grumpy from the after effects of the Tint, but he was mentally refreshed, at least from his point of view.

His week quickly descended to mental chaos and he resorted to more Tint than usual. Even to the extent that he turned over one of his shifts.

Karnock noticed and called him into his cabin.

"I know, Captain," Ven started before Karnock could. "Too many things this week."

"I've noticed that certain places have that effect on you. You need to get that under control. Traders have to go where the work takes them and you can't just avoid certain places."

"I'm working on it. I keep it to a minimum."

"And there is one of the lies that I've kept you around for. I can't stand it when you lie to me, but you do it so smoothly that you would fool any customs official. Remember my rule, in this room, you must stick to the truth."

"Okay. I'm dealing with it. I've taken as much as I thought I could get away with this week."

"Do you need some time off or professional help?"

"No. When I stick to the plan, things get better. Just lately it has been hard."

"Anything to do with the change in schedule?"

"That might just be it. Now that I think about it, I usually get lost in the routine."

"It couldn't be helped. I increased my profit by ten percent and everyone benefits by that. Work on it."

"I will."

"To help you out a bit, I'm ordering you to skip your shift and take some Tint and be ready to get off the ship and do something different. No hotels this time. Yeah, I know all about it. It comes with having a crew full of addicts."

Ven took Karnock at his word and long before his shift would have started he was laid out in his bunk.

Whenever he took enough to lay him out, Ven had to wake up twice. The first time he could barely function and usually just took in his surroundings and maybe took care of the necessary things before going back to a more natural sleep. The second time he woke, usually just an hour or two later, he was ready to go. On this occasion when he woke up the second time, the ship was deserted. He checked his comm pad to see what his shipmates were planning. He relied on that information because at this point his memory was often still foggy and unreliable. It had become habit to put anything important on his comm schedule so he could remember it when he was fully conscious. They were meeting at the Nova Trango Bar again so Ven decided to join them.

When he walked in, none of them were there. He checked the time on his comm and he wasn't more than fifteen minutes later than they had said. It was always possible they had changed their plans so Ven didn't worry. Normally his post Tint anger would flare at something like that, but the food was good and he was hungry so he sat down. He felt doubly lucky when the same enchanting dark-haired woman from his last visit came over to take his order again.

"What will you have this evening?" she asked, looking much less tired than she had the last time he'd been in.

"I don't think you ever told me what I had last time, but it was really good."

"I think it was the qadiar and pasta with baked braj. Does that sound good?"

"It does."

He took in more of the bar while he waited. While it wasn't completely full, he realized that it was a very busy place. There was certainly a wider variety of gender and species than on Karnock's ship. Ven really appreciated everything Karnock did, but he didn't much care for the all human male crew. Some variety would be nice. Ven planned on hiring the best he could, no matter what species or gender. He liked what he saw around him. He saw a table with three Zeccans, a human, and a Neathmodin. Another seemed to have one of almost every other species.

He hated to confess that due to his lack of contact with other species, he was not good at identifying gender, but among the humans, the genders were almost equally represented.

He had to consider himself lucky that Karnock had taken him on. While many of his ideas seemed backward, the help he provided his crew to succeed as traders was amazing. Ven couldn't imagine that he could have made lead pilot under any other captain, not with his problem with Tint. But he did have to concede that Karnock didn't try very hard to cure any of his crew of their problems. He worked on helping them live with it and succeed, but not on getting over it. Karnock said that was part of the lesson he wanted to pass on, but Ven was beginning to wish he could find a way to live without Tint. To do that he would have to stay put, and that wasn't in his nature. He'd left home and had been on the move ever since and had no intention of stopping any time soon.

"Taru, come back here," a woman called. Ven turned to see a toddler coming right at him. He put his hand down to block her way and she stopped and looked up at him. It provided enough of a delay that the woman caught her. She was dressed in the bar's uniform.

"Thank you, Mister," she said. "Marzi was watching her in the back and she got away."

"I've heard kids will do that."

"Did she get away again?" the dark-haired woman said as she set his food down on the table.

"I don't know what to do, Kotula. She does this to me, too."

"Try a leash," Ven suggested, "It worked for my uncle with my cousin." Ven regretted it as soon as he said it from the way the two women looked at him. "It was just an idea."

"We'll think of something, Dani," Kotula told her friend, seeming to ignore Ven's suggestion.

Ven turned to his food and, if possible, enjoyed it more than the last time. He was nearly finished when Kotula came back to his table.

"It was a good suggestion, but Dani tried it already. Taru figured out how to get out if it in less than a week."

Ven was lost for words for a moment. "I had the impression you two thought it was a bad idea."

"No, just not helpful."

"It's all I had."

"If you think of another one, let me know."

"I will. The food will bring me back."

He was looking directly at her when she suddenly bent in close and grabbed his face. She looked at each of his eyes closely. "You shouldn't use Tint," she said and stood up.

"Just from my eyes?"

"The eyes always tell the truth. You've used Tint recently. I don't hang around with Tint users."

"Even ones who are lead pilots on their ship."

"Not even then."

"And if I stopped?"

She huffed and said, "Like that is going to happen. I've seen your type before."

"You don't even want to know why?"

"There isn't a good reason, so don't bother. Too bad, other than that you seem nice. I don't get that a lot here."

"I'm a trader. I'm never in one place very long. Who knows when Captain Karnock will change the schedule again and I won't be in anymore."

"Karnock, huh. I've heard of him. I heard his crew is pretty wild."

"Are they? They love this place and have been here every time we've stopped so far."

"Where are they tonight?"

"As you noticed, I've used Tint. I have no idea. A change of plans I would imagine."

Kotula smiled and left. A few minutes later she brought Ven a desert that he had not asked for. It was as fantastic as everything else she'd recommended.

Ven lingered at the table. Kotula would occasionally come over and talk and she brought him a second desert that wasn't as sweet or heavy, but was equally delicious. She stopped over one last time to let him know she was off. Ven didn't have anything else to do so he stayed. An hour later his shipmates showed up. They had eaten elsewhere and had come to Nova Trango for drinks. Ven didn't care for alcohol, but he stayed and participated in their evening.

Ven expected the week that followed to be like any other, but his thoughts kept returning to Kotula. He couldn't seem to get her out of his head, which was not a bad thing. During his off time, thoughts of her made a pleasant change from the ghosts of his childhood. Rather than the ghosts that led to depression and drove him to Tint, he found that day dreaming about her seemed to clear his head. Even on duty she intruded with the unexpected side effect that he enjoyed being a pilot for the first time in a long time.

But the dark thoughts were not completely dispersed. He continued to take Tint at night, but it wasn't the large dose that knocked him out for long periods. In Tint culture it was called a maintenance dose. It helped keep the mind focused and not drift. Ven had heard that was one of the original uses for it when it had been developed as a medicine. When Ven wanted to sleep, he was often plagued by his memories and most of the time he took a maintenance dose as a matter of habit. If he took it and concentrated on sleep, the thoughts he wanted to keep away were blocked. It gave him control over where his thoughts could go. It also could make him extremely grumpy much of the time. His shipmates had grown accustomed to his moods, but he didn't want Kotula to see that side of him.

When the crew talked of where to go on Xinar Lamgun, it was Ven who suggested they go to Nova Trango. A couple of the others said they were getting tired of it. Ven countered that they could get food there and then go elsewhere to party and that brought full agreement.

Ven did not take any Tint after he landed the ship. Instead he went to Karnock's cabin.

"What can I do for you, Zaran?" the captain asked.

"I've been on your crew for a long time now. I'm senior pilot, but do you think there is room to move up?"

Karnock smiled. "This is the first time since you came aboard that you have asked about more. What has changed?"

"Nothing really. I made senior pilot five years ago and I'm wondering if there is more and when it might happen."

The look on Karnock's face told Ven that the old captain was not fooled. He'd always been able to read Ven like a book. Ven was a good liar. He often dealt with Customs in difficult systems because he could talk his way through a stop better than the captain or first mate. But even so, nothing ever got by Karnock.

"Jeshmar and I have been talking about that. He is getting old and never had aims to be captain except on the rare occasions when a first mate needs to take over. He is thinking about retiring and we both think you are the best one in the crew to fill that role. We've been waiting to see if you could move past your Tint addiction. Are you at that point yet?"

Ven was surprised at the information and took a moment to process it and to consider what Karnock had asked. It seemed that two things might be linked. Two things that could make his life complete. He carefully chose his words as he answered. "I think it might be time to work on that."

"I've found that when someone wants something bad enough, they can do anything. We'll keep an eye on you and if you make that final step, it will be time for you to learn how to run a ship."

For a change, Ven went with his shipmates as they walked out the port entrance and the short distance to the Nova Trango Bar. This evening they ended up in Dani's section. After talking with his shipmates, Ven ordered something different.

They all had hardy appetites and it didn't take long to plow through their food. Several of them spontaneously changed the plan by ordering a second round of drinks. It gave Ven a chance to ask Dani about Kotula.

"Marzi had a school event and I couldn't find anyone else so Kotula is watching Taru."

"She sounds like a good friend."

"The best."

"Tell her I asked about her."

"Oh? Okay. I'll tell her."

Ven didn't feel like going back to the table. He noticed that some of the walls were decorated with various images. The centerpiece was a large false color three-dimensional image of the most spectacular portion of the Trango Nebula that the bar was named for. Ven felt drawn in. It was one of the most incredible things he'd ever seen. He vowed to see this nebula in person in the near future. It was images like this in the vids that made him want to be a pilot. It was the vistas, the adventure, the excitement that had driven him to leave his old life. It wasn't the bad memories that haunted him, it was the chance at what might lie ahead. When he found Tint, he'd thought he'd found a way to break his last ties to his past. Instead, the fear of his memories was like a weight dragging him down. It would take as much effort to break that as it had to break from the past. He didn't know if he had that in him a second time, but he intended to find out.

In the middle of the next week, they had to put in at a port for repairs. That put them behind schedule and Karnock took his weekly break where they happened to end up. It was a familiar port and Ven was tempted to go to the Tint den to get knocked out for most of the day, but he resisted that. Instead he just restocked his supply of maintenance doses.

He had to ask himself if he was doing this for a woman or for his career. He thought long and hard about it and came to the realization that he just wanted the next step in life enough to go for it now that an opportunity had come along. He had no idea if he stood a chance with Kotula, but it was not her specifically that had helped him come to this decision, it was the idea of the life that could follow. Whether it was her or another woman he might meet in the future, a Tint-dazed trader would not win over someone who could live the life of a trader captain's wife.

It took three more weeks before the rescheduling from that delay worked out and they ended up on Xinar Lamgun on Karnock's day of rest. Ven didn't bother to check with his shipmates, he just went to the Nova Trango Bar.

Dani saw him as soon as he walked in. "It's been a while," she said when she came over.

"Ship troubles. One of the hyperdrive power feeds went out. Nothing serious, but it put us behind."

"Well, I know who you want to see."

Something in her eyes made Ven think there was a great sadness in her life. Part of him would love to find out what she had lived through and how she coped, but that wasn't something he would ever intrude on. He had enough secrets of his own that he respected other people's secrets.

Dani directed him to a table and then left. A few minutes later Kotula came over.

"I heard you were looking for me and then you didn't come back," she said.

Ven didn't want to talk about business so he just said, "engine issues."

"I hope that doesn't happen again."

"It probably will. It's a hazard of flying older freight runners."

"I'm starting to get the feeling you aren't coming here just for the food."

Ven hadn't given much thought to how obvious he'd been. He didn't have much experience trying to pick up women. He had pointedly avoided most relationships. Fear of the past probably. The personal relationships he had witnessed in his family had left him dreading it. At the same time, it was something he wanted. It was time to take a risk and move beyond what he had been and become the freight runner captain he'd dreamed of.

"No," he finally said, "the food is great, but you are incredible."

"You don't even know me."

"I'll tell you, after serving with traders for so many years, I've seen them at their worst. Especially on my current ship. I've gotten very good at reading people. The first time I came in, you were at the end of what must have been a pretty tough shift and you still were the most friendly, most beautiful woman I've ever met."

"I see. You think you've seen me at my worst? I'm not so sure of that."

"In one way. I think you are talking about another side. We all get crazy sometimes, but I've noticed that when we are tired our true self shows through."

"You don't mean my angry tirades?"

"No. We all have those moments."

"You are making a good point, but you use Tint and I could never get serious with that in the picture."

"What decent woman would. If I can fix that, do I stand a chance?"

"Maybe. Is maybe enough?"

Ven smiled as he replied, "Maybe."

Kotula laughed and walked away. A couple minutes she came back with food. "This is my absolute favorite and it isn't on the menu."

"Can we go somewhere to talk when you get off work?"

"Why not stay here?"

"You have the advantage. Maybe someplace else we'd be on equal footing?"

"You drive a hard bargain."

"Plus, if we go somewhere else, it will feel more like a date."

Kotula smiled at him. "Then you have yourself a date."

Ven's shipmates did not come in at all that evening. Kotula changed and freshened up when her shift ended. While she was in back changing, Dani came over to Ven.

"I want you to know that Kotula is my best friend. She has her goals and you had better respect that." The look in Dani's eyes told Ven that she was not to be messed with.

"You are a good friend. I assure you that I respect her. I'm not a playboy trader. Outside of a couple of personal issues, I am quite stable."

"Keep it that way. We have close ties with the port authorities."

The implied threat did not need to be elaborated on. To Ven, it showed more of Kotula's qualities as a friend.

Ven's knowledge of the port was limited so Kotula chose their destination. It was a drink and snack shop just on the other side of the port entrance. Ven hadn't heard of most of the selections before so he let Kotula pick. They sat and talked for long hours. Ven had expected that they might chat for a hour or two, but they never seemed to run out of topics. Ven finally called it a night when she yawned three times in just a couple of minutes.

"No," she said, "I don't have to be at work until late."

"Be honest, do you remember what I said a couple minutes ago?"

"No. But..."

"I'll be back in a week, baring technical delays."

"Once a week doesn't seem like much."

"I'm a trader. That's all I have. Though I have almost unlimited time by hypercomm."

"I didn't think that worked when you are already in hyperspace."

"It doesn't. But I can record messages and view messages I receive while I'm on duty."

"That is one way to stay in touch."

"I'm afraid it is all I have to offer. I'm a trader through and through. It's all I dreamed of as a child and I gave up everything to make that dream come true. Thanks to you, I've really seen how Tint has been slowing me down. I can be more. If I can clean up, my captain has hinted that I am in line to be first mate. That's the next step to being a captain myself."

"Your plan doesn't seem to include me," she said with a bit of an edge.

"It does include you, I'm just trying to tell you how important my work is to me. Don't you have things that you consider so important they override everything else."

"Yes. I have very specific ideas on where and how I want to raise my children."

"This is the same thing for me. You have become very important to me, but becoming a captain is important, too. It's two parts of what I've always dreamed of. In the vids, the hero gets the ship and the girl."

"You don't have small goals, do you?"

"Nope."

"Why have you let Tint get in the way?"

Ven had been dreading that question. He though long about answering, but his research on ways to get over his addiction had indicated that being honest was the best way, even if it cost. "That is not the only issue. It has been a coping mechanism for dealing with my past."

"Your past?"

"When my parents insisted I go away to a University, I jumped ship and changed my name. It had not been a good situation and I've never talked about it before."

Kotula reached across the table and grasped his hand. "The past is the past and you need to move forward. Put it behind you."

"If you are with me, you deserve to know."

"When you are ready."

Ven smiled. He wasn't truly ready. Not yet.

As he and Kotula communicated via hypercomm messages more and more often, he found he had less and less time and his memories didn't wander down the dark paths of his past nearly as often. He also found that he needed Tint less and less. He slowly worked up the courage to utter names and events that he had sworn he would leave buried forever. If he expected Kotula to live with him and his ghosts, she needed to know what they were.

It took him two months to build that courage. In part he wanted to be free of Tint. When he had managed to stay clear of Tint for a week, he took Kotula to the same little shop where they had gone that first evening, and most of the subsequent evenings on Xinar Lamgun.

He told the story backwards. He started with the easy part, his troubled career and his battle with depression before he'd found Tint to use as a crutch against those old mental wounds.

"I took my new name from a vid character and my best friend. Zaran was really my only friend untouched by my family's craziness. He was the only good part of my life and I thought by using his name that I could keep him with me in a way."

"And you haven't ever contacted him?"

"No, How could I. My family would probably find out and then where would I be."

But he hadn't told her about his family yet. He took a deep breath and started. Both his parents played mind games. It had always been impossible to know what was real and what they had manufactured. They had manipulated him until they day he left for the university. He hated to admit that to get away from them he had used the same tricks they had always used on him, but he also could not hide, as he told the tale, his joy of getting away from them at last. But Kotula still didn't know the dark truth of what he'd been running from, the demons that had driven him to Tint.

He dredged up the memories of his parents and the variety of things they had done to try and control him and about how they had lived their own lives. Both were criminals, or would have been labeled that if they had ever been caught. His father had turned a life of crime into a life of politics and had wanted Ven to follow in his footsteps. Ven had eschewed the life of crime offered as one avenue of training and instead begged for the university.

As he told the tale, going back as far as he could remember, he could not help, at times, getting emotional. Kotula sat there and encouraged him. She listened to his story and supported him as he struggled to get it out. She was horrified at times, but understanding of his situation throughout.

It was everything he had to share. Every ghost in his past, down to the first time he'd witnessed his father execute a lackey for failing in some task or the other. He had no other secrets to share and his past was laid bare for her to judge.

When he was done, Kotula looked at him for a long time. "Ven," she said with something new in her voice, "You have been through a kind of hell. I think I finally might know you. But you need to hear this. You need professional help. If you rely on me and the goal of making captain, everything you build could come crashing down one day."

"Do you think I could tell anyone else what I've just told you? Could anyone help me without knowing that? The only reason I could tell you... is... that I love you."

Kotula smiled and moved around the table to sit on his lap. "I know you do, dear." She had said it to him many times in the past few weeks, but it was the first time he had said it to her. "We'll find a way."

It was a struggle, but with her help and encouragement Ven was finally on the path to being free of Tint. But not just the Tint, but also the demons of his past. He began to build new memories and forge a new inner strength, all thanks to this lovely vision he had encountered by chance. He was determined not to let either her or the chance to captain a ship of his own get away, not again.

He put all his effort into it and in three months Captain Karnock promoted him to first mate. That was a huge accomplishment, but for Ven, that was not even the beginning. He asked her to marry him when he'd been free of Tint for six months, but she would not answer. He asked again each month, but not until he'd been free for a full year did she give him an answer. He was always sure her answer would be yes, but until she actually said it, he had been plagued by doubts. At long last his life was back on track. He was forging ahead and beyond all dreams, he had found someone to share his life with who had not run from his demons.

III
Honed and Polished
4597 GCE

"I'm pregnant," Kotula told her husband, Ven Zaran.

Ven's head swam with the implications, both good and bad. Financially this could not have come at a worse time. He was just at the point where he had enough saved to buy a ship. Not that he had one picked out, but he has saved virtually every credit he could. Now with a child on the way, that plan would have to go out the window.

While he feared the financial side of what this meant, it was the start of a family. He could fix the mistakes of his past and move forward with his new family. It was very exciting and something he'd hoped for. The timing was his only real complaint which offset his excitement at hearing the news.

His wife knew him well and must have considered all his possible reactions. She seemed to be expecting him to react as he had. He realized that she must have some plan but he wasn't prepared for what she said next.

"There really isn't anything you need to do."

"But your expenses are going to go up."

"They are, but it's covered. What do you think I spent all those years working at Nova Trango for? Besides, I have family and lots of resources here on Leywan. You don't have to worry about anything more than you have been. Maybe even less, at least for now."

"No, I have quite a bit saved up. I should use it to get us an apartment."

"Ven, it is more important that we invest in the future. You need to move your career forward. You use your savings for that. I have always wanted to raise our children here on Leywan and I have taken care of everything I'll need."

Ven couldn't argue with anything she said. He had broken from his family and had no intention of his children ever meeting the horrible people he had left behind along with the name he'd been born with. Kotula was the youngest of four and had several nieces and nephews that were closer to her in age than any of her siblings. Her eldest sister was still on Leywan and had followed in their father's footsteps with a local company. The Gaskonya name was well respected and Ven had made a place for himself in their midst in the past three years.

"You haven't said anything in a while, dear," Kotula said to him, "but I know you are really close to being able to get your own ship and that is more important right now. A ship of your own is more important to our future than you thinking you have to pay for anything right now. After you get a ship, then I'll expect a home of my own, but first the ship. You are a born trader. Old Karnock has told me that over and over."

It was true, Karnock had seen something in Ven from the beginning and had given him a chance. It had taken Ven nine years to get serious and work through his problems and then three years ago Karnock had promoted him to first mate, just before Kotula had agreed to marry him. He was working hard at getting certified for his own command and was getting very close. He'd been saving for years and was finally close to being able to afford a ship. But when he found one, it would have to be refitted and registered which would take time and money. By the time he got to that stage, he hoped he would be certified so he could get started immediately.

Ven was not convinced right away that his wife had the finances on her end handled. Starting a family was a scary road to travel. Scarier than owning his own ship. Every time he returned home, Kotula worked on him, repeating much of that first conversation.

"There are times you are stupidly stubborn," she yelled at him five months later. She sat him down at her terminal and showed him her financial statements for an hour and it slowly dawned on him that she was being serious. As much as he had wanted his own ship all these years, she had wanted a family. She and their son would be fine. She even had room for a second child in her plans. He hoped it wouldn't take that long for him to succeed. If he could get his own ship and get established with regular runs, he would finally have the captain's share to split with her. She had finally succeeded in convincing him that she was right.

Her timing was perfect as always. Three weeks later Ven stumbled on an auction. The Customs Corps was selling ships they had seized from convicted criminals. Karnock's ship was a medium freighter and Ven had looked at that size and decided that dropping to the light freighter arena would improve his chances of making good money. There on the auction block was an older light freighter. It wasn't too much smaller than Karnock's *Clarion Spectre*, but it was a light freighter class. Ships of that class were supposed to be maneuverable and able to touch down in all those out of the way places that he wanted to service.

Ven was cautious. Customs didn't evaluate or maintain the ships they seized. Many of them were damaged or in need of service after years of abuse or neglect. This ship looked like it had seen better days, but something about it seemed right so he put in a bid. At the end of the day, his bid turned out to be the highest and he won the ship. He had expected some competition and had left room to increases his bid, but it hadn't been necessary.

Since he was a certified pilot, he was allowed to fly the ship from the impound dock to the service dock. That was an experience he would never forget. Customs had been in possession of the ship for nearly eight years while the case had languished and several systems had deteriorated. They failed during the flight and he barely managed to land the old girl safely. He would need a good engineer to work on it and he'd need a good name for it. He would need to see about a repair dock first. They were far less expensive than the cargo dock he ended up in. He really wanted to get the ship to Leywan, but it would never make it that far in its present condition.

Before he did anything else, he hired a cleaning crew. The previous owners had left hastily, without a chance to clear out their belongings and the ship was a mess. Sitting for eight years had made it far worse. Once it had been cleaned up and he could really see what he had, his next task was finding an engineer.

Karnock was very understanding. When he heard that Ven had won a ship at auction, he gave him a week off to get the initial things taken care of. But only one week. He was still needed on the *Clarion Spectre* as first mate and he still had a ways to go for certification. It was not really enough time, but he made the best of it.

He immediately advertised for an engineer, but the first few people to respond weren't the type of person he was looking for. He knew he couldn't expect to be too picky, not being a new captain just reaching certification, but he also didn't have to scrape the bottom of the barrel. While he waited he took care of what repairs he could make himself. A part of his apprenticeship had been to learn the basics of repair, but it was not as easy on a near derelict ship such as this. He did manage to get several system up and running, enough that he could transfer the ship to decent repair dock.

His week was almost up when an engineer with good qualifications answered his posting. His name was Berglund and was looking for a change from the heavy freighters he'd been serving on. He wanted a more hands on situation on a smaller ship. It turned out he also wanted the increased travel a smaller ship offered. Ven quickly checked his references and after getting Karnock's advice, hired him.

With only a couple days left, it was a whirlwind tour of the ship to show him the known issues. Berglund seemed confident that he could get the ship in shape in a decent amount of time and within the budget that Ven outlined. His week off over, Ven had no choice but to rejoin his ship and leave his new ship in the hands of his new engineer.

He had an anxious week with too few communications with his new engineer for his liking. At the same time, he also had a chance to do some research on the ship's history and found out it had been somewhat famous in its day. Four hundred years ago it had traversed the hyperspace lanes as the *Star of Argent* and he was able to get schematics of the markings and was able to confirm its transponder code had not changed. He read up on her original owner and was impressed. The ship had come to him with a name, but since he was in the same line of work as her original owner, he decided to give the ship a fresh start with her original name.

The few reports he had received from Berglund were not encouraging. The ship would need some major work to go back into cargo service. With the bargain Ven had gotten on the ship in the first place, he could afford what Berglund was talking about, but he wanted to be sure. He didn't have inexhaustible resources. He had to be careful. Karnock had warned that as a new, untried captain, it would take a while to build up business to a point where money was coming in. Having as large a reserve as possible up front would increase his chance of success. On the other hand, he had to have a ship that actually worked and was reliable so he could build a business and gain a good reputation.

But Ven needn't have worried. He had struck gold with hiring Berglund. The man was a genius. When Ven explained the budget problem to him, Berglund immediately turned around and had an alternate plan that would cost about half as much and still put the ship in good flying shape. Ven went away for another week and when he came back, most of the systems were up and running. Before too long, the ship would be ready for her first voyage.

One thing Ven didn't hesitate to spend money on was the ship's external appearance. After Berglund had the hull repaired and ready, he had the ship repainted to match its original appearance, right down to the markings. It made all the difference. Although it looked a bit old fashioned, it now looked well maintained. A big plus for prospective clients.

Everything came together too quickly for Ven to keep up with it mentally. He passed his certification one week, they transferred the newly renamed *Star of Argent* to the Leywan repair docks the next, and his son was born two weeks later as he was in the midst of hiring his first crew.

He was still serving as Karnock's first mate, but with an end in sight to the repairs and his first cargo scheduled, he had given his notice. Karnock was completely understanding, even when two others in his crew decided to join Ven in his new venture. Karnock wished them all luck. Ven figured Karnock would hire a few more misfits and just go on as he had. That was just what the old captain did. Ven was on his way to be one of his success stories and he seemed to be doing everything he could to help make it happen.

Karnock gave Ven a couple weeks off when his son was born. Being able to be there made Ven about the happiest person around. He was pleased that he had managed to convince Kotula to name their son Chupardeth, after a vid character that Ven had admired. He realized later that one of her great-grandfathers had the same name, so it really wasn't much of a victory on his part. Still, that meant the name carried significance for both of them. It took them less than a week for them to shorten it to Chup.

Being on Leywan for an extended time could have been a vacation, but for Ven it was busy. Not only did he spend time with his wife and son, but with his wife's family. Having a horrible family that he had discarded years ago, he had issues dealing with her very normal seeming family. He had once thought families like that were a fiction of the vids, but Kotula's family practically walked right out of one. They all accepted him warmly and made him feel the love of family he had been deprived of in his own life. He had found his own version of it in the camaraderie of a ship's crew. It had taken him years to get used to the idea, but now that he owned his own ship and could call himself captain, it was very much what he wanted.

The time also gave him the chance fill out the crew himself. He found an able first mate and three good pilots and three good navigators, the requirement for a ship of that size. It technically fit in the mid-sized freighter category, but it carried a light cargo. He didn't mind. The more the merrier as far as he was concerned.

As the new crew got settled in and used to the ship, Berglund got the last of the systems up and running. He made them all spend some time repairing the interior of the ship. They replaced missing panels and made the cockpit look professional, a far cry from the near demolished state it had been in when Ven took possession of the ship.

Ven joined Karnock for one last run as first mate, ending a thirteen year tour with him.

As they were on approach, Karnock called Ven into his cabin.

"It has been a pleasure having you on my crew, son," Karnock told him as he poured them drinks.

"If you hadn't given me a chance and believed in me, I don't know where I would be."

"You make the twenty-seventh man who has served under me to go on to his own command. I knew you could do it."

"I haven't even gotten started yet."

"But you are starting, which is all the success I need. I hope you have a long career ahead of you, Ven. You came into my cabin just now as one of my crew. Well, that time is at an end. You leave here as a fellow captain." He handed Ven a chit.

"What's this?"

"A bonus for all the years of loyal service you've given me."

"I can't take that."

"Yes you can. You are one of a few that I've helped. Far too few. And you are the first in a long time. I'd forgotten what it felt like to have a protégée leap out on their own. It's a good feeling. Now, Captain Zaran, a toast to you and your new command."

It was strange leaving *Clarion Spectre* that way. He disembarked as soon as they had landed and it just didn't feel like home any more. The other two who were coming with him would be along later.

He had two days on Leywan before he departed with his first cargo. Things had been far too busy in the last weeks and Ven had not gotten to do one thing he really wanted to before his departure. He cleared his schedule and convinced his wife to find time in her schedule. Chup was just over three weeks old, but Kotula carried him as Ven gave them a tour of *Star of Argent*. She was fully crewed and ready to receive her first cargo and depart in just over twenty-four hours.

"It's a beautiful ship," Kotula said as she carried Chup while Ven gave her a tour. "Your cabin seems a bit stark. You should let me fix it up."

"I'll be back in a couple of months and I'll give you a week while Berglund does a maintenance check."

"Sounds like a plan. I'll have something in mind by then."

"You take care of this little guy," Ven told her as she got ready to leave.

"I will. You take care of you."

"I will. I'll be back before you know it."

"I'll play the part of a trader captain's wife and wait for you to come back."

Ven frowned. That was the only down point. He so wanted to keep her aboard, but between Custom's regulations and Kotula's insistence that she raise their son planetside, there was nothing he could do. Not yet. That would be an upgrade he would look into. This old ship had plenty of room, it just had to be configured properly and Kotula had to be convinced.

The next day Kotula didn't come to the ship to see him off. She didn't want to be a distraction as he prepared for such a momentous day. He ran through his first departure check and clearance as a certified captain and reveled in the realization of his dreams. The words "I'm pregnant" had turned out to be turning point in his life that he would never forget. He was no longer just a pilot or mate, he was the captain of his own ship and a father.

In the past three years he had commanded many departures for old Karnock, but it was totally different doing as a captain in his own right. The childhood dream that had seemed so distant not even five years ago, was now a reality.

No longer was it a dream for him to command his own ship. He stood in the cockpit and commanded his navigator to call for clearance. Once received, he ordered his pilot to takeoff. The workings of his crew were still something he would have to tweak, but in theory, he now had people he could delegate and expect to have things done.

The icing on the cake was the ship. A derelict from an auction that no one else seemed to want had turned out to be a semi-famous ship, a veteran of countless hyperspace voyages, planetary landings and her fair share of adventures. Luck was with him and he would ride it as long as it lasted.

Test of Command
4607 GCE

"Hey Stormy. You got any extra belts over there?"

"No. You might ask Bellek. And you'd better hurry. We need to be at the ship in ten minutes."

"This won't take long."

"It better not." Stormy continued to check over his armor. This was a big day for him. He was getting his first command. It really didn't matter to him that it was only for this one patrol, it was still a command. He wanted his armor to be perfect. He finished cleaning the body plates with his rank on the shoulders and put them on. The armor barely fit on his large frame even though it was the largest size that the Customs Corps had. The helmet was the last piece. He gave it a last wipe before he put it over his head. The rest of the crew would have to wear their helmets for the next sixteen hours. Since Stormy was the commander, at least on this patrol, he could take his off after he boarded a ship if he felt there was no danger. That would be a welcome change. The helmets weren't uncomfortable, but after wearing them for sixteen hours, they did start to feel confining.

Jemlon came back in the room. "Thanks," he said, "Bellek had one."

"Good. Now hurry up. I can't wait for you."

"I'll be right there."

Jemlon was a good man. Stormy had worked with him for the last couple of years. They had both transferred from the same ship a few months ago. Jemlon specialized in scanner operation which was a vital role on a Customs patrol ship. Stormy's own specialization was in flight operations which included weaponry. Both of them had served on the large class patrol ships for several years without being noticed. Stormy's command potential had been noticed right away after the transfer when his commander had been wounded and, as the senior Customs Guard aboard, he'd taken command. Now as up for a command of his own and was being given a test age his abilities.

Their quarters were a short distance from the ship which is convenient if there was an emergency. Not only did they ave to randomly inspect incoming ships for contraband, they also had to answer distress calls and just about any other kind of emergency that came up.

He left the closet he called his bunk and walked to the ship. He got there with two minutes to spare. Jekky was already seated in the pilot's seat starting her pre-launch check. She was the new one on the crew. The outcome of Stormy's promotion would determine if she was just filling in while he played commander or if she might become a regular member of the crew. Stormy had met her several times when they were off-duty. She had a cute round face and coffee colored skin. All customs guards had to keep their hair cut according to regulations to fit under the helmet. Jekky had occasionally griped about that. Before she joined the corps, her hair had been down to her waist and she missed it.

The other three seats were empty for a minute before Kirch'kal and Ullan arrived. They took their positions. Kirch'kal was about as blond as anyone Stormy had ever seen. The poor guy couldn't even get his skin to tan to give him some color. Ullan was about the plainest woman Stormy had ever met. She had medium brown hair, slightly tanned skin, light brown eyes, and features which weren't quite pretty or cute, but also weren't ugly or disagreeable. The one thing she did have was a beautiful voice, a quality that came through even over their helmet comms.

They all readied their stations and waited for Jemlon to show up. The chron had counted four minutes past the time before he arrived. It was hard to glare through the face of the helmet, but Stormy made a good try. "It's good of you to join us. Now that we're all here, give me the ship's status."

"Flight controls and weapons are green," Jekky said.

"Propulsion and life support green," Kirch'kal said.

"Defensive systems and communications are green," Ullan said.

They all waited as Jemlon rushed through his scanner checks. "Anytime now, Jemlon," Stormy said with a noticeable level of irritation.

"Scanners and docking systems check out... are green," he finally said. The chron showed six past the hour.

"Disengage docking systems, put us in launch position and inform system control that we are ready to launch."

Three people quickly carried out his orders. As the ship released its hold on the dock, the thrusters moved it into position. The comm system buzzed as Ullan negotiated with the system controller to launch and begin the sixteen-hour patrol. She transferred the beacon code to the pilot's station so Jekky could lock it in. Stormy enjoyed seeing a well-trained crew carry out their duties. If he passed this test of his command abilities, he might get a ship of his own. That was somewhat relative since it would be a command assignment and which ship he took out could change with nearly any patrol.

The signal came through indicating their clearance to launch. Jekky waited for Stormy to give the order. "Take us out, Jekky."

"Aye, Sir." She deftly followed the beacon out of the maze that was the Customs Corps section of the port.

Stormy checked the pad with his orders again. It was just a standard patrol, but he wanted to make sure he followed his orders to the letter. It wouldn't look good if he slacked off on the regulations on this patrol.

"Where are we heading?" Jekky asked as they neared the port boundary.

"We're patrolling sector fifty-seven today."

"Sector fifty-seven it is." As soon as they passed the boundary, Jekky took the ship into a steep climb that angled back over the port.

"Careful where you're going," Jemlon told her. "There are other ships up here."

"I've never hit anything. Just stop your whining."

"Both of you just concentrate on your jobs. Your little maneuver made us back the time that Jemlon cost us, but be more careful in the future. We should be on time now to relieve Chansor so you don't need to rush." Inwardly Stormy had to smile. He'd heard Jekky was a good pilot and that maneuver not only proved it, but also showed that she could think on her own. It was just the sort of thing he might have done.

Names were an interesting thing in the Corps. There were times when you didn't know the real names of some of the people you served with. A lot of his fellow guards had no idea Stormy's full name was Stormus Rolfel. As commander, even for this one mission, Stormy had access to his crew's personnel files and had checked all their names. Kirch'kal went my his family name, as did Ullan. Jekky was short for Jekkilvara Kuballen. Jemlon just used his given name. His family name was very long and Stormy had no idea how to pronounce it.

It took just over an hour to reach the patrol area and everything went smoothly. Ullan hailed the ship they were relieving. They sent back the standard acknowledgment and a request for an open line.

"Go ahead," Stormy told her.

Chansor's voice came over the comm. "Sergeant Rolfel, I hope your patrol is a success."

Chansor was a stickler for protocol so Stormy followed the book. "Thank you, Command Sergeant Chansor. I hope to have many more."

"You will if the review board likes what it sees. Good luck."

"Thank you. Have a safe flight back." Stormy didn't like these formal conversations. Most of the command sergeants kept it casual.

As part of the change over from one ship to the next, they transmitted a log of the last ten days events in the area. Stormy took a few minutes to look over the last few items and saw that Chansor's patrol had been quiet. Nothing out of the ordinary or even exciting and only seven ships had come through.

Sector fifty-seven was a little used hyperspace entry point into the system. A large nebulae blocked most traffic. That made this sector a tempting entry point for smugglers and pirates. A ship on constant patrol kept those incursions to a minimum. What little traffic there was consisted of flights from neighboring systems or traders trying to avoid the congestion that some of the entry points had.

They had been on patrol for ninety-seven minutes when Jemlon detected the first ship on the scanners. "It's a Bismina

Class Seven freighter, registered as *Harmilon's Haven* to Jissik Vattila of Arseris. Scans show it to be carrying a full cargo."

"Hail them and have them stop for inspection," Stormy ordered. In remote sectors like this one, the Customs Corps wanted every ship stopped for an inspection. Ultimately it was up to the patrol commander to decide which ships were inspected and how thoroughly. Stormy figured that this ship would just get a casual inspection; a look at the logs and a visual check of the cargo and that sort of thing. If he felt it was necessary, he was entitled to search the entire ship, open every cargo crate and individually match each item of cargo to the manifest. Stormy hated doing that and thought it only should be done if he suspected something was up. Usually it turned out to be nothing and the only thing the patrol commander had succeeded in doing was annoying the trader.

The freighter slowed and Jekky pulled the patrol ship alongside and activated the docking tunnel. "We're locked on," she said once the procedure was completed.

"Jekky and Kirch'kal come with me," Stormy ordered. They all made sure their helmets were on properly and activated the seals. There had been some incidents of stopped ships that had pulled away and killed the guards in the docking tunnel. They had made sure that the armored uniforms were tough enough to protect for a few minutes of vacuum exposure. Even though some other ships had tried it in recent years, no one had been hurt in quite some time. But that was one of the reasons they couldn't remove their helmets. It was very annoying, but they were all accustomed to it. Stormy could remove his helmet while on board a ship, but during transit the regulations forbid it, and with good reason.

They stepped out of the airlock into the freighter. It was dimly lit. Stormy checked the air analyzer on his forearm guard. It checked out as normal human quality and pressure so he took off his helmet. He got a whiff of the air and wanted to put his helmet back on. Some of these ships could really stink. In the years he'd been boarding ships, he'd never had his helmet off before and he now understood some of the weird looks he'd seen on the commander's face. The airlock had opened onto the main central corridor and there was no sign of anyone. "Hello. Anyone here?" Stormy called when he'd recovered from the initial shock of the smell.

"Just hang tight," a male voice called from the direction of the cockpit.

"I'm afraid we can't do that. We need to see your cargo manifests now."

"I'm trying to find them."

"If you don't produce them now, we will have to search your cargo."

The man growled then sighed. "Well, I can't find it so I guess you'll have too."

Stormy turned to say something to Jekky and Kirch'kal and saw Kirch'kal reach for his pistol so he dodged to the side and an energy bolt passed where his head had been. Kirch'kal and Jekky were firing back by the time Stormy had turned around and drawn his pistol. There were four men at the end of the corridor and one fell as Stormy started firing back. His lack of a helmet and the red shoulder pads that marked him as the commander were making him a target. He fired back and caught one man in the chest.

Jekky caught the third man in the leg. A chill ran up Stormy's spine and he turned away from the last standing man at one end of the corridor to see three more at the other end. "Behind you," he yelled at the others. Jekky didn't miss a beat. She turned and fired at the new targets.

The last one at the other end was being difficult to hit. Kirch'kal made sure his back was covered and fired at any movement leaving the new three to Stormy and Jekky. Stormy hit one right in the shoulder severing that arm. Jekky caught one in the knee when he didn't pull his leg behind cover. It was quiet for a minute. They were waiting for an opening. Jekky got the first shot and blew the pistol right out of the man's hand. There was no guarantee that he didn't have access to another weapon so they held their ground waiting.

Kirch'kal had the next opportunity and repeated Jekky's marksmanship by shooting the pistol out of his target's hand. But he was certain that there were no other weapons so he edged to the door. "Come out with your hands where I can see them," he called when he was close to the door.

"Hang on a sec."

"No. Now!"

The man responded by slowly sliding around. Kirch'kal was ready for any sort of weapon, but he didn't see any. "Don't worry, I'm not armed." He held out his hands to be bound. "Can I say something to my crewman down there? It'll stop this."

"Go ahead."

"Akbret. You might as well give up. They've got the rest of us."

Stormy and Jekky watched as Akbret came out nursing his injured hand. Stormy motioned for her to bind him. As soon as they both were bound, Stormy pulled his scanner out of his belt and ran a weapons, drug, explosive, and comm scan of the two prisoners. He removed several items that were on the Corps list to confiscate from prisoners. That done, he contacted the ship to have them call for backup. It would take a while and some of the injured might die, but the Corps general orders stated that if someone was shot resisting a lawful search or seizure or arrest that they could just wait for the backup ship to arrive. Innocent bystanders, on the other hand, were to be given as much care and help as possible.

Stormy stood guard over the prisoners while the other two searched the other crewmen and bound the live ones and removed their weapons and comms. They searched the crew area first and didn't find anyone else. They stood guard at the cargo bay door and waited for backup.

The backup ship was quicker than Stormy expected. It only took twenty minutes for it to arrive. When the backup ship's commander came aboard, Stormy felt a great sense of relief.

"I see you have the situation well in hand," the backup commander said.

"I hope so."

"I just need to get your report of the events and a copy of your comm logs."

"Of course." It only took Stormy ten minutes to fill out the report. He handed it and the comm log card over and he and his people left. The wounded freighter crewmen were being cared for and the dead were being removed for identification. The backup crew would search the ship and fly it or tow it back to the base. Stormy would receive a copy of their report when they were done. For now, he and his crew had to get back to their patrol. No other ships had come through so they hadn't gotten behind.

The backup ship towed the freighter off fifteen minutes later as a ship came out of hyperspace into the sector. Knowing that the eyes would really be on him now, he ordered this ship to slow for inspection. It was a larger ship running a skeleton crew and carrying very little cargo. Stormy took Ullan and Jemlon with him.

The ship was very old and the airlock seemed in need of repair. Stormy was by no means certain what he would find on the other side of the door. The fire fight had made him more nervous that he would openly admit.

When the airlock opened, he was greeted by four Halarivans. Their short stature was often to their detriment in dealing with other species, but Stormy always treated everyone equal.

"Welcome aboard kind officer," one of them said in a deep airy voice that was in sharp contrast to his small stature.

"Thank you," Stormy responded. "I need to see your cargo manifest."

"This way, if you please. We keep such things in the cargo office."

Stormy followed. He noticed that this must be an old human ship since it was too big in proportion to the Halarivans. A number of modifications were evident where things had been lowered or shortened or a ladder added.

The cargo office was furnished to their size so Stormy couldn't sit at the desk and had to sit on it. He looked over the offered pad and knowingly checked it for any sign of tampering of falseness. With pad in hand he asked to verify the cargo. The one who appeared to be the captain took him into the large cargo bay which was virtually empty except for ten pallets resting against the forward wall. He quickly scanned the crates and checked their numbers with the manifest. He was satisfied and hoped his superiors would be too. "Everything looks in order. You may continue on your way."

"Thank you good sir. If there is anything we can do for you, do let us know."

"I will." Stormy proceeded back to the airlock with the Halarivans following. It was a relief walking down the connecting tunnel to the patrol ship. "Something about those guys was really creepy," he commented to the others.

"I know," Jemlon said. "They were way too polite"

"It's not that. It was just the way they kept staring at us."

"It's just how they are," Ullan said. "They are always staring at something. Usually it's each other."

"Really? How do you know so much about them?" Stormy asked her.

"There were a lot of Halarivans on the station where I grew up. There were always staring and being nice and polite. Most of us kids were used to it, but it freaked a lot of the adults. They just didn't like it."

"This is probably the same thing," Stormy said. When they got back aboard, Jemlon disengaged the docking tunnel and they resumed their stations. Stormy wrote up his report while they waited for another ship. Each one had a different way to spend the long hours waiting. Jemlon gathered statistics on the frequency of arrivals and departures. The scanners could pick up ships from several beacons away in every direction. Ullan chatted with other bored comm operators at neighboring beacons. Kirch'kal spent his time making sure the ship was running properly. He was really the only one who was always busy. Some of these patrol ships were old. With each system having at least a hundred and twenty of them that meant millions of ships with some working better than others. This ship seemed to be in good shape, but Kirch'kal was intently monitoring it to keep it that way.

Jekky was doing the same thing to pass time that Stormy had always done. She was flying simulations to keep her skills sharp. The command station didn't have that option so Stormy spent his time trying to find some way to spend his time constructively. He made sure all his reports were caught up and reviewed the logs of the previous days. He found that this beacon had been busier than normal lately.

"Finally," Jemlon said. "We have a personal cruiser that just came in." The ship's chron showed that just over two hours had passed since they had come back aboard from the last ship.

"Hail them and have them slow for boarding." Stormy started a report and listed all the ship's particulars and who the owner and captain were registered as.

Stormy didn't mind these slow sectors, but it was only minutes of activity breaking the hours of boredom. There was only so much you could do to keep busy before even that became boring. As the cruiser slowed, Stormy let his mind wander. He'd been hoping for a command of his own for years.

This was what he had been aiming for when he joined up. Some of his commanders had given him a turn at the command seat in the last couple of years, but no promotion. He'd been on the larger ships for a while, but had requested a transfer to the smaller patrol ships for a better chance at promotion. Someday he might have a shot at command of a larger ship. On the larger patrol ship, the crew lived aboard and it was permanently assigned to one captain. Someday maybe Stormy would have his own ship, but for now command of a patrol ship was good enough.

Stormy knew something was up the moment he came out of the airlock. Kirch'kal and Ullan could sense it too. This ship was very opulent but there was something that just wasn't right. This was going to be a long boarding.

"Greetings," a uniformed woman said to them as she came into the room just inside the airlock. "Welcome aboard. I am Captain Dan'ernar. How can I be of assistance?"

Stormy took his helmet off as was treated to a surprised look as Dan'ernar admired his features. He really hated when that happened on the job. "We need to see your manifest including a listing of all personal possessions worth over twenty thousand credits."

"That might be difficult. I don't know that the owner or his guests even have such a list."

"It is required by Confederation law. If you don't have a list, we will have to search the ship."

"That's not acceptable."

"Nevertheless, it is the law."

"Can't we come to an agreement that would avoid a search?"

"I'm afraid not."

"Is there a problem, Captain?" a gracefully aging man asked.

"Customs needs a list of all valuables over twenty thousand credits."

"Oh dear. I didn't know we were required to. I don't believe we have any sort of accurate list on board. It's been so long since we were last stopped by customs that I'm not up on the current regulations."

"If you don't have a list, we are required to search your ship." They were going to be here a while. Well, at least the air smelled good.

"Well, if you must, but I'd prefer if you didn't."

"I'm afraid I don't have a choice."

"Please assist them, Captain. I think you know this ship better than I do."

"Yes, Sir. I'll get you the manifest and an old copy of the valuables list," she said to Stormy.

Stormy wondered how old it might be and when she handed it to him he saw that the date was over fifteen years earlier.

"I think this is the list they made for me when I started."

"You know, if you stick to the more common beacons you probably won't get stopped again for another fifteen years."

"Thanks for the tip."

The manifest indicated that there was a crew of ten and five passengers. The ship was owned by Jasoph d'Harrel Auberken, the retired owner of a large AI manufacturer. AI's were expensive and it wouldn't take selling too many to make a company rich.

The trouble started when Kirch'kal went to search the private rooms of the crew. Stormy was personally seeing to the search of the passenger's possessions. "Commander," Kirch'kal called over the comm.

"What is it?" Stormy asked.

"One of the crewmen refuses to let me search their room. He's armed."

"I'll be right there."

"What was that?" Auberken asked.

"It seems one of your crew doesn't want his quarters searched."

"We'll just see about that." Auberken started to go but Stormy stopped him.

"It would be better if you let me handle it. He's armed."

"Perhaps you're right. I can be a bit hasty. And I no longer have the same bearing that I did when I was younger."

Stormy found Kirch'kal at a standoff with the crewman at the entrance to his quarters. Both held their weapons pointed at the other. The distraction of Stormy's arrival was just the opening Kirch'kal had needed. When the crewman's eyes strayed to Stormy, Kirch'kal fired a single shot. The crewman fell to the deck unconscious.

"Good job, Kirch'kal. Now let's see what he was hiding." Stormy stepped over the collapsed crewman and went into the small room. He pulled out his scanner and swept the room. The initial sweep didn't show anything unusual, but Stormy swept the room again and found something that they would likely have missed if the crewman hadn't made a fuss. He pulled the thin case from behind the bunk and set it on the small desk. It didn't look like it could hold much, but when he finally got it open, Stormy found that it was filled with valuables. His scanner estimated the value at over twelve million credits. Some of the items had tags on them indicating that they were to be delivered to someone. Two of the items had tags indicating that they were to be delivered in this system. There were a number of credit chits. When Stormy read them the total was an astounding eight hundred and forty-five million credits.

Stormy chuckled. This was quite a find and it made him think of his best friend, Jimmed. Where Stormy was aspiring to captain a patrol ship, Jimmed wanted to get into undercover work. Stormy knew that the Customs Corps would have an agent try to deliver these items to catch the buyers and that was just the sort of thing Jimmed would love to do. He was halfway across the galaxy stuck as the pilot of a larger patrol ship. The only way he'd get an undercover assignment was if he was in the just right place at just the right time and if they were in need a pilot.

He called the ship. "Jekky, call for backup. We have a smuggler operating off this ship. Inform them that we have a couple of packages scheduled for delivery here and they might want to follow up on them."

"Right away," was her response.

Stormy closed the case and scanned the room again just to make sure he hadn't missed anything. Kirch'kal had the crewman bound. Since it was a single crewman, they'd take him aboard the patrol ship and let the cruiser get back underway just as soon as they finished the search. It took Ullan over an hour to go through all the valuables that the passengers had with them. They did have the proper papers on all the jewelry on board so the only hassle was finding and cataloging everything. The rest of the crew had nothing to hide and they didn't find any more contraband on the ship.

The crewman was still unconscious when they carried him back to the patrol ship. Stormy fined them for not having a list of valuables, but the fine was a paltry fifty thousand credits compared with the millions in valuables that had been cataloged. "Have a good trip," Stormy told the captain as he was leaving.

"Thank you, Commander," she replied. "You didn't make it too painful."

"Keep a list and stick to the main beacons and you won't have this problem again."

They detached from the cruiser and watched as it proceeded on its way. They held station waiting for the backup ship or another ship coming out of hyperspace. An hour and a half later the backup ship finally arrived to take the prisoner and his cargo back to the base. Stormy checked the chron and saw that their shift was over half over.

Sometimes Stormy wondered why the small patrol ships worked all the out of the way and seldom used beacons. It would make more sense for the small ships to work the more common beacons so there could be several ships and one backup ship. As it was, the bigger ships tended to work the common beacons. The reason given was because they made so many boardings and one ship often could stay on station for weeks. The problem that Stormy saw was a class of ships was missing. They had the small patrol ships and the large patrol ship, but no medium. They needed one that was big enough for a permanent crew and to take care of prisoners and small enough so that they didn't waste manpower. But no one would listen to a mere sergeant. They only listened to officers and only the larger ships had officers. Stormy didn't see himself being an officer until he had gray hair.

They had a boring two hours after the backup ship picked up the prisoner before another ship showed up. Before they had boarded that ship a second one appeared. This was the main reason why they didn't board every ship at the busy beacons. They had the second ship hold and docked with the first one.

It was an old freighter that had seen better days. The hull was scarred and their docking tube didn't seal properly. They wasted precious air finding that out. They energized the energy seals on their armor and went across in a vacuum. Stormy had no idea why the docking tube didn't have the same energy seals. Jekky was always nervous being in a vacuum. She much preferred to be behind the controls in the pilot seat.

"Don't worry, these suits are safe," Jemlon told her.

"Coming from you that isn't very comforting."

"They are safe, Jekky," Stormy confirmed. "Just try not to think about it."

They couldn't get the airlock hatch to open. "The captain says that sometimes it sticks. He'll try to open it from inside." Suddenly the hatch opened and the contents of the airlock spilled out. The airlock had failed. It was the first time Stormy or the others had seen something like that. Stormy looked back at the patrol ship and saw a sickening patch of red splattered on the hatch. If their boots weren't magnetic, they would have flown too. The docking tube showed signs of damage.

"Ullan, you'd better call for backup. We have a problem." So much for a good report. It wasn't good to have accidents. Not involving Customs Corps property. They wouldn't like that someone had gotten themselves splattered all over the side of the ship. The scanners didn't show anyone else on board the old freighter so Stormy left it for the backup ship to take care of. But according to regulations the patrol ship couldn't move until the backup ship arrived. That meant that they would have to float over to the other ship and hope that they weren't getting into lots of trouble.

The freighter was drifting and had left a gap that Stormy, Jekky, and Jemlon went through. They jumped from the tube and drifted over to the second ship which had pulled close after Ullan had explained the situation to them. Jekky was very scared and was trying to pretend not to be.

This airlock worked at their request and they entered the second ship. The captain met them. "Welcome aboard. Do you need anything before we start?" She asked.

"I don't think so," Stormy said after taking his helmet off. "Thank you for asking though."

"Here are our manifest and logs," the captain said handing him a pad. Stormy took it from her and checked it. "Everything should be in order. We were stopped a few days ago at Jendar Seventeen."

"It looks in order. We need to see your cargo though."

"Certainly. Right this way." She led them to the lift and took them down to the cargo hold. It was a large capacity ship and it was fully loaded. "If there's anything I can help you with just let me know."

"I will if there is," Stormy replied. They spent thirty minutes checking the cargo. The backup ship still hadn't arrived when they were finished.

"What do we do now?" Jekky demanded. "I'm not going back out there."

The captain overheard them. "We aren't on a tight schedule. We can wait here for your other ship to show up."

"We shouldn't impose on you like that."

"It's no imposition, sergeant. I have some time. None of my cargos are due until tomorrow anyway. Please, come to our common room and relax for a few minutes."

Jekky had taken off her helmet and the look she gave Stormy with her dark eyes seemed to remind them that he hadn't gotten his promotion yet and they were still equal rank and he'd better do it or she'd make trouble.

"I guess we can stay. It is a large cargo after all."

"That's the spirit," the captain said. She lead them to the common room and had her steward get them some refreshments. Jemlon took off his helmet as he sat down. "It's a shame you guys have to wear those helmets all the time. It's so much nicer to see your faces."

"Nicer, but not safer," Stormy commented. "They're not only armored, they provide vacuum protection as well."

"That's an ingenious idea. Someone must have made a fortune."

"The design is old and well tested."

"Your commander isn't much of a conversationalist."

"He's like that when he's on duty," Jemlon told her. "Problem is he isn't much better off duty."

Stormy glared at him. "Oh stop it, Stormy," Jekky said. "You know you are. You're always business. The only time we ever see you loosen up is when that friend of yours comes to visit. You never even give us ladies in the Corps a chance."

"I never know when I might serve over or under one of you ladies in the Corps in the future. I don't want things like that causing problems. The only women I associate with are civilians."

"You ought to think about what is important to you, your career or your life." The captain looked at him sternly. Her fading hair indicated that she might be fifty to sixty, but it was hard to tell. "If your life is important to you, you should give every woman an equal chance. Unless you like men?"

The frown on Stormy's face answered her question.

"Well, you never know. It's good to hear though. It gives us men loving women something to chase after."

"No one is chasing after Stormy right now," Jekky said. "But a few have thought about it and might do something if he'd just show a little interest."

"Like you?" Jemlon teased.

"No! I have Harkel. You know that, so does Stormy."

Their banter was interrupted by the comm. "What is it?" Stormy answered.

"The backup ship finally arrived. They say that the cleanup might take an hour or more," Ullan told him.

"Are they going to pick us up?"

"They said they were cleaning up and if the captain isn't in a hurry they'd like you to remain there until they have finished."

The captain nodded that it was okay. "Yes, we can do that," Stormy replied.

Typical of some backup ships, the cleanup took almost twice as long as they'd said. It was just over two hours after the backup ship arrived by the time the patrol ship was able to dock and Stormy and his crew were able to get back to work.

"Thank you for your hospitality, captain," Stormy said as he entered the airlock.

"You're quite welcome. I hope the rest of your patrol goes well."

"I do too." The airlock cycled and they passed through the docking tunnel to the patrol ship.

"Welcome back commander," Ullan said.

"Thanks. There's nothing quite like being bored while boarding a ship." With their helmets on Stormy couldn't see their expressions, but he could sense the strange looks anyway. He just ignored it and sat in the command seat. "I think we all have some reports to work on. Resume stations and continue monitoring for incoming ships."

This time they didn't have long to wait. Within fifteen minutes a sleek new freighter arrived. Stormy took Kirch'kal and Ullan with him when he boarded it. The captain greeted them with the proper paperwork in hand and they were out of there in under half an hour. Stormy hadn't gotten his other two boarding reports finished so he finished those first. He was just about to start on the report for the last boarding when the next ship came into range.

"It's not answering our hails, commander. There's no ID signal either." This was very uncommon and Ullan seemed disturbed by it.

"Don't worry about it, just pull alongside and prepare for boarding. Kirch'kal and Jemlon, check your weapons. We might need them."

They pulled alongside and could see that the ship was heavily damaged. It had been attacked and after seeing the damage Stormy was amazed that it was flying. The scanners showed life on board, but the ship was barely functioning. The airlock appeared undamaged so they docked.

It took several tries to activate the airlock. They finally had to override it and just open it as a hatch. They found out why as soon as the outer hatch opened. The inner hatch had been blow in. There was some thin smoke in the air creating a haze over everything. Stormy motioned Kirch'kal to head aft and he and Jemlon went forward.

They checked every cabin and found two dead in one. The hand scanner showed life signs in the area of the cockpit. They found another one dead in a side corridor. Unlike earlier boardings, Stormy had left his helmet on. He wasn't going to take that risk here. It was a good thing because the door to the cockpit was just discernible through the haze when someone fired at them. They ducked into a doorway the offered some shelter.

Stormy activated the loudspeaker on his helmet. "We're Customs Corps Guards. Put down your weapons."

"How do we know you are?" A voice called.

"The uniform is a dead giveaway. We aren't asking you to disarm, just put your weapons away."

"How many of you are there?"

"Two here and one checking aft." Stormy waited for some sign that it was safe to move.

"Okay. Our weapons are down."

Stormy and Jemlon cautiously approached the cockpit. They saw that the safety hatch had been cut through. "Who's in charge here?" Stormy asked.

"I am," said the man who had spoken to the before. "I'm First Mate Li'egis Zi. Our captain is dead."

"What happened here?" Stormy was pretty sure he knew the answer.

"Pirates. They attacked us and held us in a tractor beam. They killed the captain after they'd taken our cargo. Then they shot at us again before they left. The main engines are damaged and most of the systems are dead."

"Where were you headed and where were you when you were attacked?"

"We were headed here. Our navigator had just finalized the course when we were attacked. We didn't even have a chance to jump to hyperspace. We had stopped in the Rabbada sector to come around this nebula. We never even saw them on the scanners."

"We'll get you taken care of. We'll get a ship here to tow you into the port. Are there any injuries that need to be taken care of right away?"

"No. They killed everyone they shot."

"What were you carrying?"

"It was a load of refined Kwandish. They must have known we were carrying it."

Stormy was surprised. Kwandish was very rare and expensive. Li'egis offered him the manifest. Stormy stared at the amount. It was definitely a cargo worth a lot of money. The pirates might just reveal themselves if they tried to unload it somewhere. Unless they already had a buyer.

"The Customs Corps will do what it can to apprehend and punish the pirates."

"A lot of good that does our poor captain."

The backup ship took just over an hour to arrive. By the time everything was taken care of and Stormy and his guards were back on the patrol ship, there was barely an hour left in their patrol. Stormy just knew that a few minutes before their relief arrived that a ship would come in and he was right. It was a small personal cruiser and when Stormy checked his chron when he keyed the airlock it was two minutes before their patrol was to end. He had this feeling that it wasn't going to be a simple check and he was right.

The owner had no records or papers of any kind. Not even the registration. The ship's registration had come up with the owner's name and that matched the identification the owner had, but none of the rest. It was a reporting nightmare. He had to check everything and verify everything independently. The ship's registration signal could be tampered with so the Corps insisted that everything be independently verified.

Their relief arrived just minutes after Stormy found himself in the middle of a mess. He had to finish the boarding before he and his crew were off, but the relief ship took over immediately waiting for any additional incoming ships.

After almost an hour sorting out the owners nonexistent records, Stormy, Jekky, and Ullan finally left. Stormy signaled the relief ship that they were done and were heading back to base. They transferred the logs of the last ten days and left.

By the time they reached the port, docked and shutdown the ship and turned it over to the prep crew, they had been on duty for about twenty-one hours. They had a day off before they had to go out again. The ship would probably be back out in just a few hours depending on what kind of repairs it needed and how fast it was refueled and how many other ships were ready to go. At least the ship had made it through. Some of the others had been feeding him horror stories of the things that could go wrong including destroying the ship. The Corps didn't like that too much and a prospective command sergeant usually didn't get their promotion if they were at fault for something like that.

"Well, you survived your first command. How does it feel?" Jemlon asked him as they were going back to their quarters.

"It was a nice change. I'm just worried about the promotion."

"I'm sure you'll get it. You're a good commander."

The road to promotion was a crazy thing. It all depended on getting noticed by your superiors. That was hard to do on the larger patrol ships, especially if you weren't in the lead position for your field. Stormy had been just one of the pilots and Jemlon just one of the scanner specialists. They had transferred together, even though Jemlon could be very annoying at times, because they both thought that they would stand a better chance on a small ship.

The team they had been assigned to was under the command of Yaskis Meliaska, a forty-something command sergeant who was content with that. He'd been injured in a firefight a week earlier and Stormy had stepped up and captured the ruffians who had started it. They'd been on two patrols since with a temporary commander before Stormy had been assigned to command this patrol and Jekky as pilot. If things went well, Stormy might even get command of this team. He hoped so. They were good people. He'd met Jekky right after he transferred to the unit and they become friends. She was probably the best pilot around and if Stormy ever got the chance to command a larger ship he'd ask for her as his lead pilot. That would be years down the road.

Stormy didn't know how long he'd have to wait to find out how he did on this patrol. Sometimes they really liked to make people wait. But with Meliaska out for who knew how long, they might rush things and let him know sooner if he was going to get it. Stormy knew he hadn't done a bad job, but he also wasn't sure if he did well enough to get the promotion. He had originally just been aiming for the lead pilot position on a large patrol ship. Several years as pilot on the small patrol ships would have given him a good shot at that. If he didn't get this promotion, that would still work.

As the commander on this patrol, Stormy had to file all his reports and logs before he could get any sleep. He'd kept that in mind and only had to finish his final patrol summary report since he'd already done all the boarding reports right after they'd done them. The last one had taken too much time to do more than start the summary. It took him an hour to finish it.

It was then that he realized that he hadn't eaten all day. He'd seen the rest of the crew eating their meals and had thought about it, but never gotten around to it. Before he tried to get any sleep, he had to get something to eat. It must have been his nerves that had kept him from feeling the hunger pangs. Now that he'd thought about it his stomach was telling him to have a feast. Fortunately there was food available all the time. He went to the common room where the food replicators were and ordered a large filling meal. There were a few other people in the room, but not many. It was the middle of the duty shift or sleeping time for almost everyone.

Stormy sat in silence and ate his meal. He felt some of his weariness and hunger fade as he filled up. He was finished and ready to leave when Chansor came over to his table.

"How was your first command of a patrol?" he asked.

"It went well. I don't know if it went well enough for my promotion to be approved."

"I bet it did. You deserve the promotion."

"Thanks. I'm glad you think so."

"Everyone who knows you thinks so. Your old commander, Keffel, thinks so too. I talked to him a week ago when I was on Nejak-Felhak."

Stormy wanted to ask what he'd been doing there but didn't pry. Chansor had been in the Corps for so long that he had friends everywhere. Besides it was only a few hours away by hyperspace. "How's he doing?" was all Stormy asked.

"He's good. He was complaining about having to find a good enough pilot to replace you. He really misses your reliability on boardings."

"I'm a Customs Corps Guard. That's my job."

"Some people don't have your commitment to the Corps. That's why you'll get your command. You're committed and we all know it. It's not just a job to you, you believe in it."

Stormy wasn't going to argue with him. How his personal beliefs appeared to other people wasn't his concern, especially if it helped him. He actually did think of it as just a job. He just believed that he needed to do thing right the first time. He also had ambitions. He didn't just want this promotion for the responsibility and prestige, it paid better too. There were things he wanted to do with his life when he was done in the Corps and the more money he could earn the more he could do when he retired. He'd sometimes thought of buying his own ship and seeing the galaxy. "I do my best. Now, if you'll excuse me, I've been up for almost twenty-four hours and I need some sleep."

"Sorry to keep you, Sergeant. Good luck."

"Thanks."

Chansor finally left and Stormy put the remains of his meal in the recycler and headed for his quarters.

Six hours later, Stormy awoke refreshed. He always slept six hours no matter how tired he was. Only when he was injured did he let himself sleep longer. He checked his messages and found that he was to report to the command offices in twelve hours. That meant there would be some news.

He went to the common room and grabbed some breakfast. It was packed with people from the day shift having lunch. He sat by himself but he was soon joined by Jekky and one of her friends. "Good morning," Stormy said as they sat down.

"I hear you have to report to the command offices. Think it's going to be good news?" Jekky seemed very cheerful.

"I'm not sure. I have to report and at a strange time so I'm not sure."

"We've been talking this morning and Niffy here thinks you're going to get it."

"But I really don't think I did anything yesterday that really warrants a promotion."

"C'mon, Stormy," Niffy said, "you didn't screw anything up and you did everything right. You'll get it."

"I'd say you did a lot of things that deserve a promotion," Jekky added. "You always keep your head and you calmed me down."

"That's not easy to do, either," Niffy commented.

"Thanks," Jekky bit back.

"Well, we'll see. The timing of the appointment worries me." Stormy wasn't as sure as Jekky and Niffy. He read the signs differently and it gave him doubts. He had the day off and didn't really know what to do with it.

As if on cue Jekky asked, "So, what are you doing today?"

"I really don't know. I'm too preoccupied with this promotion to really enjoy anything."

"What do you say, Niffy? Should we take his mind off things?"

Niffy looked a bit worried at what Jekky might be planning. They'd known each other for a long time. They came from the same planet and had struck up a friendship when both had joined the Corps and ended up with the same first assignment. "What did you have in mind, Jekky?"

"We should take him out and show him the city. I know he never gets out and does anything fun."

"There's a reason for that, Jekky," Stormy said.

"Sergeant Stormus Rolfel, you don't have enough fun in your life. Live a little."

"I don't see how I can say no. You're too stubborn."

"He knows you, Jekky."

"I'm not that stubborn, Niffy."

Niffy and Stormy both nodded and said almost in unison, "Yes you are."

They were all dressed in the plain gray uniform that everyone who wasn't on patrol wore. Jekky dragged Stormy right out of the common room and the three of them caught the transport to the city.

"Promise me you'll try to have fun and not think about your promotion," Jekky demanded.

"I promise."

"Good. You need to have fun sometimes. You can't just bury yourself in your work all the time."

Being a port city, it was full of strangely dressed humans and non-humans. They were close to the Zeccan sector so there were more Zeccans than any other non-human species. They averaged about the same height as humans, but had dark green skin, a round heads, and webbed hands and feet which looked more like flippers. The adult males had white whiskers that went down each side of their chin in two vertical rows from the corners of their mouth. The older they were the longer they were. They also tended to dress in bright colors. Orange, blue, and red were the most popular.

The three of them made an odd sight. Jekky and Niffy were about the same height and build. They were both a little short although Niffy was a hair taller. Stormy on the other hand was a little taller than average and was extremely muscular. It was a trait of coming from Powa-Fevna'han where the high gravity had given everyone more muscles than they really wanted. It wasn't as pleasant for the women to have large muscles but most managed to turn it to an advantage. These weren't the ultra-defined muscles that some humans deliberately cultivated, but they were still bulky and tough.

The two women dragged Stormy all over the city. It reminded him of his childhood when his older sister would drag him around with her. He put up with Jekky and Niffy stopping to check out the latest fashions. They didn't buy anything. There wasn't much point since they didn't have any place or time to wear them or any place to store them. The Corps didn't provide much storage space and you had to be an officer before you had your own private quarters.

At one point, Niffy was looking at something a ways off. "You know, Stormy," Jekky said, "Niffy is single. She isn't seeing anyone right now. You could..."

"Don't try to play matchmaker, Jekky. I know the type of person I'm looking for. Niffy's nice, but she's not it."

"Her looks or her personality or what?"

"All of the above and none. There's nothing wrong with her, she's just not what I'm looking for."

"Aren't you being a bit picky?"

"Maybe, but until I become an officer I can afford to be picky. Thanks for the thought though."

"No problem. If you ever want help meeting people, just let know. I know most of the women in our unit and a lot more on the base."

"I'll keep that in mind. For now, let's just have fun."

A couple hours later they all agreed that they were hungry and it was time to get something to eat. "Do you two like spicy food?" Stormy asked.

They looked at each other and Jekky said, "Yeah. How hot are you thinking?"

"I grew up on spicy food and one of my old crewmates told me that there is a great place to get some here."

"Do you know how to find it?" Niffy asked.

"I think so. He said it was right next to the power relay station that is across from security office."

"Oh, that place," Niffy said. "I've always wanted to go there."

"Then let's go," Jekky said.

They found it right where Stormy had been told it would be. It was called Solar Spice and it offered a variety of dishes spiced at four different levels. Jekky was daring and tried the second most spicy. Stormy went straight for the spiciest hoping that it would be hot enough to answer the craving he had right then. Niffy wasn't feeling daring at all and tried a sample of the two mildest ones before she ordered the slightly hotter of the two.

"Live a little," Jekky complained.

"This is plenty spicy for me. I don't want to burn my mouth."

The two women staring in wonder as Stormy finished his dish and ordered a second complaining privately to them that it wasn't quite as spicy as he was used to.

"So how do you eat the bland stuff that the Corps feeds us."

"I've been in the Corps for quite a few years and I've gotten used to it. Most of the time I just don't think about it. Once in a while I pick up some spicy sauce and cover my food with it. This was much better and much hotter."

"I don't want to even think about how spicy you're talking about," Niffy told him.

"No, you don't."

After eating, Jekky conned them into walking on the open air plaza in the old part of the city. There were a number of novelty shops. Stormy dragged them into one that served frozen desserts. "What, you burn your mouth then freeze it?" Jekky asked him.

"Of course." Jekky didn't like that sort of thing so she passed, but Stormy bought himself and Niffy a dish that was sweet and creamy. Niffy was hooked. They spent a couple more hours looking around the plaza. Stormy looked at his chron and thought they should get back so he could clean up before he had to report to the command offices.

Back at the base, Stormy thanked them for a fun day.

"No problem," Jekky said. "Consider it bribery if you get the promotion and if I stay on as your pilot."

Stormy laughed. "I'll keep that in mind."

The women left to spend the rest of their free evening relaxing and Stormy went to his quarters to shower and change.

Stormy showed up at the command offices fifteen minutes before he was supposed to be there. The receptionist asked him to have a seat. Typical of the Corps, the seats were all hard and uncomfortable. He waited the fifteen minutes and then waited another eight before he was called in to the offices.

The conference room he was taken too had a long oval table with five chairs on one side, each with a command officer sitting in it, and one chair on the other side that he was asked to sit in. He didn't recognize any of the officers. They were independent reviewers who didn't know him personally. They were supposed to evaluate his performance based only on what he'd done in command of the patrol. Stormy briefly feared that they'd come to a decision too quickly and were going to decline his promotion, but it was soon obvious they had not yet decided and he was here to be interviewed for the promotion.

"Welcome, Sergeant Rolfel. We have a few questions for you." The woman speaking had gray hair in one of the traditional regulation styles. Her rank and nameplate identified her as Colonel Hanzin.

"I'll answer as best I can."

"Good. First, we'd like to talk to you about the patrol where you took over for your injured commander."

Major Welkaire was the first to raise a question. "What led you to believe that it was your place to assume command? Why take over and why you?"

"The commander was unconscious so it was obvious he could not command at that moment. I had checked on the seniority of the rest of the crew when I joined them and found that I was the most senior both in time in the Corps and in time as sergeant. By the regulations the most senior crewman is supposed to take over."

"Why wouldn't seniority refer to time serving under that commander?"

"If that were the case, a newly transferred lieutenant with twenty years in the Corps and five at lieutenant would be junior to a newly promoted lieutenant who's been in the Corps two years and been on that ship the entire time. That's not that way it's done."

"Sergeant," Colonel Jessik began, "Why didn't you consult your fellow crewmates before taking over?"

"There wasn't time. The situation required that someone take charge. I've always checked the seniority status on every assignment I've been on. It's good to know for cases like that."

"Would you have taken charge if someone else had the seniority?" Major Jehnshan asked.

"Only if they failed to act promptly enough."

"What do you mean by that?"

"If they panicked or froze. There are people who are ready to command and people who aren't. I was ready and by regulations I was entitled. If someone isn't ready or capable, no amount of seniority will make them ready."

"So, what you are saying is that you would have ignored seniority and taken command anyway." Senior Colonel Hapshekish stated. "That would have been considered mutiny and you would have been ejected from the Corps in disgrace."

"If I would have saved lives and done my duty to the Confederation and my crewmates I would have taken the punishment and known that I had done the right thing even if it wasn't according to regulation." Stormy was nervous about being so frank, but it was what he truly believed and he wanted to get this promotion on his own merits.

None of the officers smiled or frowned. They continued grilling Stormy on his actions on that occasion for almost an hour. Then they began tearing apart his action in command of the patrol ship the day before. They went over his actions in detail. They were especially intent on the firefight on the freighter and the trader who was killed when his airlock failed. An hour and a half passed slowly.

"I think that will be all, Sergeant Rolfel," Colonel Hanzin said. "We will contact you when we have made our decision. You are dismissed."

It was over like that. Stormy got up and left. He saluted them from the door as custom dictated and exited. He forced himself to leave the command offices before he let the exhaustion and tension show. That was the most stressful two hours of his life. He quietly returned to his quarters and changed from his dress uniform to his casual uniform than then went for food.

The cafeteria was not as empty as it had been the night before. He got his food and sat at and empty table. He had just finished when Kirch'kal and Ullan came over.

"How'd it go?" Ullan asked.

"I've never been through anything that bad before in my life."

"What kinds of things did they ask you?" Kirch'kal inquired.

"They asked questions designed to make me doubt my actions. And they picked apart everything I did."

"You did everything by the book, didn't you?" Ullan asked.

"I think so. They didn't cite any regulations that I broke."

"They would have pointed that out. The promotion boards really don't like that." Kirch'kal came from a long line of Customs Corps officers. He was aiming for that himself but hadn't served long enough to qualify for officer training.

They all had an unspoken question on their minds. The next day they had been tentatively scheduled to go on patrol again. They had no word about the command and pilot positions. Either Stormy would command or pilot depending on the decision or lack thereof on his promotion.

They could tell that Stormy really wanted to be alone so they didn't stay long. Stormy went back to his quarters and climbed into his bunk. Two hours later he was still awake. The night was getting short and he couldn't sleep. Too much was riding on what the board would decide.

Stormy didn't know when he'd fallen asleep, but he was awakened to the sound of the comm unit going off. He struggled to sit up and sound awake. He answered in voice only mode. "Sergeant Rolfel," he said.

"Sergeant, this is Colonel Hanzin. I'm calling to inform you that effective immediately you are promoted to Command Sergeant. For now, you will have command of the same patrol crew. Do you have a preference on who is assigned as pilot?"

For a second Stormy couldn't speak. "Yes," he managed to say, "I'd like Sergeant Jekkilvara Kuballen as pilot."

"I will make the arrangement. You are to leave on your scheduled patrol at the scheduled time. Your crew will be informed by message. You should receive your official documents in a few hours."

Stormy glanced at the chron and saw that it was still early and he had two more hours to sleep before he had to get up. "Thank you, Colonel."

"Good luck, Command Sergeant."

Stormy boarded the patrol ship with a different feeling that day. It was his ship and his crew. The next step was to earn a command of a larger ship but that would be a number of years down the road.

Jemlon was on time for a change and managed to smoothly carry out his pre-launch checks. "Scanners and docking systems are green," he said.

"Disengage docking systems, put us in launch position and inform system control that we are ready to launch."

For the second time the crew followed his orders, but now they were his crew.

Overture of Friendship
4609 GCE

The low end starliner came out of hyperspace at Vedder and Ven Zaran groaned when he saw that it would be three hours still before they landed. Normally he would have come in his own ship, but Alderin Balerio had asked to meet this way as a favor and Ven hadn't been able, in good conscience, to say no. He wasn't sure what Balerio wanted, but he would find out soon enough.

Curious, he got on the hypercomm and checked other starliner schedules and found the three-hour time frame was typical when they landed on the surface. It had been nearly thirty years since he had last traveled this way and he certainly hadn't missed much in the intervening years.

Vedder was a strange place to meet. It was one of the few worlds that didn't belong to the Galactic Confederation. That also made it somewhat dangerous for casual visits. But he had worked for Balerio on and off for a couple of years and the man had done him several favors, so it was time he repaid the debt. He just had lots of questions about how coming to this out of the way corner of the galaxy fit with that.

As a trader used to long boring hyperspace voyages, it wasn't hard to find a way to pass the three hours until landing. Then he had to fight the long lines to disembark and get through the local customs. Ven traveled light, so he didn't have the wait some of the others did and was soon making his way through the port to the meeting location.

Leave it to Balerio to find the highest quality hotel this backward place had to offer. If it hadn't already been obvious from the exterior, Ven would have been able to tell the moment he walked in the door. The fact that there were very few locals only confirmed it again. It was a strange mix of off-world visitors and rich natives visiting from other cities.

Vedder as a whole was very dry. Legend had it that they picked this planet for that very reason. That's not to say it was a total desert, but the majority of the population lived in the dry regions leaving the more temperate regions free for farming the crops the fed the population. Some of these wealthy Vedderites at the hotel likely were some of the large estate farms owners he'd heard about.

Ven found his way to Balerio's suite and knocked on the door. The man who opened the door was not the calm professional that Ven was used to seeing on Quetle Station. Balerio looked haggard and stressed and Ven knew right then that this was serious and not just a social visit.

"I'm so glad to see you, Captain Zaran."

"Please, I really prefer being called Ven."

"Of course."

Ven sensed that their professional relationship stood in the way, but even as haggard and on edge as Balerio must be, he followed the protocol to the letter. He escorted Ven into the lounge where a small snack was laid out. Ven followed along.

"How's Nelmon doing?" Ven asked, curious about his former first mate and guessing it was a safe subject.

"He's thriving. He's stayed current on all his bills and is making a nice sum for he and Carrella to live on. That ship you sold him, on the other hand, seems to be on its last legs."

"Don't let it fool you. It is high maintenance, but it has a lot of life left in it yet before it sees a scrap yard."

"My maintenance staff cringe every time Nelmon comes back. There is always something to fix."

"*Star of Argent* has quite a history, but we aren't here to discuss my old ship or my former crew. You called me here for a reason and my curiosity is getting the better of me."

Balerio sighed before he started talking. The weight of his problem colored his tone. "My cousin Joratio's daughter, Monsara, has gotten herself involved with gangsters on Shimoxra. She's in hiding and hasn't been in any immediate danger, but they won't let her leave. Like Vedder, Shimoxra is not part of the Confederation so there isn't anything we have been able to do through official channels. My cousin has not had dealings with gangsters or syndicates before. I unfortunately have so it has fallen to me to find a way to get her out. But I need your help."

"Why me, Balerio? Surely you know a bunch of people who could help with this."

"Well, yes and no. I know a bunch of people I could hire and I know quite a few traders who would do this for a price, but I don't trust them. I know you and I know how you feel about gangsters and syndicates. I know you would never let it slip and endanger her life."

"That is all true. You have to be very careful that the syndicate you are rescuing her from doesn't get wind of it. But to be honest, this sounds dangerous and you aren't providing a persuasive reason for me to help."

"You know my position, Ven. You know how tight I have to run things to stay on top at Quetle. I don't have much time to be me, except with my wife and family. You have always made me feel comfortable. I could offer you a sizable sum of money to help, but I'd like to ask you to do it as a friend."

Ven looked at the man in front of him for a long time. They were from different worlds, but there were things in their lives they shared in common. Ven considered himself just an average trader eking out a living, with a few smuggling jobs thrown in to get ahead. Balerio was a corporate executive and practically ran Quetle Station, but had to walk a tightrope with the other executives on the station. He could hire just about anyone he wanted, but they were not people he could trust. Most of them weren't people Ven would trust, either.

Being a trader was a lonely business. His crew and a few long time acquaintances were his closest friends. Balerio was asking to be included in that number. He hadn't know the man for very long, but his actions with Nelmon had shown that he was the sort of person Ven would like to count among his friends.

"You put me in a tough position. But there is only one answer. I'll do it."

"Thank you, Ven."

"And with the way you put it, there is only one way I can do it. As a friend, I can't let you pay a single credit. I'll have to think of some other way for you to pay me back."

"When the time comes, I'm sure it won't be a problem. I value friends as much as you do."

"You've done your homework on me."

"Not really, it was pretty obvious with the way you helped Nelmon."

Ven laughed. He had given away his true self when he'd done that. It couldn't be helped. He valued his family and friends and would always bend over backwards to help them. "I hope you never regret this."

"It's not likely."

If Ven was going to help, it sounded like there was no time to lose. "Now about your cousin's daughter, do you have a plan yet?"

"No. The extent that I have been able to think about it is to try not and get found out by the syndicate. That is one reason I wanted to meet you here on Vedder, it is decidedly non-Confederation, but also not a place the syndicate can control. I thought it would be a good place to start."

"I can't fault your logic there, plus it is close to Shimoxra. The true benefit will be our being untraceable here and being able to get through here with your cousin's daughter. It will be getting her here that will be the hard part."

"Do you think we can do it?"

"With something like this, small numbers are best. The two of us with a few people tricked into helping us along the way and we should be good. Give me the evening to find us some local identification and we can probably head for Shimoxra tomorrow."

"So soon?"

"No sense waiting"

Ven did not frequent Vedder, but he had been here enough times to know his way around. The people of Vedder followed an ancient religion that was very prevalent, almost to the exclusion of any others. It meant they followed a different year than the standard year or the planetary year. But it was indicative of their independent nature. They had not ever been part of the Confederation or the previous dominions that had controlled this sector.

Ven used his knowledge and within a few hours he had false identification and clothes to make them look somewhat the part of two Vedderite traders. Balerio's features fit quite well, but Ven's did not. It would work as long as no one looked too close. Ven didn't intend to use this charade for anything more than traveling back and forth.

Balerio had his own simple preparations to make. To cover their absence, he arranged to hold the room and added his cousin's daughter to the occupancy. Then he arranged an open-ended liner passage for the three of them that they could use whenever they returned. No need to hide any of that. He thought about going to the effort of hiring a trio of actors to play the rolls and really cover the rescue attempt, but that opened up too many holes and there really was not enough time to pull that off so Ven was able to talk him out of it. Then he arranged for some money that could not be traced back to him. A local bank was more than willing to take his Confederation credits and convert them to Vedderite credits, for a fee, but it was a small price to pay.

The next morning they were off. Shimoxra was only a few hours away by hyperspace. Ven thought it interesting that here along this one galactic arm, in the middle of human space, were found the highest number of worlds that had refused membership in the Confederation. Each world had a more distinct culture and had been independent for a long time. Many wild theories existed for just why this was the case. Ven attributed it to their location. If it was not well charted, a world could be lost amidst the star forming regions that surrounded the sector. That probably had led to long years of isolation during the times when the rest of human or galactic civilization had collapsed. It made a good deal more sense than the crazy alternatives.

The cultural difference of Shimoxra was even worse for them having come from Vedder and pretending to be Vedderites. Where Vedder was distinct but amiable, so long as you didn't violate any of their local laws, Shimoxra seemed wild yet oddly familiar. They noticed it in seconds at the port where the number of people carrying weapons was higher than Ven had ever seen. Several things that were criminal in the Confederation were openly available.

Ven was recovering from a relapse of his addiction to the drug Tint. Instead off dens being hidden away in the back alleys as they were on most planets, here they were clearly labeled and openly operating. Ven had to steel himself and ignore them. They had a mission and he was here to do his part. Besides, his wife would have his hide if he slipped up now. That didn't change how tempting it was, but he fought it as they headed to their hotel.

"You can get your drug of choice right here in the open," Balerio said. The look he gave Ven showed that he was aware of Ven's struggle.

"It's one way of keeping the people in line. If these drugs are available freely, it prevents crime. It's hell on having an efficient workforce, but I don't think the local authorities care much about that."

"Probably not."

Ven was sure that Balerio was appalled at the hotel he'd booked, but he had picked it for location. Besides, it fit better with their guise as travelers from Vedder. Ven was confident as they checked in that no one would question their identities. Over the years he had used a number of alias's. The people he'd dealt with had always raved about the quality of forged ID's available on Vedder and Ven had to agree, these were some of the best he had acquired. Even though he didn't match the typical Vedder appearance, the clerk never questioned it.

Once they were in their room, Ven used a special scanner to check for eavesdropping devices. In this level of hotel, he wouldn't expect to find any and he didn't. Once he knew it was clear, he sat Balerio down and they got to work on the next step of their plan.

A change of clothes and another set of ID's and they were ready to go find Monsara. It was from this point the danger began. There was always a chance that as off-worlders they would be followed, and they did not want to lead any of the local syndicates to Monsara.

Balerio was lost when it came to knowing how to plan an operation such as this, but he was excellent at following instructions no matter how bizarre they sounded.

They left the hotel and walked along the street taking in the sights. Two off-worlders coming out of a hotel should be like a magnet for having gangsters on their tail. This part of the city was pretty busy, it was still early in the evening and not too busy to spot if someone started following them. Ven had the same plan either way, but being followed now could work to their advantage later. He didn't tell Balerio when he spotted the tail. He wasn't going to take evasive actions. He was headed to a bar more known as a locale for exotic prostitutes than for its quality of drinks. While most of the girls were human, there were a few of some of the other species for those who liked to experiment. Ven didn't quite understand because the equipment didn't quite function the same, but to each their own.

It only took moments for the crowd to close in around them and Ven quickly executed the move he had warned Balerio of. In seconds they were able to get lost in the crowd and sneak out the back entrance.

Ven was still a bit paranoid. They walked a few streets over and hopped a transport to a different part off the city. Ven found the sort of place he had been looking for, an abandoned retail location. He quickly broke in and dragged Balerio through and out the back. They wandered down a few alleys before they reached the next transport station. As they came out of the alley Ven signaled Balerio to act normal. They stepped onto the platform to wait for the transport as if they were just going about a normal everyday errand.

Even such public transportation could be bugged, so Ven had insisted that they remain quiet. Ven could tell Balerio was dying to say something, but they couldn't risk it. Paranoia was their only friend until they were in hyperspace again.

Monsara's coded signal had been safe enough for her to give her location, but they didn't dare risk contacting her again to tell her to be ready. Coded or not, the signal could be used to trace her. It wasn't as seedy a location as Ven would have guessed. It was a tall apartment building with doors that opened onto open-air walks on the outside of the building. Monsara was on the sixteenth floor. Ven found the whole layout dangerous, but there wasn't much they could do about it now. Neither of them made a sound until they pressed the buzzer.

"I'm Jek, and this is Ren," Ven said to the camera and nudged Balerio to do the same. Moments later the door opened and a young woman motioned them to enter. Ven could see in an instant the family resemblance to Balerio. She quickly closed the door behind them.

"Did anyone see you?" she asked.

"No, no one followed us," Ven told her. "How soon can you be ready to go?"

"I'm ready now. I can't believe you actually got here."

"I've had a bit of experience with this sort of thing."

"Yes, it's all about who you know," Balerio said.

"Well, Ren," she said, using the alias, "I wasn't sure you would be able to come, as busy as you are."

"Business is one thing, but family is something else. I couldn't let you sit here without doing my best to help you."

"I hoped you picked someone you can trust," she said eyeing Ven. "These guys have spies almost everywhere."

"I have a deep hatred for these people, young lady. Rather than stand here talking, we should be going."

For all his precautions Ven knew that he had not covered every base. There just hadn't been time. The key to avoiding any unforeseen trouble was to move as fast as possible. Ven led them away from the apartment building by a different route. They got on a transport heading in a completely different direction.

Several times Monsara tried to start a conversation, but Ven silenced her each time. Any conversation, no matter how seemingly innocent, could give them away. He was under no illusions that just because he could not see the surveillance equipment that it wasn't there. He was sure it was.

Ven was leading them through a series of alleys to reach the second of three transports he had plotted out to get back to their hotel when his senses told him they had company.

"Now is where the fun begins," Ven said to warn the others. Balerio instantly got the meaning. Monsara did a moment later when a man stepped out of the shadows in front of them.

"Now where to you three think you are going?" the man asked. "Raxan hasn't said you can leave yet."

"Who is Raxan that we should need his permission?" Balerio asked.

"He runs these parts. In fact he runs this whole side of the city. You must not be from around here to not know that."

"We don't get out much," Ven said.

"Or you are just plain stupid," another man said from behind them.

Ven sighed. He tried to avoid violence. His whole plan had been to avoid any conflicts like this, but he had feared that with the limited time he wouldn't be able to avoid all of them. "Don't move," he whispered to Monsara. Moments later he was in motion. His pistol was out in a flash and the man in front of them dropped with a dark burn covering his chest. He rolled and came up and fired at the man behind them. The beam of energy clipped the man's shoulder. He fell, alive but injured and out of this fight.

Ven knew there were more. A gangster as powerful as this Raxan would not send just two men. As he paused listened for more, he heard the sounds of two men running away in different directions. Four against three was not out of the question. It also occurred to Ven that these men might not have been sent by Raxan personally, but might be after whatever price Monsara had on her head.

"That was lucky," Balerio said. "Only four and two of them ran off."

"It wasn't luck. It means we are in real trouble," Ven replied. "We need to get back to the bar pronto. And no talking," he told Monsara. "Audio surveillance is much easier than video and much harder to spot. Voice pattern recognition isn't that hard."

Monsara gasped, but did not utter another word.

Ven revised his whole plan. They had to get out of this sector, and fast. They would be looking for three people now. Ven decided they should catch the nearest transport. It was going in the wrong direction, but that really didn't matter. He instructed Balerio to go through one set of doors and proceed back to the bar and enter the same way they'd gotten out and head back to the hotel. Ven and Monsara went through a different door and then they got off at the next stop. Ven had evidently scared her into silence because she didn't say a word the entire time.

Balerio should be able to connect to a transport going in the right direction in a stop or two. Being alone and nondescript should work to his advantage. Ven wasn't so sure that he and the girl had as good a chance. It looked like it was going to be a long night. Ven was able to divert over to a transport heading in the direction he wanted and they had disembarked and were on their way through a fairly busy business district when Ven's senses warned him in time to duck and pull Monsara down, narrowly avoiding a beam of blinding hot energy.

As Ven assessed the situation, Monsara glared at him and said, "So much for them tracking us by my voice."

"My apologies, but that is one of the many ways they can track us. The more you talk, the more likely it is. But they have other ways. I just hope Balerio is all right."

Ven finally spotted their attacker and opened fire. He hit his target with his second shot, but he had not been alone. Ven had to deal with two more before quiet descended. He looked around at where they found themselves and added one last shot to blast through the lock on the door behind them. Ven led Monsara through the deserted shop and out the back into the alley. He concentrated on moving them in the right direction as he broke into a number of places to weave their way to a transport station.

Somewhere along the way he must have gone the wrong direction, because when they rounded what he thought was the last corner, there was no transport station in sight.

"Are we lost?" Monsara asked.

"I'm a trader, I never get lost. I just took the wrong route. It's not like anyone has been shooting at us or anything."

Mercifully she stayed quiet after that while Ven reassessed his plan. According to the map on his comm unit, they were close, but time was becoming an issue. The only real option involved being more reckless.

Now sure of where he was and where he needed to go, Ven set out in a different direction. It was mercifully quiet as they headed for the neighboring sector of the city.

"Do you even know where you are going?" Monsara asked him.

"Yes. We are going to steal a ground transport."

"And how is that going to do us any good."

"We won't be taking public transports and are less likely to be seen or followed."

"I'm beginning to think you aren't qualified to be in charge."

"Maybe, but your life is in my hands, not to mention my own, so you'd better hope I'm either qualified or very lucky."

Luck definitely did not seem to be with him. Moments later they were ambushed by six armed men. Ven was able to take two of them out right away, but the others found better cover and he couldn't get in a clear shot.

"Raxan isn't pleased about you trying to come in and take away this young lady," one of their assailants said. "What happened to the other one of you?"

"Your guys got him. He lasted about half an hour before he died. I was sort of hoping that with just two instead of three, we might escape your notice. It didn't seem to work."

"You are on Raxan's turf. There is no where you can go where he can't find you."

"Then how did my young friend elude you until we arrived."

"Can't give away all our secrets."

Ven swore under his breath and took a few pot shots in that direction. He checked the charge on his pistol and found he was down fifty percent. One against four were not good odds. He wasn't that good a shot.

They traded pot shots for several minutes as Ven tried to figure out a way out. He finally heard one off them move and opened fire. He heard the truncated scream and a grunt as the body collapsed, followed by the pleasant sound off a gun sliding across the pavement. Ven caught the movement and saw how close it as and it gave him an idea. He hadn't lasted so long as a trader without being willing to take a few risks and this was certainly a time for it. He darted from his cover, rolled and managed to grab the gangster's weapon. He landed hard against the wall, with a hail of blinding energy beams trailing behind him. But now he had two guns.

He repeated the first part of that move again, but when he rolled and came up, he jerked back, the gangster's beams passing through where they assumed he'd be. He took aim and fried two of them and tried to get the last one, but his shot hit nothing. He ducked under cover and called, "come out, so we can talk," but all he heard was the distant sound of something falling followed by running feet.

Ven cautiously went to take a look. He found the four men dead. He picked up their weapons just in case. We went back to where Monsara was hiding and said, "It doesn't look like I'm having much luck tonight, so the answer is that I must be qualified."

"Not much luck?" she asked. "What do you call what just happened?"

"Skill. Luck would have been not being caught by them in such a bad location in the first place. Let's go."

Ven had a new plan. From the events that had transpired so far, he had a feeling they were being followed or tracked. Either way, he did not want this Raxan knowing what he was planning on doing. He had made sure to take steps to avoid any overhead tracking that he might not be aware of and he had seen plenty of video surveillance cameras placed around the city and had been avoiding those. Sound wasn't an issue because they had been very quiet during that one long stretch and it had made no difference. That left a tracking device or a tail. He was pretty confident it was a tail. Most syndicates did like to keep their gangsters busy and provide a variety of ways to test their loyalty. But it must be a good tail to not have given themselves away yet.

As Ven led Monsara toward their next goal, he was more concerned with what lay behind them than what lay in front. Hopefully it made for a very confusing journey for their gangster shadow. It was evidently confusing enough because they were not attacked again.

Ven also finally got a glimpse of the person tracking them, confirming what he suspected. Man or woman he could not be sure. They were tall and thin and dressed in concealing clothes. Ven was determined to get a look at them before he tried to lose them. He set about designing a plan.

Balerio had a very quiet ride on the transport. He watched Ven and Monsara get off and he continued on to a remote station where he changed to a different transport that would get him where he needed to go. At the third stop a couple of suspicious looking men got on. They were not overt, but they were watching him. Balerio did his best not to pay direct attention to them while still keeping track of them.

After a few more stops, they moved closer to him and he was sure danger was looming. Rather than react to their presence, Balerio pretended to doze off. It wasn't hard, the motion of the transport along the mag rail was soothing. They didn't seem to be making any moves, just watching. Probably with instructions just to follow. He didn't intend to let that happen. He pretended to sleep as they pulled into the next stop. Some people got on or off in other sections of the transport. Balerio carefully timed it to the automatic closing of the doors. At just the right moment he jerked like he just woke up. He looked at his chron and the station information scrolling along the walls and jumped up and ran for the door, muttering all the time about being late. He slid through the doors just as they were closing. They snapped shut behind him, but to keep up with the pretext he didn't turn to look. He kept running out of the station.

When he finally felt it was safe to look back, there was no one there. He'd ditched them. That did not mean he was safe. Far from it. He would have to be very careful to make it back to the bar safely without anyone else following him.

This station didn't offer any other options than the one transport line. He weighed his options and decided that hiding for about half an hour and then proceeding down the line as he'd intended would be the safest way. It was the direction that they would least expect and likely wouldn't be watching as close.

The minutes ticked by slowly as he laid low at the station. Several times he thought someone was there, but each time the person mercifully passed by. When the allotted time had passed, he quietly emerged and made his way to the platform, arriving just moments after the doors opened. The seats were all pretty much the same so he picked one near the doors. He was alone in the section except for a young woman toward one end. He continued to scan the platform until the transport pulled out and it was no longer visible.

He forced himself to calm down. Panicking would get him nowhere, except maybe caught. He needed to follow the plan and give Ven and Monsara a chance to get to the bar by a different way. All he should have to do was change transports one more time and avoid any of the syndicate goons and he should be fine.

For his plan to work, Ven needed Monsara to do exactly what he told her to. Their lives depended on it. She had done a good job so far. He carefully instructed her on what they would have to do and had to trust she would do the right thing.

There had been precious little time to plan and there was no margin for error. Ven set things in motion. The first part was a simple misdirection. He led Monsara around a corner and then back, through a building to the alley. He waited to exit until he saw the thin figure of the gangster pass by along the street. He counted the time it had taken them to walk from the alley to the corner and then motioned Monsara to follow him.

Then there was the trap. He had no hope that such a simple misdirection would ever work so he set two of the pistols he had picked up to overload. There was no guarantee on the timing so as soon as it was set, he told Monsara to run.

Back down the street had been a place where they could take cover and wait for the explosion. Not far away had been a personal transport that he hoped to steal. They had not made it to the hiding place yet when the first pistol blew early. They had just made it around the corner or the concussion would have thrown them to the ground. He grabbed Monsara's arm and rushed her into the dark alcove he'd seen earlier. They had barely reached when the second pistol exploded with considerably more force. The building vibrated with the concussion and debris rained down on the street.

There were no guarantees their tail had been caught in the blast or would be fooled by the attempt. Now it all depended on moving quickly and a bit of luck. Ven motioned to Monsara to follow him and moved out. The transport had some debris on it, but had not been damaged. It wasn't new by any means and if it had a security system, it wasn't activated. Ven was inside in seconds and had the transport functioning seconds after that. He motioned to Monsara to strap herself in and quickly drove the transport on a short but winding route that would put them heading in the right direction, but not looking like they were driving away from the explosion.

Five minutes later, he pulled onto the main road heading south. He constantly checked the rear display to see if they were being followed, but there was no sign of anything. It looked like luck might finally have turned in their favor.

Ven did not let Monsara speak, neither did he speak himself. He forced them to maintain complete silence as they traveled south. It probably wasn't necessary to avoided a possible eavesdropper, but it helped him concentrate on the next move. It would be great if they could make it back to the bar without further incident, but nothing about this mission had gone perfectly yet so he expected some sort of company at least once before they reached their destination.

Balerio reached the back door of the bar that they had come out of hours earlier without a problem. After a quick assessment, he could see that that it would not be quite as easy to get in again. They had arrived at the bar barely after dark and some of the security measures must not have been in place yet. Now the back of the bar was as busy as the front and there was no way in except past several armed men, each one bulging with muscles. By now the front entrance was so crowded that it could take hours to get in if at all.

But he needed to find some other way in and then wait to help Ven and Monsara get in when they arrived. He carefully circled the building, trying not to be noticed. None of the guards appeared to be equipped with any sort of night vision so he hoped that by sticking to the shadows he was staying out of sight. It took him twenty minutes of searching before he found what he was looking for, an unguarded roof access. It didn't take him long to realize that it didn't need to be guarded because it required security access to uncover the ladder. He wasn't the best at bypassing such security measures, but he had done it a few times.

He tried looking like he belonged there, but no matter how he tried, with the way he was dressed it just didn't seem right. He felt like he was sticking out worse than if there was a spotlight trained on him. It took an agonizing ten minutes to unlock the lower gate, but once he'd done that, it only took seconds to repeat the same steps to unlock the ladder. He started up and then reached down and carefully positioned the cover panels so that from a distance they still looked closed, and then he climbed up to the roof.

Finding a way in turned out to be nearly as hard. There were no direct access hatches, only the air-conditioning machinery. He used the camera on his comm pad and a length of wire he found lying on the roof and tried lowering it down several of the air shafts. Five of the shafts were exhaust vents and they seemed the most promising, but the first four he checked all led to busy parts of the bar. He didn't come on the fifth one until after he had checked several of the conditioned air shafts. It was silent where the others had sound echoing out of them from below. The rooms it emptied into were dark.

It was a good find, but it still wasn't useful unless he climbed down to check it out. The wire was thick enough to hold his weight so he tied it off securely and lowered the other end of it down. Climbing back up would be tough, but he was in shape and should be able to do it. He'd better be able to do it or Monsara might not get out of this alive.

He slowly lowered himself down. The first vent was high in a wall and of no use. The second vent emptied on an closed room. He tried the grate and found it moved easily, probably for cleaning and access. The room was some sort of office and looked lived in. The question he couldn't answer would be if it was going to get used on this night. He had no way to answer that question, he could just hope.

The door led into a dimly lit hallway. Balerio went down it both directions and quickly determined that one way were only more offices, but the other led to an elevator and they should be able to get to a lower level. At worst, they could claim to be lost. He back tracked and made sure nothing looked amiss and returned to the roof to wait. He didn't want to make that climb more times than he had to. The wire was a little too thin and had cut into his hands and legs when he'd climbed back up. He hoped Ven and Monsara would arrive soon so they could leave this planet.

The ride was quiet. There was little traffic at that time of night and no one seemed to be following them. Ven was strict about the silence. He had no way of knowing whose personal transport they had stolen or what recording devices might be active. On most sane planets that would not be an issues, but this world was known for the constant surveillance by the syndicates. In many ways, they were more oppressive than any world government he had encountered. Even Customs didn't spy on people without good cause.

They were running out of time so he didn't take any alternate routes to hide from potential tails. His backup plan was to get lost in the shuffle of people in the bar. They just had to get there in one piece. So far it was looking good. He pulled off the main road and found the arterial road he was looking for.

As they drew close to the bar, Ven broke the silence by using his comm to signal Balerio with a text only message. Balerio replied back that he'd had to find a different way in and was waiting for them on the roof and would be looking for them.

Ven parked the transport a couple streets over from the bar, hoping that the transport would fit into the surroundings. As he walked away and looked back, it looked as normal here as it had where it had been parked originally.

"We're close," he told Monsara in a low voice. "We have a short walk and a short climb and then it should be like passing through a gate and we should be able to get lost in a throng of people and get you out of here."

"Just let me know what I need to do."

"When the time comes, I need you to change clothes. You need to look the part."

They had not gotten much further when a familiar thin figure appeared in front of them.

"That was a nice trick, overloading the guns." The voice still did not help Ven identify the gangster's gender.

"I have a few tricks."

"Stealing transports is not one of them. You didn't even change halfway, which would have delayed me."

"It seems I underestimated you. It won't happen again."

"You are right there," the thin gangster said as Ven stared at the wrong end of a pistol. He though for a moment of shooting, but he heard the unmistakable sound of several other weapons and assumed they were trained on him or Monsara.

Not the best situation, but not the worst either. Ven's mind churned, trying to find an idea that would lead out of it. The question of doing or not doing something really didn't enter into his mind, it was only a question of what he would do and how fast he could think of it. As his mind settled on a course of action, he gave the thin gangster a sly smile. His first action was not what any of them expected.

He dodged to the side and plowed into Monsara, knocking her to the ground and in almost the same motion opened fire on the thin gangster. He missed, but that hadn't been the purpose of the move. He quickly turned and shot one of the other gangsters, ducked, fired again. He kept moving and kept shooting and kept their attention on him. The thin gangster kept escaping the beam of Ven's pistol, but in just a few minutes they were the only two standing.

"You are crafty," the thin gangster said. "Where did they find you?"

"Me, I came from out of nowhere and I'm always on the move. I know my way around."

"That you do, but your road will end here." His finger flexed as if to pull the trigger, but instead he fell to the ground as

Monsara rolled into his legs. Ven took the shot and the thin gangster's cry was cut short by his death.

Ven helped Monsara to her feet, all the while she was glaring at him. "You took a big risk there," she said.

"It was either do something or let them take us prisoner, and I think we both know how that would have ended. Knocking you down was the only way to get their focus off of you and solely on me. Now come on, we need to get to the bar before someone sees us here."

It was amazing that they could be just a couple of streets over from a busy bar and for it to be so deserted. The moment they reached the building, it was practically surrounded by crowds. Even the back side was busy. Ven scanned the roof line and soon located Balerio's shadow and they found their way to the ladder just below him. He had Monsara go up first and followed behind her.

"Glad you could make it," Balerio said when he reached the top.

"I am, too. The excitement may not be over just yet."

"I heard from here, but it's a lot quieter up here and I bet no one on the ground noticed."

"I hope not. Where are we going to change?"

"Follow me."

Balerio led them to the air shaft and led the way down. Monsara needed help making it down, but they managed to reach the office Balerio had found earlier without incident.

When Ven told Monsara how she needed to dress she refused. "I'm not a prostitute and I don't want to look like one."

"If you do dress like that here, no one will notice you. They'll think you work here."

"Isn't there another way?"

"I'm afraid not. It's the only way out. We have to change, too."

Ven could see she was not happy, but was resigned to it. Since the room was L-shaped, Monsara went around the corner to change and Ven and Balerio went toward the door to change. They were all ready to leave in short order. Monsara now looked the part and seemed very nervous and embarrassed.

"To pull this off I need you to do two things," Ven said. "I need you to smile and never let go of me. That will show everyone here you are taken and are happy about it."

"I'll do my best," she replied.

Ven nodded and Balerio opened the door. They made their way down the hall, found the elevator, and headed to the main floor. The doors opened to blaring music and a crowd of people with little room to move between them. It was too loud to talk so Ven pulled Monsara after him and let Balerio lead the way to the exit.

They were nearly there when an obnoxious pair of young men went dancing past, stirring up the crowd. Somewhere in the turmoil Ven lost Monsara and he called Balerio who somehow heard him over the din. Ven turned back and was looking for her when he heard her scream and rushed toward the sound.

"Hey, come with us. We know the rates and you won't find better in here." The young gangster obviously thought highly of himself. "You can't refuse."

"She can. She is already with me," Ven said, putting enough power behind his voice for them to hear him.

"Hey, man, you let her go. She fair game now."

"Hasn't your father taught you that you don't mess with old men and their needs? She's what I like and we already settled on the terms. Let go of her and there won't be any trouble." Ven left no room for mistake in his determination, showing a flash of pistol in warning.

"Okay, old man. Take her. I can do better."

Ven nodded and pulled Monsara away from them and caught up with Balerio. He took no chances as they proceeded to the exit and put his arm around her waist. No one else bothered them and they were soon leaving the building. There was a private taxi company offering their services and Ven jumped on it. Moments later they were on their way to the hotel.

No one at the hotel questioned them as they came in with a girl who so obviously looked like a prostitute. Ven could tell their eyes were on he and Balerio and they were ignoring Monsara. They made it to their room without incident and all collapsed in relief.

"We aren't done yet," Ven said, "but I think we need to get some food before we change and leave."

The room had a decent replicator, but it was expensive to use. They each ordered up a decent meal and sad down to eat. Everything was quiet until they had finished.

"Do I have to wear this all the way to the port?" Monsara asked.

"No. I have something else for you to wear. We were pretending like we came from Vedder and we have a fake ID for you. You'll need to dress like a boy."

"That's at least better than this," she said.

Ven handed her the clothes that he had brought and the wig to disguise her hair.

"Do you think this is going to work?" Balerio asked after Monsara went into the bathroom to change.

"It has to. We don't have any other options. But no one downstairs is going to remember that two guys arrived with anyone and then three people from Vedder are going to leave. I think it will take them a long time to figure it out. We should hurry; the liner should be boarding in an hour."

Ven and Balerio changed back into the Vedder costumes they had arrived in and as soon as Monsara was ready, they left. If you looked too close, she still looked like a girl, but no one should have a chance to look.

Their departure was right on time. A throng of gangsters came through the front door of the hotel as they walked across the lobby. Outside a couple of sideways glances, the gangsters didn't pay the three of them any attention. They went out the front door and headed for the transport station and the port.

They didn't break character as they went through the port or when they boarded the liner. Ven warned them that it wasn't safe until they had disembarked on Vedder. There was a sizable tourist business between the two worlds, but Vedder did not tolerate any gang or syndicate activity. They had the death penalty for violent crimes and it kept the gangsters from causing trouble.

Once back in the hotel on Vedder, they could at last relax. Balerio was paying for the deluxe suit so Monsara made use of the shower and clothing replicator and came out looking like the stunning young woman she normally was.

Ven was against them spending too much time on Vedder. While the gangsters did not typically pursue anyone to Vedder, there was always that chance. Balerio agreed. He and Monsara headed out on a indirect route to Quetle station. Ven stayed in the suite for two more days before he checked out and headed back to his own ship. When he arrived and checked his messages, there was one from Balerio that read, "Thanks, old friend. I don't know how I can properly repay you for this. My whole family thanks you."

Ven replied back, "That's what friends are for. I'll be on Quetle Station next month and I'll stop by and say hi." He was truly happy with how things had worked out. He valued Balerio's overture of friendship far more than money. He could pick up a smuggling job almost anywhere that would pay more than any sum Balerio might have offered. His friendship was priceless. Ven had few friends as it was and being able to count Balerio among that number had made the danger he had faced on Shimoxra well worth it.

Race On The Rim
4609 GCE

Jimmed Albanis grunted as the Customs shuttle set down hard on Neskellior. The pilot had better go back to school, he thought to himself. It took several minutes before he and the other passengers were told they could disembark. Jim really hated taking the free customs shuttles, but there'd been nothing else coming this direction.

Neskellior was a busy thriving world. It was the hub of a large trade network that webbed its way through the inner systems including the capital, Seri Theosis. That meant that the number of customs ships needed to patrol it was higher than average. Jim's best friend, Stormus Rolfel, or Stormy to his friends, commanded one of the smaller patrol ships and should still be on patrol. Jim had a few hours to kill before he got back.

Stormy hadn't said what they would be doing while Jim was here, but knowing him, it would be a blast. They hadn't spent much time together in years. It was about time they did something fun.

Jim was good at using up spare time. He'd had lots of practice in his seven years in the Corps. He quickly found a good place to eat and took his time.

Stormy finished his post flight check. He'd managed to finish his command report before they'd gotten back to port so once he left the ship and turned in his reports, he was on leave for ten full days.

Stormy saw the engine warning and looked over at Kirch'kal. When the engineer shook his head, Stormy sighed. The ship had been acting up during the patrol and Stormy had hoped it wasn't anything serious, but it was turning out to be a major repair that he would have to report personally when he turned the patrol ship over to the service crew.

After an hour of talking to the idiots on the service crew trying to explain the problem Stormy thought that maybe they'd finally got it. He looked and his chron and knew that Jim would be waiting at the Ruby Nebula, which was just outside the Customs base.

Stormy and Jim stood out from most humans. They were from Powa-fevna'han where the gravity was higher. On their homeworld they were just average, but average there was extremely muscular to the rest of the galaxy. They looked like a pair of body builders, but they weren't quite as sculpted.

"It's about time you got here," Jim complained.

"The damned ship was having engine problems and the service crew didn't seem to understand."

"That sounds familiar." Jim had served on a few of the larger patrol ships before getting his transfer to intelligence.

Stormy sat at the table and ordered a drink from the food processor. "So, how was your trip."

"By customs shuttle? You can guess." Jim had been in suspense about what Stormy had been planning. "Come on, Storm. You've kept me in the dark long enough. What are we going to do for the next ten days?"

Stormy laughed. "You'll love it. We are going on a cruise."

Jim's only reaction was to stare at his friend. "You call that a vacation?"

"What's wrong with it?"

"Would you like the full list? How about the bare bones? Those cruises are full of old people and children. They don't even go anywhere interesting."

"That is the typical thinking. But this cruise is different."

"Yeah, right," Jim said. "I'll go, but I'll bet you that this is the most boring vacation either of us has ever had."

"You're on."

"When do we leave?"

"In two hours."

"Are you packed?"

"That's the beauty of this. They will provide everything for our whole trip."

"What's the catch?"

"No catch. Someone owed me a favor, that's all."

Jim shook his head, but agreed to go. "How come you don't have any bags?" Jim asked him.

"You'll see. It's why I told you to pack light." Stormy was silent for the rest of their short trip, first to the cruise line's shuttle and then to the boarding station in orbit. "There she is," he said as they passed a large port. Beyond was one of the largest cruise ships Jim had ever seen. It was covered with reflective ports and was docked at no less than twenty arms. The multicolored hull markings made no sense to him with the confined and brief view he had.

"Well, it is big," was Jim's only comment. Stormy smiled and said nothing. Boarding had commenced so they didn't have to wait. They had their boarding passes checked three times before they were allowed to walk across a docking arm to the cruise ship.

"Welcome aboard," one of the crew said in greeting, "may I see your boarding passes?"

Stormy handed them to her and gave her a big smile. She didn't take any notice and gave them directions to their suite.

"I don't think she was interested," Jim teased his friend. Stormy grunted in response. He wasn't used to women ignoring him.

They found their suite without any problems. Jim was quite impressed when he saw it. The entrance opened into a large living area complete with a well-stocked food processor and an entertainment center. Their suite was on the outer hull and had several large ports. Right now they only revealed the station. To either side was a bedroom, each with equally impressive ports.

"What do you think?" Stormy asked.

"Nice. It's really impressive. How did you manage to get such nice rooms?"

"It wasn't too hard. Almost all of the suites are this nice. Getting one with the ports was a little challenging, but my connections came through."

A little more exploration told Jim why they hadn't had to bring along any clothes to speak of. Each bedroom had a tailoring processor. Jim read the instructions and found that it worked in conjunction with the shower. When activated it would scan the body and produce perfectly tailored clothes of any style desired. Since Jim hadn't had a chance to do more than eat, he thought he'd give it a try. Twenty minutes later he was clean and dressed in one of the current elegantly casual styles.

Stormy had also showered and changed. The tailoring program had taken their physiques into account. "Not bad," Stormy commented when he looked at Jim. "Now you look like you belong here."

"So what do we do now?" Jim asked him.

"Usually, nothing happens until we undock. Then the fun begins. The lounges open up and there is partying and dancing nonstop until the cruise is over. Some of the dining rooms are on set schedules and some are always open. So we really have our pick of things to do, but not until we get going. Which should be in just a few minutes."

"Just partying and dancing?"

"No, there's a bunch of other things too. Sports, VR games, special vid presentations, side excursions, tours of the ship. You name it, they've got it. I'm here for the women."

Jim smiled. "And to find them we need to go to the parties. I see where you're going now."

"I thought you would."

As soon as the cruise ship was underway, Stormy dragged Jim to what was supposed to be the best party for singles on the hunt. The party room was huge. People were just starting to arrive. Stormy snagged a good seat for the two of them. Before long, the room was crowded with people in search of a companion for the night, for the trip, or even for life.

It wasn't long before Stormy saw his first target. She was a tall willowy red head and really filled out her jumpsuit. Stormy caught her eye as she wandered near them and she came over.

"What brings two such handsome men here?" she asked them in a sultry voice.

"We just got here and were feeling a little lonely," Stormy said with his smoothest style. "Why don't you join us?"

"I'd be happy too, but there's only one of me and two of you."

Jim looked at Stormy and they exchanged a look that, after years of friendship, conveyed many meanings. Jim began to rise. "Why don't you take my seat, I want to take a look around."

"Don't leave on my account," the red head said in a way that indicated that she wanted Stormy all to herself.

When he was out of sight, Jim shook his head over Stormy and his red headed women. Stormy always described them as fire.

Just a few minutes told Jim that Stormy was quite right about this cruise. There were plenty of single women. Some of them were looking for other women, but there were plenty others who had men on their minds.

Suddenly, Jim was soaked. He looked down at the apologetic face of a young woman. "Sorry," she said meekly.

Jim was a bit angry, but she was too cute to growl at. "Well, you lost a drink and I lost a shirt. I'd say that makes us even." She apologized again before she disappeared into the crowd.

Jim was winding his way to the door when a woman intercepted him.

"I see my sister got you pretty good," the brunette said.
"I'm just a bit wet."
"You'd better watch it, Jess likes spicy drinks."
"I was just headed to change."
"Mind if I tag along?"
"Okay. I'm Jim."
"I'm Soriya."

They chatted as they went back to Jim's suite. She wasn't as tall as Stormy's red headed vision, but she was prettier. They both avoided too much about their backgrounds, concentrating on what they wanted to do on the cruise. She and her twin sisters were there to celebrate the twin's seventeenth birthday. She just wanted to enjoy herself while her sisters wanted to make the cruise one long party. Jim could sympathize since Stormy had a similar attitude to Soriya's sisters.

Jim asked her to wait in the living area while he changed his clothes. He didn't want to mess with thinking about what to wear, so he just punched up the same clothes again, and changed as quick as he could.

"You two didn't bring anything with you, did you?" Soriya asked.

"No, we didn't. My friend said everything would be provided and so far it has been."

"My sisters wouldn't dream of doing that. They had to bring half their wardrobe with them."

"You mean on a chit?"

"No, they had to bring luggage filled with clothes."

"That's a little strange."

"They get that from our mother. She is a bit extravagant. I have all my clothes programmed at home and all I do is make a chit."

"That's the way to do it. I get to do that at work, but I tend to like nice lived in clothes so I usually bring my own."

"I wish my sisters and mother just liked their clothes broken in. They have to have hand tailored clothes. Mom just can't stand the thought of her clothes coming from a machine, so she has cloth, from a machine, handmade into clothes."

Jim got the irony of that and chucked softly. Soriya smiled in response. "Shall we head back?" he asked her.

She nodded and they headed back. Partway there, Soriya stopped. "Isn't there someplace else we can go?"

"What would you like to do?"

"I don't know. Something different. Maybe something...."

"Romantic."

Soriya smiled shyly, but didn't say anything.

Stormy looked into Brizea's eyes. They were both getting a little buzzed from the drinks. "When are we going back to your room?" she asked him.

"Whenever you're ready."

She got up and pulled Stormy after her. "Let's take a walk." She led Stormy from the party room. When she looked back at him and saw his confused look she added, "Come on, put some effort into it." Stormy followed her up to the observation deck.

At this time of the day, the observation deck was practically empty. The ten meter by five meter observation ports glowed with the light of the hyperspace streams. Since it was ostensibly night, the lights were dimmed and the glow of the streams lit the deck. Brizea pulled Stormy along the deck until they ran into the railing around the pool on the deck below.

"I know what we both want," she told him, "but we're in such a romantic place I just can't help it."

Stormy smiled and pulled her to him. "I know exactly what you mean." He didn't kiss her immediately. He looked into her eyes and caressed her face. Something behind her caught his attention and he briefly glanced at it. He had to smile when he saw Jim with a slender dark-haired girl. He managed to turn his smile into the prelude to a kiss and tried to ignore his friend.

Jim caught Stormy's glance just before he kissed the redhead. He grunted and shook his head.

"What is it?" Soriya asked.

"Don't stare, but see that guy over there?" She took a quick glance in the direction he indicated and nodded.

"That's my friend Stormy."

"He doesn't waste much time, does he?"

"No, he doesn't. He's strictly hands off with the women he works with, but all other women seem to be on his list."

"Even me?"

"Probably. Don't you want to be?"

She blushed slightly when she said, "I'd rather be on your list."

Jim smiled and pulled her close and said, "You are on my list." The light from the streams changed from green to a golden orange close to firelight. It made a very romantic glow as Jim and Soriya shared their first kiss.

By the time Jim cared to look, Stormy and his redhead were gone. "Where'd he go?" Soriya asked him.

"Probably back to the suite."

"Where does that leave you?"

"It's not a problem, that's why we have a suite. I'll just wait a while before I go back."

"Well, you don't have to wait alone."

"Remind me to thank your sister for running into me."

"I'll thank her for myself, too."

"Do you have a couple of hours or do you have to get back?" Jim asked.

She frowned and leaned into him. "I have to get back pretty soon, but lets drag it out."

To drag out their time they went a couple of decks down to one of the restaurants. Neither of them were really hungry so they just had a small snack and some drinks as they talked for over an hour before Soriya reluctantly brought the evening to an end. They parted for the night after Jim escorted her back to her room.

"Well...," she began to try to say goodnight.

Jim smiled at her and gently kissed her. "Call me when you get up, okay."

"Okay," she replied.

"Goodnight," they said almost together

Jim managed to avoid Stormy and his redhead, though he could hear them laughing as he went through the suite to his room. He was asleep in minutes and woke up the next morning very refreshed. He cleaned up and got dressed and was thinking about food when Soriya called.

"Good morning," she said sleepily over the comm.

"Morning. Did you just wake up?"

"Yeah. Why? When did you wake up?"

"Over an hour ago. When can you be ready?"

"If it's just for breakfast, I can meet you in twenty minutes at that small bar just down the corridor."

"Perfect. I'll see you in twenty minutes."

Jim detected the sudden rush of wakefulness as she realized what he meant. "Just be patient," she begged.

"I will be. Bye."

"I'll hurry. Bye."

Jim chuckled as the connection ended. She was cute. She'd really thought he'd take twenty minutes the exacting Corps way. Well, he could use the few extra minutes.

The first thing to greet his eyes as he left his room was Stormy's redhead, in all her natural glory, standing by the food dispenser. He tried to sneak out without attracting her attention, but the sound of the door closing behind him gave him away.

"Oh hi," she said without any additional modesty. "You must be Jim. Nice to meet you. I'm Brizea. Storm said I might run into you."

"Nice to meet you," Jim said with all the politeness he could muster. "I have to meet someone, so if you will excuse me." Jim exited as fast as he could.

"It was nice meeting you," he heard Brizea call after him.

Jim went to find a member of the crew to get some information before he went to wait for Soriya. Fortunately, by the time he found someone, they had the answer he was looking for or it would have been him who was late. As it was, his chron said nineteen minutes had passed by the time he sat at the small bar near Soriya's room.

She rushed in a few minutes later and Jim just couldn't help teasing her. "Twenty-three minutes. Not bad."

"Oh stop it. I told you to be patient."

"I am. I'm just teasing you."
"Well, behave yourself or I won't kiss you today."
"I'll be good. What do you want?"
"You."
Jim laughed. "I meant to eat."
Soriya ended up picking a small gourmet breakfast. Jim opted for his more typical large Corps breakfast. Soriya was amazed at the amount of food that he could put away. "Don't they feed you in the Corps?" she asked him.
"Of course. I'm going a bit light since I'm on vacation."
"You mean you normally eat more than this?"
"Yes. I also work a lot harder."
"I just can't imagine it."
A short companionable silence followed as they both enjoyed their respective breakfasts.
"So what do you want to do today?" Jim asked her.
"I don't know. Why don't we just wander around and see what we find?"
"That sounds like a fun plan."
An hour later they were outside the Folei game courts, but there were already too many people waiting for an open court so they just went up to the viewing deck to watch. They had a good view of three of the courts. "I'd much rather watch anyway," Soriya told him.
"Not much of a player?"
"Oh, I can play and I'm pretty good, but I tend to just watch my sisters. They are really good. I wouldn't be surprised if they are waiting down there to get on one of the courts. Since they are identical twins, it makes keeping track of who's winning very challenging."
"Identical?"
"Even though I've known them all their lives, I still have a problem telling them apart sometimes. At least they never dress alike."
"That would make it impossible, wouldn't it."
"The worst thing is that they can act exactly the same. Jess usually acts as reserved as Mel really is. They have fooled so many people."
"I might be able to tell them apart. I have some experience with that. I've always been good at seeing through people."

Soriya laughed. "I'll tell them you said that. They'll take you up on that you know. They will put you to the test."

Jim smiled and took the challenge.

Stormy woke up alone. He hadn't really thought Brizea would stick around. He got up and looked around, but didn't find any message from her. He had the most rotten luck with women. Sometimes he thought he was cursed. True he enjoyed his pleasures with the ladies, but he did want more deep down. He let out a long sigh and turned to the autochef and asked for his favorite breakfast.

It seemed that every time he really enjoyed an evening with a women, it was she who was after the night of passion more than he was. He kept hoping that one of these women would be after more and stick around for a while, but he had time yet. He wanted to try to at least make the early retirement age before he worried too much about finding a permanent companion. Stormy had to admit that those women he was truly interested in were a small percentage of those he took to bed, but still, everyone he had the slightest interest in seemed to vanish with the morning.

He and Jim had both taken to the typical Custom Guard playboy lifestyle when they'd first joined up. Jim had quickly tired of that scene and become a bit choosier with the women he dated. Romanced would be a better word. Jim hadn't had any luck finding a long term partner, but those women he dated certainly remembered him fondly. Stormy pondered over breakfast why he'd never changed; why he still seduced women instead of romancing them. He guessed romance just wasn't his style.

In lieu of female companionship, Stormy decided to find the gym and work out for a while. He checked with the ship's information network to make sure he found a gym with adjustable gravity. His home planet of Powa-Fevna'han had a much higher gravity than most humans felt comfortable with and he preferred to work out in that higher gravity to try to stay acclimated to his homeworld, even though he hadn't been there in years.

The gym was fully equipped and in the comforting feel of the higher gravity, Stormy made use of most of their equipment during his hour long intense workout. Then he took advantage of the VR treadmill to take his usual cool off run.

Jim and Soriya had a marvelous afternoon. They were on their way to dinner when the deck shook under their feet.

"What was that?" Soriya asked.

"That felt like a missile attack."

The deck shook harder this time throwing them both off balance. The lights dimmed then steadied. It was quickly followed by another, smaller, shake and a slight fluctuation of the gravity. "I believe we are under attack?"

"By who?"

"There have been reports of Pirates in this area, but I have no clue why they would be going after a cruise ship. That makes no sense."

Their conversation was cut short by Jim's comm unit. He didn't need to answer it to know it was Stormy. As soon as he activated it Stormy started talking. "You should see the sleek lines of the attacker. It's a custom job."

"Pirates then?"

"Definitely. They're closing in for boarding. Let's meet up."

"How's the executive rec room sound?"

"Perfect. See you there in five."

"Come on, we're going to meet Stormy and figure out what to do." Jim practically dragged Soriya as he rushed to the executive rec room. They entered through one door moments before Stormy entered through another. Soriya was practically breathless while the two men weren't even winded.

"Do you think we have a chance?" Jim asked Stormy.

"That depends on how many of them there are. We'll know after they board. There really isn't much we can do until then." Stormy looked carefully at Soriya. "Why did you bring her here?"

"She's with me so I intend to look after her. Why, did you get dumped again?"

Stormy just grunted in response.

"Can we," Soriya began as she got her breath back, "make sure my sisters are okay, too?"

"I think so. We have a few minutes before they board. Try to call them on the ship's comm. It might still be working."

Fortunately it was and Soriya was able to track her sisters down. Stormy had tersely warned not to hint at the real danger so she used a private code the sisters had devised to signal a troublesome man. When Mel and Jess arrived minutes later, they were ready to defend Soriya from Jim and Stormy. It took several minutes for her to calm them down and explain the real danger. Then the two younger girls became really worried.

In the meantime, Stormy had been hacking into the ship's systems to try to gain the upper hand when the time came. He was making little progress and getting very frustrated. Jim, for all his undercover training, couldn't be much help when it came to hacking into a ship's system. Stormy had been doing this for a long time and he regularly had to slice through layers of security that the criminal elements thought would protect their ships from the prying eyes of the Customs Corps patrols. This cruise ship was proving to be a bigger challenge than he anticipated.

After she had calmed down, Jess took note of what Stormy was doing and was watching his progress, or rather lack thereof. After a several minutes she became frustrated. "That's not how you do that," she blurted out. "You are going about this the wrong way. That might work on some small trader's ship, but on a cruise ship they do things a little differently." Jess spoke from experience. She and her sisters had practically grown up in such surroundings and Jess had long ago learned how to hack into the ship's systems to circumvent many of the safety protocols and age restrictions. Stormy just glared at her in response. "Do you want to let me try? I might actually get somewhere," Jess suggested.

"What have we got to lose, Storm?" Jim pointed out. "You aren't getting anywhere as it is."

Stormy's glare deepened, but he motioned for Jess to give it a shot. She sliced through the layers of security almost like they weren't there. "Not bad," he said grudgingly. "Can you get into the ship's environmental systems? I'd like...." Stormy was stopped by the grins on the other two girls and the slow blush spreading on Jess's face.

"Yea," Mel said, "Like that time you turned off the gravity when Kashuk dumped you and was dancing with that Wishva girl."

"You didn't have to bring that up," Jess complained.

Their amusement was erased as the ship shook again reminding them of their impending problem.

Now that Stormy had access to the ship's main systems he set up a back door using tricks that Jess couldn't even fathom. When he was done, he would be able to make changes from almost any control board on the entire ship. He pinned a view of the approaching pirate ship to one corner of the screen while he worked.

"Now," he began, "there aren't any weapons to speak of on this ship and I'm sure our friends there will be bringing their own."

"So what do we do?" Mel asked.

"We take them from them. We have to disarm them anyway so why not turn around and use their own weapons against them. The first couple might be hard, but we will have surprise on our side."

"What do you want us to do?" Mel asked.

For the first time Stormy took note of who he was talking to. "There isn't much you can do except stay out of the way."

"Really?" Mel began. Jess looked like she was ready to back her sister up.

"I think Stormy's right," Soriya interjected. "But I bet there are a few things that we can do to help them out."

Stormy looked about to argue, but Jim followed Soriya's lead. "We do need someone to watch our backs and handle the security systems," he told his friend.

As Stormy was a very practical man, he could see where this was going and how useful a team of five would be as opposed to two so he shrugged and agreed with the division of labor.

Half an hour later, the pirate ship docked and the first boarding team boldly came through the hatch onto the cruise ship. The met no resistance as the cruise ship captain had followed their instructions to the letter and warned the passengers and crew of the impending boarding. In doing so everything had played right into Stormy's plan.

The boarding party split into three groups of four. Stormy had easily predicted where one of those groups would head and had selected an ambush location. The four pirates never knew what hit them as the two heavily muscled Customs Agents used brute force to knock them flat as they hurried to the bridge.

Stormy sent one man flying down a side corridor. He landed in an awkward position with the unpleasant sounds that indicated a serious, if not mortal, injury.

Jim dispatched the two on his side of the corridor with fluid attack moves backed by his muscle strength. They careened into a bulkhead as Jim came away with their side arms in his hands.

The fourth one almost got Stormy. He lunged as Stormy was mid throw dispatching the other pirate. Stormy saw him at the last moment and avoided the long silver blade that this particular pirate preferred to his pistol. Stormy's training took over and he caught the knife wielding arm. The pirate grinned as he pressed his advantage and tried to drive the knife into Stormy's chest. Stormy smiled back and used his superior strength to turn the knife back on the pirate and seconds later the pirate lay dead on the deck with his own knife sticking out of his chest.

"That was a bit messy," Jim commented.

"Yeah, but it got the job done. Let's put these two away for later," he said indicating the two that Jim had at gunpoint. They stripped them and put them in a supply closet down a side corridor. They sealed the door with one of the pirates pistols.

"Now lets see what the girls have for us."

"The other two groups went about where you thought they would," Jess said over the comm when Stormy contacted her a few minutes later. "The second team went straight to engineering and the third to life support. That third team almost got themselves lost and have been arguing for several minutes."

"They have any other problems?" Stormy asked.

"No, the crew went to their quarters so they didn't meet any resistance."

"Who do you want to face next?" Jim asked. "I'd say the ones in life support."

"I think you're right. Should we face them directly?"

"I have another idea if Mel or Soriya would be willing to help?"

Mel smiled impishly as she volunteered.

The Life support team had just gotten a call from their captain who was worried that the first team hadn't reached the bridge when Mel, looking very scared and much younger than she really was, stumbled into the Life Support control room. She took one look at the pirates and screamed.

"Look what we have here, boys," one of them said with a devilish grin on his face.

Stormy, looking his least intimidating, came in behind her. "I told you not to run...," Stormy stopped cold when he saw the pirates. "I just came to get my daughter," he stammered.

"She's ours now. I suggest you just run...," and he never had a chance to say another word as Jim shot him through the head from the corridor. A second one dropped from Jim's second shot before the other two even moved. One lunged for Stormy and tried to draw his pistol at the same time. The other went after Mel and fell dead from Jim's third shot at Mel's feet. The evil look on Stormy's face and the pistol that had almost magically appeared in his hand froze the last pirate in his tracks. Mel had the pleasure of taking his gun, and then gathered the guns from the three dead pirates. They locked the lone survivor in a closet, as they had the other three, and disposed of the dead pirates.

"We've got four more...," Stormy began when his comm interrupted him.

"Hey guys," Jess called over the comm, "we've got twenty more pirates that just came on board. Half are heading to the bridge and half have spread out. I think they are looking for you."

"Sounds like it's time for target practice. Shall we?" Stormy asked.

Stormy and Jim loaded up with four weapons each. One of the pirates had a smaller second gun that Mel grabbed. Stormy was about to argue with her but her determined expression and the outstanding way she'd already handled herself stalled him into silence.

"Just watch our back, Mel," Jim said. "You'll help us out most by making sure no one shoots us from behind."

With the help of Jess and Soriya relaying what the ship's security system showed, they were able to avoid two pirate boarding parties and cornered the third in a deadly crossfire. Stormy opened up on them first taking out one before they ducked under cover. While they were turned away, Jim jumped out and mowed the other three, but not before they had radioed their comrades.

"You have two pirates coming from aft," Jess called over their comms. Mel was the first one to see them and got off a lucky shot hitting one of the pirates in the middle of the chest. Stormy quickly turned and clipped the second one in the leg just as he tried to duck out of sight.

"I don't think you got him," Jim said.

"No, I just nicked him." Stormy cautiously edged down the corridor until he could see the alcove that the pirate must be in. He could hear muted whispering and assumed he was calling for help. In a much practiced maneuver, he jumped across the possible line of fire and shot twice into the alcove. When he stopped on the other side, all was now silent in the alcove except for a faint murmur from the pirate's comm.

When the comm abruptly stopped, they both instinctively knew that the person on the other end had guessed what had happened and would be sending more pirates their way. There was only a moment's hesitation before they both decided that they would wait in ambush.

The seven pirates who came to investigate moved with great caution. Even so they weren't prepared to be ambushed. Stormy dropped into their midst from where he had hidden in the ceiling. They were momentarily surprised allowing Stormy to take three of them out in mere seconds. Just as the others regained their composure to start fighting back, Jim on one end and Mel on the other opened fire. Stormy figured Jim could take care of himself so he concentrated on the two left standing between him and Mel. Once had taken cover and there was no way Mel could get him from her location. Stormy acted fast and took a flying leap. He impacted the pirate, but not before the pirate got off a shot that hit Stormy's thigh. The other pirate was distracted and looked like he was about to take advantage of Stormy's predicament when a blast from Mel's pistol hit him in the chest. He was the last to fall.

Jim had no trouble dispatching the other two. The first fell to a direct shot and the second after Jim rolled down the corridor and came up shooting. He checked to be sure all the pirates were either dead or out cold before he turned to find out how Stormy was.

"It's not bad," he told them, "It just hurts like hell."

"Let me have a look," Jim told him sternly, knowing how Stormy didn't like to admit how bad things could be. But Stormy was right, it was just a minor injury. The pirates weren't using very deadly weapons. But they were good weapons to take over a liner and take hostages.

"We do need to recapture engineering," Stormy commented. "They should be the next group on our list."

"Are you up to that?" Mel asked him.

"Of course. I've been hurt worse than this and still done what I needed to."

"You guys need to get out of there," Jess called over the comm. "There are three groups of pirates headed your way."

"Engineering it is then," Jim decided.

Getting into engineering proved to be easier said than done. Stormy's plan was to sneak in from a different direction and take them by surprise, but the hatch he needed to get through to do that was sealed and nothing Jess could do had any effect.

"You know," Jess started, "with what the engineers locked down before they left and with what I could lock down remotely, there really isn't anything they can do from there. You still have thirteen other pirates running around to deal with."

"Jess has a point," Stormy agreed. "Let's get the others first."

Mel chuckled.

"What's so funny?" Jim asked.

"Just that if there are so many pirates on board the liner, whose guarding their ship."

"I think the girl has a point."

The airlock was guarded by three pirates, one of higher rank. Jim and Mel watched as Stormy came into view opposite the airlock from them, swore, and ran off.

The higher ranked pirate motioned for the other two to go after him. He was still looking in that direction when Jim slammed into him and broke his neck.

"You two are frighteningly efficient," Mel commented.

"It's just good training."

They waited a few minutes for Stormy to return. "They think I went up a deck. It'll be a while before they give up."

They locked and sealed the hatch into the pirate ship and cycled the airlock. There wasn't anything they could do from there to disconnect the docking mechanism. Mel wasn't as good as her sister, but she did know a few things about hacking into a computer to find things like maps and other information not usually considered critical. It took her less than five minutes to get a full display of the ship and even less time for Jim and Stormy to memorize what they'd seen. Mel tried but failed to get a crew compliment for this trip.

"Try checking the life support status?" Jim suggested.

"Why?" Mel asked.

"If we know the capacity and how long they've been out, we can guess at how many there are and be pretty close."

"How close?"

"Plus or minus two is what the Corps figures."

"You picked up some interesting things in your intelligence training," Stormy commented.

After Mel brought up the figures, Jim did some quick calculating and arrived at an estimate of forty to forty-five pirates. The left five to ten left on the ship.

"You two go to engineering," Stormy suggested. "I'll head to the bridge and if I need help I'll call."

Jim looked like he was about to argue when he guessed Stormy's concerns. "And we'll call you if we run into anything we can't handle."

The bridge wasn't on the same deck as the airlock. Stormy tagged along with Jim and Mel partway back until he found the gangway going up. Once on the right deck he cautiously made his way forward. He didn't encounter anyone until he was almost there. He and one of the pirates surprised each other and the pirate received a fist in the face and unconsciousness for his troubles. Stormy tied and gaged him quickly to make sure he wouldn't be surprised later.

Jim and Mel had better luck getting to engineering unnoticed. Jim sealed the door behind them to prevent reinforcements and then they started looking for the engineering crew. After a thorough search, they didn't find anyone.

Jim brought up the power stats and found that the pirate ship was taking advantage of the umbilical connections to the liner to leach power. There wasn't anything Jim could do from engineering as those functions were strictly controlled from the bridge.

The bridge wasn't all that small and could house most of the five to ten people Jim had estimated were still onboard. Stormy cautiously approached the door and found it sealed from the inside. It would require a code to open. For most people that would be the end of the plan, but Stormy took a more forceful approach. He smashed the controls and yanked out the wires. He'd done this a few times before and hopped that he could do it now when time mattered as fast as he had before. He crossed the wires in sequence and the door clicked and slid open.

As he expected, the pirates took a few pot shots as the door opened. He had one shot at this. He lunged through the door and landed rolling. He knocked over two pirates and came up next to a third who was so surprised that he didn't move for the couple seconds he had before Stormy grabbed him and tossed him into a fourth. A fifth pirated jumped out the door and used it as cover as he opened fire on Stormy.

Stormy managed to dodge every shot, but the controls and viewport weren't so lucky. When one shot punctured the innermost layer of the viewport, the klaxon sounded. Stormy's view down the corridor showed three unhappy people enter from a side room. Their weapons were drawn.

Stormy smiled and shot two of them before ducking to the side of the door. When the Pirate at the door tried to fire around the corner, Stormy grabbed his arm and threw him across the room where he landed on the main control panel. Since it had already been shot to pieces, it didn't matter. He closed the door to give himself a few seconds to prepare. He grabbed the pistols off the bodies lying around the bridge. One was an older model with an interesting flaw that Stormy took advantage of.

When one of the pirates opened the door a minute later, something clattered to the deck at their feet which was in itself nothing to worry about, but they instantly panicked when they detected the slowly building whine. One jumped through the door and closed it behind him and Stormy detected that at least one other was running the other direction before the closing door cut off his view.

A small explosion rocked the corridor and kept the pirate's attention off Stormy. When he did remember and look around, it was just in time to face a fist flying at him. Stormy took the few minutes the explosion bought him to finish securing the bridge. He took stock of the controls, now partially damaged in the fighting. It was mostly functional, but the comm system and navigation interface were both non-functional.

Jim and Mel had completely secured the Engineering section and sealed all the entrances. From Jim's perspective this was to give Mel a safe haven while he went back out and finished taking the ship.

"But you need someone to watch your back," Mel complained.

"I can't leave Stormy to do it all and I can't be worrying about keeping you safe at the same time. Please just stay here and keep this area secure."

"You don't have to be so protective, but I'll stay right here. For now, anyway."

Jim didn't leave through the main entrance, but chose one of the smaller ones and had Mel seal it after him.

He found himself in a small crawlway that extended forward between the main deck they'd come in on and the one below. It contained various life-support and power systems. Had he known what was what, he could have easily disabled the entire ship from here.

He went forward until he was almost in the bow of the ship. He exited into a small room on the main deck that looked like a crew common room. It was deserted. Recalling the layout, he exited to port and went aft to the main gangway. He was debating about where to go when he heard and felt a small explosion from the deck above. He rush up the gangway and almost was knocked over by a pirate running down past him. He turned and tackled the pirate and knocked him to the deck. There was a sickening crunch that indicated something had been broken and Jim suspected the pirate might be dead. But then piracy still rated such a punishment in the courts.

"You didn't have to kill him, you know," a voice said from behind. "And don't try anything or you'll be dead."

Jim sensed the truth in the Pirate's words and turned slowly. This wasn't the just an ordinary pirate. He was dressed more ornately and sported a moustache. "Are you in charge of this rabble?" Jim asked.

"I never thought of them as rabble. But you and your friends seem determined to make this difficult."

"You could say it comes with the territory."

"You'd be some sort of government person then, wouldn't you?"

"I just really hate pirates."

"Pirate is such a harsh word."

"But very accurate."

"But we need to end this. I can't have you killing off my entire crew."

"Are you the captain?"

"I'm Brehl Dar and this is my ship. At the moment, I'd like to escape this situation with my ship and my life. I'm not prepared to give those up without a fight. But I will concede that you have kept me from my mission."

"That was our primary goal. But I don't think my partner will be so willing to stop at that."

"It is worth your life? I bet it isn't. I'm sure we can agree on something. Your friend has the bridge. Let's go talk to him."

Jim shook his head and followed Dar's instructions. They stopped outside the badly scarred hatch that lead to the bridge. "Very resourceful," Dar commented sadly. "These were good men."

"What now," Jim asked.

"Get him to open the door."

Jim only had one option. The door was likely soundproofed and air tight so he called Stormy on the comm.

"How's it going out there?" Stormy asked.

"It could be better."

"You got careless?"

"You could say that."

"What does the captain want?"

"He wants to concede the liner but leave with his life and his ship...."

"And don't forget what's left of my crew," Dar added.

"And the rest of his crew."

There was a pause as Stormy pondered. "We really shouldn't allow them to get away. There are ways to finish this."

"But are they worth it, Stormy?"

"That is the question." Silence followed as Stormy gave it some thought. Being in the intelligence arm of the Corps had given Jim a sense that there were some battles you chose to lose in order to win in the end. Stormy's line of work in the daily grind of system patrols didn't share that philosophy. Stormy was trained to look at only the immediate incident and he might not see the big picture.

"As much as I'd like to kill or capture every one of your crew, Captain, I think it might be prudent to agree with you on this. But you'll have to surrender to Jim if you want me to let you go. I won't agree to anything as long as you have a hostage. But you have our word that you and your ship will be allowed to leave."

Dar thought about the choice he was being given. Jim didn't get the sense that he was the hardened pirate type. He seemed to be more a corporate flunky. He likely worked for someone else.

"I'll take you up on that, Mr. Stormy." He handed Jim his sidearm.

"It's just Stormy," he said as he took the weapon. "Now if you could get all your people back aboard, we will send you on your way."

Dar nodded in agreement. Both he and Jim got on their comms to carry out the terms of the agreement.

"So we aren't going to finish them off?" Mel asked when Jim told her to meet him at the door to engineering.

"No, we aren't. We've put a good dent in their numbers. That's good enough."

They met back up with Stormy and Dar at the main airlock which was still sealed. Dar had contacted his men aboard the liner and Jim opened the airlock to let them in. Dar gave them some terse instructions and they headed deeper into the ship.

Jim nodded to Stormy that they were all accounted for. Stormy motioned for Jim and Mel to go back to the Liner. When they were safely off, he turned to Dar. "You've kept your end so we will keep ours. I hope we don't meet again. I'd have to finish what I've started here."

"I don't think you and I will meet again. Stay away from I'ab and I'vo and I'll guarantee it."

Stormy backed through the hatch and closed it as he went. Mel was already working on what Stormy wanted done. She over pressurized the airlock and ran the sequence of commands to disconnect the pirate ship. When the board said they had a soft dock, Stormy said, "Do it."

"Initiating," Mel said.

They all felt a slight lurch as the airlock suddenly opened and decompressed. The air created a strong thrust that pushed the pirate ship a considerable distance from the liner. With their controls damaged, they wouldn't be able to correct it right away.

Jim got on the comm with Soriya and asked, "Are our prisoners still tucked away?"

"They didn't find them and they haven't gotten out on their own. There aren't any cameras so I can't tell you if they are still tied up or not, but they haven't moved from where you put them."

"Good. Then we have come away with something besides just beating them off the liner."

Stormy and Jim gathered the prisoners and the dead pirates. They made a makeshift holding cell in a larger storage closet and made sure the prisoners were secure. They debated about the dead pirates, but finally decided a simple space burial would be best. The liner didn't have any supplies for that purpose, so they just dumped them in space from an airlock.

The captain was quite grateful for their help, but didn't seem surprised that it had happened. Soriya asked Jim about that as the liner returned to port.

"They weren't after money or cargo," Jim told her. "There was a very special passenger on board."

"So it was a kidnapping attempt?"

"I think so. There was nothing else on the liner that should have tempted a pirate."

The last day, the five of them met for lunch before going their separate ways. Soriya, Mel and Jess were headed home and Jim had to catch a Corps transport.

"Thanks for meeting us for lunch," Mel told them. "We wanted to thank you for giving us the best vacation we've ever had."

Stormy almost choked on his drink while Jim just laughed. "I'm glad you had fun," Jim told her. "Most people would be glad it's over."

"Oh, that's not what I meant. I mean, most vacations are just so boring and this one wasn't. I wouldn't want to go through it again, but it was something I'll never forget."

Mel still looked worried so Soriya added, "I'm sure he knows what you mean, Sis. I think we all feel that way."

"You know," Stormy began, "We couldn't have done it without you three. There are things the two of us are good at and there are things we aren't."

"Next time I hear of a pirate threat," Jim suggested, "we can take another vacation together."

"I have a better idea," Soriya said. "Let's just take a vacation and skip the pirates."

They all agreed that it might be fun and Jim warned the three girls again about Stormy's womanizing habits.

"You never did tell me who was on the cruise that the pirates were after," Soriya reminded Jim.

"Monnel Safi was onboard in a private suite near the bridge. They could have practically written their own ransom check if they'd succeeded."

The three girls were in shock. "Not the Monnel Safi?" Jess asked.

"With the number of people in her party it couldn't have been anyone else. I think she owes us a favor. Too bad we can't collect."

After an enjoyable lunch, they parted ways. Jim had time to reflect on the trip as he waited for the transport. Stormy had been right to agree to let the pirate go. It gave them some information that might lead to the rest of the organization. Someone else would probably be the lucky agent assigned to that case. Jim had other, more interesting cases. It had turned out to be a very good vacation after all.

Chased by Shadows
4614 GCE

"Captain," First Mate Hilum called down the gangway. "We've got company."

Captain Alluren Beldaras kept her door open most of the time for just such emergencies. In a flash she was out of her cabin and across the common room and racing up the gangway. Hilum was silent as they stopped at the control panel just behind the pilot. On the screen the scanners showed a ship coming up fast behind them. It was still too distant to get a positive ID on it.

She checked their stats and saw they were at maximum power and their shields were configured to protect from any attack from behind.

"I never would have thought this cargo would be that important. Henges warned me, but I never believed him."

Hilum didn't dare smile. The Captain might make that claim, but she had ordered them to proceed with caution and run at top speed and with *Lehra Aur's* shields at full. Part of it was her natural paranoia, but she had listened to some extent. "What should we do?" he asked her.

"There isn't anything we can do right now. We are going fast enough that they won't catch up with us for at least half an hour. I want to see who they are before I make any plans."

Hilum waited a moment for her to do something before he realized that she fully intended to stand there until there was a change.

Captain Beldaras was an intense woman. She wasn't very tall, but she made up for it with her dominating personality. She couldn't really call any of the four in her crew friends.

Hilum didn't know if she really had anyone she could call a friend. She was very much a loner. He'd served with her for six years now. Only Loris, the senior navigator, had served with her longer. They were very much alike, but outside of their navigator-captain relationship, they never associated.

Loris had a sordid past. She'd learned late that she had an aptitude for navigation. Before that she'd lived planet side and had an ordinary life. Something had happened and her husband and two children had been killed. She'd drawn a line in her past and never talked about it with anyone, but she did have a picture of them in her bunk. She had a talent for finding the best route through the densest of star clusters. As near as Hilum could tell, Loris had been on the ship when Captain Beldaras had bought the ship sixteen years ago.

Hie, the pilot currently at the controls, was the newcomer. He'd only been with them for a little over six months. He still hadn't gotten used to the Captain's hard manner. He took her barking personally. Hilum was still trying to show him the ropes, but he wasn't sure how much longer Hie would last.

The other navigator hadn't shown her face since her shift had ended seven hours ago. Hilum knew that Urazid was awake and knew what was going on. She only slept four hours a day. But if she wasn't in the cockpit, she was on the lower deck with her music. She was almost obsessed with keeping up on all the latest music. She didn't talk about it much, but Hilum had gotten hints that a relative of hers was in the music industry and sent her all the music she could possibly want. She was the least experienced of the crew, but she had an instinct for navigation that came a close second to Loris. She still made rookie mistakes on occasion, but what she could do could be considered music of a different sort.

"There we are," the Captain suddenly said. Hilum looked and saw the ship following them on the scanner. It was larger, but it wasn't a Customs ship. It didn't look armed, but that didn't mean much. Hilum knew from experience that most armed ships carried their weapons concealed.

"Any idea who they are?" Hilum asked when the Captain didn't volunteer anything.

"Not yet, but I know who they aren't, which is a start."

Their cargo was completely legal; Captain Beldaras wouldn't carry anything that wasn't. She was up-front with every client that she opened every crate that came on board her ship. Their current cargo shouldn't be an unusual target, but Hilum guessed that there was something he wasn't getting about the real value of the cargo. His mind was on the danger that they were being followed by pirates. The last ship he'd served on had had a serious run in with a band of pirates near the Felkil sector. Captain Beldaras avoided that sector for that very same reason.

"Yes," the Captain said as she thought about their follower and what course of action she should take. "I don't think they mean to attack us. They won't have intercepted us by the time we make orbit and they wouldn't dare attack us under the gaze of the Customs patrols. I think they mean to follow us down and intercept us on the surface. The rules are different down there."

Captain Beldaras was referring to their destination, Metajis Orom. It was a wild world and crime was rampant. An attack on the cargo there would likely go unnoticed and, in the scheme of things, would fall through the cracks. If they were to deliver the cargo safely, they would have to avoid any traps on the surface. Loris would love this. She always relished any mission that allowed her to carry a gun.

"What course of action are you thinking of, Captain?" Hilum asked.

"I'm working on it. I have some ideas, but I'm still working through them. Land as if nothing is wrong. I'll tell you what we are doing by the time we touch down."

They both watched the scanner as they approached the planet. Their shadow kept closing until they reached the Customs perimeter, then they slowed to a similar velocity.

It wasn't until they had landing clearance and had hit the worst of the ionization of atmospheric entry that Captain Beldaras smiled. She had her plan.

The ship slipped easily into the atmosphere and the glow of ionized plasma against the shields quickly faded. Metajis Orom was not naturally habitable and required constant atmospheric replenishment. The side effect was a fast entry and a dirty orange sky. The surface was covered with normal greenery and they could see the silver spires of the city as they approached the port.

Captain Beldaras keyed the comm to the local network. She had their client on the line before they were on final approach to the port.

"We are having a bit of a problem, Henges," she said. "I wasn't too worried until we picked up a shadow after we came out of hyperspace."

"What do you intend to do about it?" Henges asked.

"If we are quick, we can have your cargo off the ship before they find us. How soon can you get a transport to the port?"

"It'll be at least ten minutes. You'll have landed by then."

"Well, how important is this cargo to you? I was under the impression it was pretty important."

"It is. I'll see if I can arrange a transport to meet you. I'll be there as soon as I can."

The connection closed and Captain Beldaras gave her full attention to the view out the front port.

"I'm confused," Hilum said. "You never told him what our berth assignment was."

"No need. He already knew, just as I'm sure he knows who is following us. He didn't show any surprise that we were being followed. I think he expected us to fight them off. Go down and get Urazid. I'm going to need all of you to help with the cargo to get the hold emptied in time."

Hilum didn't waste a second heading to the lower aft deck. Urazid wasn't in the common room so he checked the crew cabin. He wasn't surprised that she didn't hear him, she was listening to music in her bunk, like he'd guessed. She saw him and paused the music.

"Captain wants you to help with the cargo. We're being followed and she wants to get it unloaded as soon as we land."

A hard to read look crossed her face before she answered. Hilum guessed she was looking for a way to say no, but there really wasn't any way out of it. "I'll be right up," was all she said.

She wasn't dressed for work, so Hilum assumed she needed to change. He went back up to the flight deck and waited. Urazid took a little longer than he would care for, but she did arrive well before the ship landed.

Captain Beldaras didn't move until the ship touched down in the assigned berth. She checked the status of their shadow and estimated they had fifteen minutes to move a cargo that would normally take more than twice that long.

"Hie, finish the shutdown procedures. The rest of you are on cargo duty. We should have a transport here to load it on any minute." She led the way to the main hatch and extended the ramp. The cargo completely filled the hold and blocked the internal access hatch so she had to extend the cargo ramp from underneath the ship. She keyed the lower hatch open and jumped on the cargo ramp before it was fully down.

The crates were large and awkward, but weren't very heavy. They had the first two down the cargo ramp by the time the transport had arrived. "Hilum, take over," the Captain said as she headed down the ramp to verify the identity of the new arrivals.

Hilum took over sorting the cargo and moving it to the top of the ramp while Loris and Urazid moved them down the ramp and arranged them outside.

Captain Beldaras was cautious and verified the identity of the cargo handlers before she let them start loading the cargo. Hilum checked his chron quickly and saw they only had about five minutes before their shadow might arrive. "Keep up the pace," he said to Urazid and Loris. They both nodded and stepped up the pace.

The first row of cargo cleared the internal hatch. They were on the second row when Hie came through the hatch at the back of the cargo bay. He got right to work and they started moving twice as much cargo. Hilum thought that they just might finish.

The last crate was moving down the ramp with one minute to spare and Hie and Hilum followed behind it in case there was trouble. One of the cargo handlers appeared and picked up the last crate and carried it to the waiting transport. Hilum closed the cargo hatch behind them as he and the rest of the crew stood in front of the ship.

Captain Beldaras looked over at Hilum and gave him a brief nod. Their pursuers could arrive at any moment. She continued to finalize the manifest and payment, not something that took long, but this time, when they wanted to be done as soon as possible, it seemed to take forever.

They heard the commotion before they could see anything. Weapons' fire echoed back from the street as Henges' guards opened fire.

"Hilum," Captain Beldaras yelled, "shift change, get her started and get clearance."

"Yes, Captain," he called back as he grabbed Urazid and headed for the main ramp. Hilum understood the shift change. On several previous occasions, Urazid had proved that as outstanding as she was as a navigator, she was incompetent when it came to weapons. Hie and Loris were both outstanding and already had their pistols drawn.

In the cockpit, the two worked in unison to get the ship ready for flight. Without a specific destination, there wasn't much Urazid could do to plot a course, so she proceeded to get the hyperspace engine partially charged and helped Hilum by calling for departure clearance. They both had a clear view of the gate and the back half of the transport and saw when the guards outside were overpowered and the people who had been following them entered the bay. Captain Beldaras, Hie, and Loris opened fire. It was times like this that made Hilum disagree with the laws that kept trade ships from carrying any armaments. A small anti-personnel weapon could solve all their problems in just a few moments. He had to admit that the three hand-held weapons that belonged to the ship were making a good show of themselves. Their attackers were trapped at the gate.

"We have conditional departure clearance in ten minutes," Urazid said. She didn't finish the thought that Hilum could see on her face. She was worried about their crewmates just out of view under the bow of the ship.

As firefights went, this one wasn't all that serious. The transport itself provided good protection from the gate and their attackers were trying to avoid hitting it. Hilum wasn't too surprised when the ship's comm beeped. It was their client. He'd guessed what was happening and had people on the way and was calling to check the status of his cargo and, almost as an afterthought, on its defenders.

"Right now we have them pinned at the gate and there isn't much going on. They aren't making any drastic moves and they are just trading a few shots now and then."

"We'll be there in thirty seconds."

The comm went dead. "Looks like he's bringing in backup to rescue his cargo," he said to Urazid.

"Good."

They had front row seats to see what transpired on the other side of the gate. At first all they could see was that the attackers were distracted. Then they could see the energy bolts flying across the gate as their client's people attacked in full force. The return fire slowly diminished and then suddenly stopped as the attackers were killed or ran away.

Captain Beldaras wasn't taking any chances, she marched around the transport and met their client's representative. After several minutes she turned and headed back to the ship. A couple of minutes later, Hie and Loris came in the hatch followed by the Captain. She retracted the ramp and closed the hatch behind her before joining Hilum and Urazid in the cockpit.

"It looks like our part is over," she said. "Do we have clearance?"

"We have conditional clearance," Urazid said. "Let me call and get final clearance."

Hilum glanced at the chron and saw that they'd been on the surface for less than half an hour. The chron passed the half hour mark before port control got back granting clearance for immediate departure. He didn't wait a second to confer with the captain, he knew her mind and it was time to go.

He was surprised when the comm beeped just as they were clearing the atmosphere. He was about to answer it from the pilot's console when Captain Beldaras keyed it from the secondary panel. She started to give her customary greeting when the voice on the other end cut her off saying, "Tradeship *Lehra Aur*, change trajectory for parking orbit and prepare to be boarded."

"What reason do you have for this action?" the captain asked.

"You are under suspicion of carrying contraband."

"Nonsense," she replied. "We just delivered a completely legal cargo to a reputable merchant. Our holds are now empty. You have no cause to detain us."

"We have a report stating that you received a large parcel of Gurvig powder in payment for your delivery. We will have to do a thorough search of your ship."

"That is preposterous. It will take hours, if not days for a thorough search. I am an honest trader, my record speaks for itself. I won't stand for this."

"I will remind you, Captain," the Customs Agent said over the comm, "that information from a credible witness trumps everything else. You are required by Galactic law to follow our instructions."

The captain said nothing as she closed the comm. Hilum knew better than to say anything. She would be weighing her options, but he was sure she would follow the instructions so he prepared the course change for orbit instead of escape and waited for her orders.

When they came several minutes later, they were not what he expected. "Hilum, maintain course."

He slowly turned to look at her, not believing his ears.

She saw him and just looked at him for a moment before she said, "We have nothing to hide and have acted aboveboard in all of this, but someone is playing dirty and I don't think the Custom's ship will have a chance to reach us. Did you check your scanners? We are being followed again."

Hilum checked his instruments and mutely nodded as he saw the familiar shape behind them. If they headed for orbit, their pursuer could easily catch up. He hadn't even thought to check for that.

With clear orders, he deleted the alternate course and slowly boosted the power. He altered the course slightly to give an indication that they were aiming for orbit, but that only served to put him in a better trajectory for a quick escape to hyperspace. "Get cracking on a hyperspace course," he told Urazid. Now that they had a final escape trajectory, she worked quickly to plot their course. Hilum smiled at her skills. For all her issues as a crewmate, this was why she was here and she excelled at it. He caught a glimpse of her course and wasn't surprised to see that it only took them a few parsecs away and wouldn't take more than a few minutes. As soon as she had that one done, she was plotting a proper course to their next scheduled destination.

When it was clear that they weren't diverting to orbit, the comm started beeping and their pursuer, who had been aiming for an orbital intercept, changed course to follow them. Hilum's trick had put them just far enough ahead that there was no chance that they would catch up before he turned the ship over to Urazid.

Their pursuer got far closer this time than when they'd approached the planet initially. Hilum started feeling a bit nervous that they were getting in range of any weapons their pursuer might have. His instincts proved right and he just had time to dodge their energy beam and avoid any damage.

"That was far too close, Hilum," the Captain said. "Are we almost far enough out?"

"Almost."

"We still have two minutes before the hyperspace capacitor is fully charged," Urazid added.

"Does it need to be fully charged for your course?" the Captain asked, fully aware of the answer.

"No, it is a short jump and it is sufficient for entry."

"Then don't wait."

Moments later they were far enough from the planet. "She's all yours," Hilum told Urazid. She nodded and just as she activated the hyperspace engine, they all felt the unmistakable impact of their pursuer's energy weapon. There was no indication of any serious damage immediately and the space in front of the ship was ripped open by their engines to let them slip into hyperspace.

The Captain didn't swear often, and when she did it wasn't a good sign. She let out a string of language that would have gotten them kicked out of any decent establishment on most planets. Hilum's board didn't show any problems, but when he turned to look at what the Captain was looking at, her board was covered with orange warning lights. He looked over at Urazid's board and it was clear as well.

The Captain saw him looking and said, "We have a problem. The main power converter has been hit. We are going to loose life support and we won't be able to recharge to enter hyperspace again."

"Ever changed a hyperspace course mid-flight?" Hilum asked Urazid.

She shook her head. She had turned white.

"If you want to live, get cracking at it."

Loris came up and spoke softly with the Captain for a moment and got wide eyed. Changing destinations while in hyperspace was not something most navigators ever had to do.

From her expression, Hilum guessed that Loris didn't even want to try and was glad Urazid was in the hot seat. Even Urazid looked back, hoping Loris would pull rank as Lead Navigator, but quickly went back to her panel when it became clear everything was in her hands.

The navigation computer was programmed to make it difficult to change course once it was engaged for a very good reason, it was not something that should be done except in an emergency. That programming made it doubly difficult to do when it was vital like it was now. Urazid had to resort to hacking the navigation system to disconnect it. She finished with five minutes to spare before the previous course would have ended. They were now flying blind in hyperspace.

With the eyes of the rest of her crew on her, she linked one of her screens to show their relative position to real space in a live picture. She added a course projection and it flashed showing a collision alert. She zoomed in on that location and found that it was not a true collision, but a near miss that would be far too close for safety. She went back to the raw course data in the navigation computer and put in a course change setting for three minutes and then adjusted the course after that to the extreme limit of what was possible and then checked the collision location again and found it just at the edge of the danger zone. It would have to do. She set a new course change point and searched for a known planet along the route. There wasn't anything. She widened the search parameters to the maximum she could deflect their course through hyperspace and tried again. There were now four matches. She checked each in turn for a location where they could land and service the ship. The first two only offered outposts to dock at but lacked any facilities. They needed more than that.

Hilum started to worry when the third destination turned out to be abandoned, but habitable. They would live, but would have to be rescued. With their recent encounter with Customs, they likely would be arrested if they depended on that scenario. He looked on anxiously as Urazid pulled up the fourth match. He smiled when he recognized it as a port with full facilities where they would be able to make proper repairs. Urazid double checked the listing and the coordinates and plotted the course. She rechecked the entire course before she told the navigation computer to initiate it. "Now we just have to get there," Urazid said quietly, breaking the silence.

"Good job," Captain Beldaras told her. She went back to her control board and frowned. "We are going to need to reduce our power consumption to make it that far. Hilum, what systems can we safely shutdown so we can make it there?"

Hilum checked his board and made some quick calculations. They had to leave most of the systems on at least standby in order for them to keep functioning. He checked off several items mentally before he turned around and told the Captain what they needed to do. "We need to turn off the lights, heat, comm system, food replicators, and all auxiliary systems. We have to leave the flight systems on standby and reduce the gravity, but leave the grav system operational. That should give us enough power and keep everything operational until we land."

The Captain nodded. "Everyone should remain on the flight deck to minimize the impact to life support. Loris, Hie, go below and gather all the blankets you can find. And bring up three chairs from the common room."

They quickly left the flight deck to follow the Captain's instructions, and very shortly returned with two chairs piled with blankets. Hie went back down and came back with a third chair.

The Captain keyed the aft control panel to activate the power saving measures and soon they were all feeling lighter. She closed the internal hatches, separating each compartment, including dividing the upper deck halfway aft. It left the smallest portion of the ship for them. Hilum knew that she hoped that the small space would give them the margins to survive and still stay comfortable. The calculations he'd done indicated it wouldn't really matter.

"At least with these course corrections it won't be easy to follow us," Urazid pointed out.

"Looking at the positive side of things is the best approach," Captain Beldaras said. "Now we should all rest quietly to conserve air." Hilum could tell she shared his thought that being followed on this course might be harder, but not impossible.

They were all used to spending time with little or nothing to do, but usually they had the advantage of doing it in their bunk or planet-side. There was little to do and only Urazid and

Hilum had comfortable seats. The chairs from the common room were designed for activities around the common room table, not for trying to bundle up in a blanket to stay warm.

The nine hours to their revised destination seemed to last for eternity. Each of them kept glancing at one of the displays showing the course and time to destination. Their normal jovial conversations never appeared. They were all very aware that they were sailing through hyperspace on a dying ship. The systems had to last long enough to get them to their destination. Hilum tried not to think about the ship that may or may not be following them that had inflicted the damage. It was better not to dwell on something worse than a dying ship.

The display showed their first course change was successful. It was the full 1.16 degrees this model hyperspace engine was capable of. Hilum could tell it was close by looming darkness that mirrored the star in real space. There were legends of things that lived in the gravity echoes and that if you got too close you'd never be seen again. Hilum preferred to believe that the gravity echoes disrupted travel and were best avoided for less mythical safety reasons.

By the time their second course change completed, they were all very tired, but unable to sleep. The silence of the crew and the minimal sounds of the ship's systems made every breath seem loud. At one point Hilum thought he could hear his own pulse. They had no choice but to wait and watch the systems. The hyperspace display showed their progress to the new destination and the life support display showed how long it estimated until the air would become unbreathable. The numbers were way too close the entire flight. The combination of stress and boredom only got worse as the display counted down the final minutes.

Hilum caught Urazid's slight smile as she worked the controls that would end their flight through hyperspace. She was up to something, but he wasn't sure what. She had better be very careful and sure of what she was doing. At the huge distances they covered every second in hyperspace, it required very precise calculations to arrive at your destination without arriving in your destination. He guessed she was going to deliberately overshoot the hyperspace beacon. With the crazy course they had taken to get here, that worried him.

The final seconds counted down and the navigation computer initiated the return to normal space. Hilum found himself tensing as they dropped out of hyperspace.

He had to give Urazid credit, she was good. Now that they were back in real space the rest of the landing was in his hands. She had managed to bring them halfway to the planet. Hilum quickly activated the comm and broadcast that they were having technical issues and needed to immediate clearance to land. It was granted in seconds.

When he set the course, he found the ship was positioned in exactly the right place for them to make a direct descent to the port. He'd have to get Urazid a special gift for the fantastic job she'd just done of not only getting them to this planet, but coming in and shaving more than half an hour off their approach time.

The captain was very vigilant. As the atmosphere gripped the ship's shields, she quietly said, "and there they are." They all knew what she meant.

With the power reduced to several systems, the atmospheric entry was rough and jarring. Hilum took advantage of the friction to reduce power and slow the ship. Port control had given him a vector that necessitated making a large spiral for the final approach to the port. As the ship started to bank into the spiral, the life-support alarm sounded.

Behind him, the Captain quickly turned off the alarm. "Now we have just what is in the cabin," she said then made several adjustments to the systems as the autopilot brought them in on the port's approach course.

Hilum saw the power readings change. He knew they still had enough air to make it down, but power was another thing. He checked the systems on his board and shut of what he could.

The autopilot beeped, indicating it was time for him to put the ship down in their assigned berth. With one eye on the power levels, he quickly took the controls. He cross referenced the planet's gravity with what the knew of the ship's capabilities and brought the ship in quickly and as hard as he dared.

The gravitic thrusters lost power a fraction of a second after the landing pads made contact, causing the ship to settle much harder than he'd hoped, but well within what the pads were designed to tolerate.

They all breathed for a moment before Hie asked, "What do we do about our shadow?"

"You and Loris get outside and get the umbilical connected so we have some power. When they get that done, Hilum will contact Customs and ask for help."

"With what happened back there," asked Loris, "won't that put you at risk?"

"It's better than what our shadow is planning for us," the Captain stated.

Hie and Loris were out of the ship moments later. The Captain had to join them when the port agent showed up and started chewing them out for the hard landing.

Hilum turned to Urazid and said, "Great job. I have never seen work like that before. That approach was daring, but I think you saved our skins."

"Thanks. I hope the Captain thinks the same way."

"I'll be sure to tell her what I think."

With the Captain taking care of the agent, Hie and Loris quickly had the umbilical connected and Hilum was immediately on the comm with Customs and asked for help. He got back the first piece of bad news, that the other ship had landed, but the girl he was talking to then stressed that she had dispatched a squad who should arrive in five minutes or less.

"Think they'll make it?" Urazid asked.

"I hope so. I guess it all depends on how close our shadow is." Hilum quickly contacted the port to arrange for the ship to be serviced. They'd arrive in about an hour, probably well after the excitement was over. Hilum privately hoped that they'd be here to go over the repairs.

"Why don't you stay here in case Customs calls back or if we need you to call them again. I'm going to join the Captain."

Urazid nodded.

He checked the master control panel as he stood up. He reset it to normal so the ship could draw air and power from the umbilical. Even before he got to the hatch, he could tell the difference in the air quality.

Outside, the Captain had placated the agent and they were discussing what the ship would need. Hie and Loris were already in position to face their shadows and Hilum joined them. According to his chron it could still be three minutes before Customs arrived.

The three didn't speak as they waited. The only sounds were the distance sounds of ships taking off and landing and the agent talking, occasionally punctuated by the Captain's terse answers.

They waited out the tension, pistols at the ready. The seconds dragged on before they heard anything. First they heard voices followed by the discharge of energy weapons. Nothing gave any indication of what was happening until the squad of Custom's Guards led a small group of bound prisoners into the berth.

Hilum quickly holstered his gun and went to meet the squad.

"Are you on this crew?" the squad leader asked him.

"Yes, I'm the first mate."

"Are these the ones you called us about?"

"I think so. Did they come from that ship I called in?"

"I'm pretty sure. We've put a lock on it. My sergeant should be here shortly. These four are guilty of firing on my squad so I've called for a transport to take them to detention."

"I didn't fire on you," one of the bound prisoners yelled. The squad leader pointedly ignored him.

They didn't have long to wait for the sergeant. He arrived with an uncomfortable look on his face and headed straight to the Captain.

"Captain Alluren Beldaras?" he asked.

"Yes, Sergeant?" she replied.

"We have apprehended several people who apparently were on their way here to attack you as you feared. We also received a message that you are to be arrested for breaking orbit in violation of a direct Customs order to remain in orbit. I'm sorry, but you will have to accompany me."

The Captain was silent for a moment. "Will it affect my first mate seeing to the repairs?"

"No. It only affects you specifically, as the captain."

"He can handle things. Let's go." She gave Hilum a nod as the sergeant led her away.

Hilum, Loris, and Hie stood there for a moment in shock before the port agent said, "That was unprecedented. Now we can't finish."

Hilum went into action as the Captain had indicated. "In Captain Beldaras's absence, I am authorized to conduct all business for our ship. I believe you were discussing the repairs and maintenance we need to have done. I wasn't listening to your conversation so let's start with a quick rundown of what she had covered."

Hilum spent the better part of an hour working things out with the representative. In the end a repair crew would be sent in for a preliminary check later in the day. The restock crew arrived shortly after the agent left.

With the ship out of the way, always the Captain's first priority, Hilum set about finding out what he could do to get her released.

The Captain had been processed and was being held in the local detention center. He wouldn't be able to see her or get her released until at least the next morning, but he was able to arrange to meet with her appointed advocate.

The man was neat and tidy, but had an air of someone who didn't get out much. "Holtov Salrot," he said when Hilum was shown into his office. "You must be Herkon Hilum, the first mate. What can I do for you?"

"How can we get this situation cleared up?"

"That is going to be difficult. Your captain violated a direct Custom's order. There are severe penalties for that."

"It wasn't her fault. Have you had a chance to speak with her?"

"No, nothing will happen until the hearing tomorrow morning. Would you care to fill me in on what you know?"

Hilum proceeded to tell him about their cargo delivery, being followed, the firefight, their hurried departure, the sudden charges of smuggling, the attack in orbit and the attempted attack here. He had brought in a data chit with the cargo manifest, the Captain's logs, and the automated ship logs of the landings and damage sustained.

"This is all quite interesting," Salrot said. "I'll have to verify this. Do you think I can contact your client about the cargo? I probably will need his statement. As the firefight occurred on the planet, that really isn't in Customs jurisdiction. I think we can get the charges dismissed based on this. The ship data files clearly show the ship was hit as it was entering hyperspace which clearly shows that Captain Beldaras's orders to break orbit were for self-preservation. Plus the other ship was ID'd following yours during the initial landing and departure and then the landing here. Meet me at the court tomorrow and I'll see what I can do."

Hilum returned to the berth and met with the repair crew and showed them the external damage and system diagnosis of the other issues. They did some scans and confirmed the damage. There were a couple of parts that they couldn't manufacture so they needed to return to their office to locate them. They would return the next day to begin work and have a better estimate on how long the repair would take. The parts might cause a delay if they couldn't find them locally.

Hilum knew there wasn't a lot to celebrate with the Captain detained, but he invited his three crewmates out anyway.

"The Captain always says that it is important to recognize an important achievement right away. I wanted to do that for Urazid, who showed tremendous skill today in getting us here safely. So, the drinks are on me."

"I didn't really do anything," Urazid pleaded.

"Nonsense," Loris said. "Remember who's lead navigator here. You did something I would have been scared to do. You deserve the praise. There are still a few things I can teach you, but you've got natural talent. You could go far, kid."

"I can't believe how quickly you did that," Hie added. "I watched you do it and I still can't believe it. And then coming out so much closer to the planet, that was even more amazing."

"You're not a navigator or you'd know which part is really amazing," Loris told him.

Hilum made sure he didn't overdo it so he could meet the advocate at court. Urazid eventually got into the celebratory mood and really overdid it. Hilum and Hie had to help her back to the ship.

The next morning Hilum was on time to the court. Salrot was already there and told Hilum to have a seat and stay quiet unless he was called on.

Hilum had never been to a court before and hoped he wasn't called on. He sat toward the back and waited.

The Captain's case was up first. The prosecutor went over the evidence that Customs had, which Hilum had to admit was pretty damning. But Salrot then presented the evidence that he had gathered, both from Hilum and the Customs records. He presented the documentation to the court.

The judge called for a short break and reviewed the information both sides presented for several minutes before he said anything. "It seems to me," the judge said directly to the prosecution, "that the real case in this is not Captain Beldaras, but the captain and crew of the ship following her. The evidence against them is quite compelling. If that evidence were presented against them, this would go to a full trial this afternoon. But for Captain Beldaras, this is sufficient to drop all charges per the emergency and threat to life clause. Captain, you are free to go. Please stay in port for the next couple of days in case we need your direct testimony."

The Captain joined Hilum in the back of the court and they watched as the captain and crew of the other ship had to go through the same situation. Their advocate had no evidence to back up his claims. The prosecution leveled several charges against them including filing a false report with Customs and attacking a Custom's squad. The judge found the evidence compelling and ordered the trial to begin after the lunch break.

The Captain and Hilum returned to the ship and found the repair crew hard at work. Their foreman reported that they had found the parts locally and unless they uncovered some unexpected damage, the ship should be ready in two days.

The Captain nodded her approval at the time schedule as it matched the judge's orders.

"I think we need a change of scenery, Hilum," she said. "When they have our girl back in shape I think we should head for the Lamgun sector and see what we can find there."

"An excellent idea. It will be good to be close to home for a while." He hadn't seen his sister in several years and hoped it wouldn't be too much of a shock for her.

Just before the repair team had finished, they got word that the crew of their shadow had been convicted of the charges and the ship was impounded and would be auctioned off, after it had been stripped of its illegal weapons.

When the repair crew certified their work complete, Captain Beldaras ordered their immediate departure. It was time to do something different.

A Night At Nova Trango
4614 GCE

Taru hesitated before she entered the back door of the Nova Trango Bar for her shift. This was her first shift back since her mother had died and she wasn't sure if she was ready for it yet. She had to pay the bills and to do that, she had to work.

She prayed she wouldn't have any troublesome customers, she didn't think she could deal with them yet. She went in and changed into her uniform.

Being the first bar travelers found when they left the space port meant that Nova Trango had a varied clientele, but they also had their regulars. After she had changed and found her section on the board, she started running into her co-workers. Burz gave her a hug and patted her shoulder in sympathy. Aren had her hands full and just gave her a big smile in passing.

Marzi, the owner, saw her and said, "I'm so glad you could come in. Gargi is out today, she had another fight with her boyfriend and they broke up again so she is too upset to come in." Taru appreciated Marzi just getting down to business. She had been very sympathetic when she called earlier, but here at the bar she was all business and that made everything feel normal.

She glanced around as she took over the tables and saw several familiar patrons, but her section was full of strangers.

Some people wondered why Marzi didn't upgrade to some of the new systems that tracked the biodata of patrons to cut them off when they'd had too much. Taru hadn't had to hear the answer to know. People had a much finer touch. Sometimes what was chemically within the biodata limits was too much for some patrons while other times a patron might need to get inebriated beyond what the biodata would indicate they could tolerate. Marzi relied on her staff to monitor every patron and keep their consumption from getting out of hand.

Taru quickly fell back into the routine of the evening. She had one table of humans from one of the outer systems who seemed quite out of their element. Another had a group of Zeccan traders. From the dark green of their skin and the length of their side whiskers, they were older and they were drinking very slowly. She tried to talk them into some food, but they declined. She hoped they tipped well.

As she made her rounds, a couple of the regulars came up to her. Papa Riz was the kindest, he just said he was glad to have her back and left it at that. Her first hour flew by and before she knew it she had a new set of tables, although the Zeccan traders still hadn't moved.

"Are those guys ever going to eat?" the cook, Halzon, asked her.

"I've been trying. They just want to sit and drink in peace. They aren't even talking that much."

"Just be careful, they might not be just traders."

"Not everyone has to be a spy, Halzon," she chided him.

"Is he going off about those Zeccans still?" Aren asked as she came up for her order. "He was bugging me about that when I first seated them."

"What? Do you have a special Zeccan dish you want to try on them?" Taru guessed. Halzon's guilty expression was all the answer she needed. "Give it a rest," she told him. "You aren't the greatest chef in the galaxy. Not everyone has to try your specials."

"I've gotten virtually every species that has come in here to rave about my food. I just can't get any Zeccans to like what I've made for them."

"I don't think this group is a good sample." Taru picked up the order that Halzon had just finished and took it out to the table.

Marzi had called her in for the evening and night shift. Being near a port meant that except for the dead of night when the port was mostly closed, that they were busy all day. Marzi was only there during the day and evening and Halzon kept the same hours. They would both be leaving before long. Once Halzon went home, they would rely on the food replicator.

Marzi had it programmed with all his dishes plus those of his predecessor. Since Taru and the rest of Marzi's employees ate at work, they had all noticed and complained to Marzi that the versions in the replicator were not as good. She just chuckled and blamed it on Halzon. Her father had tweaked the replicator so it was nearly flawless and Halzon hadn't liked that so he always left something out.

When she had a minute, she went back to the kitchen. "Halzon, could you make me something fresh so I don't have to use the replicator."

"For you or a customer you are expecting."

"For me? Why would I be expecting anyone?"

"Since it is for you, I will whip up your favorite before I leave. Just don't get busy and let it sit too long."

"I won't."

When she went back out, the table of Zeccans was getting up. Marzi had a pay-as-you-go policy, so they were paid up, but one of them motioned her over.

"I want you to know," he said in a deep raspy voice, "how much we appreciated your service. You were quite kind and pleasant." He put a credit chit in her hand.

"Thank you," was all she had time to say before he turned and left. She put the chit in her order pad and processed it. It was a tip of two hundred credits. She didn't know quite what to say. Most tips were only twenty to fifty credits; this was way more than they should have given her.

Marzi gave them a good wage and told them to do the best they can and they could keep any tips. Not every customer left a tip, but those that did gave them a nice bonus. It wasn't regular, but it helped.

Her first thought of what to do with it was to take it home and add it to the medical fund, but her mother was gone and there was no need to do that anymore. She found herself crying and went to the restroom to compose herself.

Aren came looking for her a couple minutes later. "Are you okay, Kiddo?" she asked.

"I thought I was, but those Zeccans left me a big tip and it made me think of my Mom."

"I'm sorry. I can't imagine how hard it must be. It was just the two of you and now you're alone. You can come stay with me anytime. With my daughter off to school, we have an empty room."

"Thanks, Aren, but I'll be fine. I've gotten used to the house now, but just the thought of what to do with the tip set me off."

"I got you. Stay in here as long as you need, I'll make sure things get covered."

"I should be fine, don't worry."

She took a few minutes to compose herself and went back out.

Marzi knew what Taru was going through; her father had died three years ago. Nova Trango had been his creation and he had run it for forty plus years. She'd been crushed and the need to keep things going had gotten her through it. Taru was one of her best employees and she needed to get back to work and make new patterns for herself.

She wasn't too good at being soft, it had never come natural to her, but she did know how to handle people. When Taru came out of the restroom, she cornered her.

"I get what you are going through, but I need you here to work, not cry in the bathroom." From Taru's initial reaction, she thought she might have gone too far, but the girl just nodded in agreement. "Good," she said with a smile. "Go work and don't let the customers get to you. I've seen you handle a table of drunk off-route traders without batting an eye."

She normally left about this time, but she was worried about Taru and decided to stay a while longer. There was a pile or two in her office that could use her attention. She'd wait until it slowed down a little to make sure Taru would be okay. Halzon would be leaving shortly himself and sometimes the patrons didn't care for the replicated versions. She knew he'd left things out to protect his recipes and didn't mind. It helped business during the day that all the locals knew he had the best food. Even the replicator versions were better than most of their competitors.

After the Zeccans left there was a lull for a few minutes and she had a chance to eat. Halzon's food was as good as ever. Taru checked the schedules and saw that port control had a liner and eight small traders on approach and a dozen others expected at any time. In about half an hour they would be really busy.

"It's been like this a lot lately," Burz told her as she came to look at the screen, too.

"What are they trying to do? It's so much better when there is a steady stream."

"I don't know. I haven't checked, but maybe Customs is doing something."

"That could be." There really was no way to check. Customs did not release any schedules like the port did because part of their job was to do the unexpected. Smugglers were savvy enough without any help of that sort.

"It's good to see you back," Uvik, one of the regulars, said when he caught her attention. "It's not the same without you."

"Thanks. I wasn't gone by choice."

"Yeah, sorry to hear about that. Herzil wanted you to know he's been thinking about you."

"Tell him he needs to come in with you one of these days. It's been forever since I've seen him."

"I'll do that. He's been working late hours and I seem to be just hanging out here more rather than spend time at home alone."

Just then a customer walked in. Taru looked, but Aren as taking care of him so she turned back to Uvik just as Aren called for her.

"Taru, this gentleman is here to see you."

"Sorry," she said to Uvik and bounced over to see what the newcomer wanted.

"You are Taruba Murask, Danoray's daughter?" the man asked as she reached him.

At first she didn't know how to respond, but she slowly nodded her head and said, "Yes."

"I am Wyas Dek. Your mother asked me to handle her estate. While it isn't large, there are some details to take care of. Is there a place we can talk?"

Taru, fortunately, did not have to answer that question. Someone had told Marzi and she had come out in time to hear his questions. "You can use my office," she offered.

"I had hoped to reach you at home," he said when they had both sat down in Marzi's office, "but it seems you are back at work already."

"They needed my help and I was ready."

Dek's face remained expressionless as he pulled out his legal pad. "Then I suppose we should get down to business and not keep you too long from your work. Your mother had some small investments that come to about thirty thousand credits. As her heir, you can keep them or liquidate them. In your current situation I would advise liquidating. In addition, she left you the house and everything in it."

"That is what I thought, but why did you need to come all this way for that? We could have handled this over the comm."

"That part we could have, but your mother left some additional instructions that I have been charged to carry out in person. There is some sensitive information that she was afraid to give you while she was alive. She very much wanted you to know as soon as possible should something happen."

Taru was having difficulty holding her composure. Her mother's death was still too close. She felt like she was on the verge of breaking down. She took advantage of his silence, as he waited for her to respond, to try to focus. She needed to get back to work and while what he was going to tell her was important, she needed to work. The tears she would save for when she was home alone. "What did she want me to know?"

"She never told you about your father."

"She knew?"

"Apparently. She set up these provisions when you were three."

Taru took a moment to digest this. She was about to find out who her father was. "Mister Dek, please go on."

"Sorry. I am trying to judge how you are taking this news, and I sense that you are still grieving. Unfortunately there isn't another time for me to tell you this."

"I'll be fine. Sometimes it is just better to get it over with."

"Your father is Sevam Pondelur. She had a short relationship with him and found out while he was away that she was pregnant. She wanted to keep you and her parents wanted her to finish her education. When she refused, they kicked her out. She had a friend who had moved here so she moved in with her and started a new life."

Taru absorbed it. Sevam Pondelur was a familiar name. He had been a musician popular when she was little. Her mother had all his recordings and had played them often. Now that she thought about it, she had played his music right after she had asked about her father a couple of times. Lately she'd been listening to his music to feel closer to her mother.

"Are you all right Miss Murask?"

"It is a lot to take in. I know who Sevam Pondelur is."

"Unfortunately that is where my information ends. Since your mother cut ties to her parents and left so abruptly, she had no way to contact him. She never did hear if he was looking for her, but when she made these arrangements, she did refer you to the lyrics of a short list of his songs." He handed her a data chit. "It's all on there. Everything she had that she never shared with you. She called it her previous life. Your grandparents contact information is in there as well."

"Did she say if anyone ever tried to contact her?"

"No one. When I talked with her originally, she said her parents should have been able to find her or direct anyone else on how to find her, but no one ever did to my knowledge. She kept in contact with the friend who first took her in. I made sure she was informed of your mother's passing. She sent her condolences, her message is on that chit as well."

"Thank you for everything Mister Dek. If I have any more questions, can I contact you?"

"You can contact me, but I tried to make sure everything you might need is on that chit."

"I think I would like to liquidate the savings."

"She thought you might. I will transfer the money to you as soon as I return. That really does conclude everything I came here for."

"Thank you again. I really appreciate this."

"You may be in shock right now, but your mother really did have your best interests at heart. She didn't want you to know because she didn't want you growing up dreaming of someone who would never be around. We can debate the merits of her decision, but her intentions were for your benefit."

"It is quite like her. I agree with her reasoning. It was better for me not to know."

She tried to get him to dine on her, but he refused. He hoped to catch the next return flight and be able to transfer the funds to her in a couple off days.

Marzi came over into the office after he'd gone. "Do you need anything?"

"She knew all along who my father was. You'll never believe who."

"Not unless you tell me."

"Sevam Pondelur."

"The singer?"

"Yes."

"I never would have guessed. You do look a bit like him. I've always thought you had your mother's eyes, but your skin and hair are darker than hers. I never would have connected that to him."

"I never did either, and I've spent my whole life listening to him. It makes so much sense. She always put on his music when she was sad."

"Knowing your mother these past twenty-two years, I can tell you that I never had any reason to disbelieve anything she said."

"I think I'm in shock."

"Do you need to go?"

"No, I'm fine. I know I keep saying that, but I really am."

"Then you'd better get back to work." Marzi was suddenly very serious. Taru was worried for a moment and then Marzi winked at her.

Danoray had originally worked for her father and she and Marzi had become good friends. Marzi had appeared to go through the normal interview processes to hire Taru, but she wondered if Marzi had just done it for show like she'd just done in telling her to get back to work.

Aren and Burz were swamped when Taru rejoined them. She quickly fell into the swing of handling the rush from the port.

One of her tables was the crew of a freighter who were somewhat regular. She'd never asked if this was the whole crew, but it was always three humans and two Hilven who came in. They joked with her as always, but she was too busy to really give them the attention she usually did.

Halzon had gone home and they weren't happy about getting replicated food. Taru pulled up the old menu on her pad and suggested they order from that menu out of the replicator. The oldest one said he remembered some of the dishes and made suggestions to his crewmates.

Her other tables didn't make a lasting impression except for two Ka'rhe'eran. They ordered a lot and ate it all down. She wasn't fond of their table manners, but it wasn't her place to judge. With their large build and sharp teeth, it didn't seem out of place. She didn't know how they handled all that fur. She had enough trouble keeping the hair on her head under control and they seemed to have it everywhere.

When the rush died down, it looked like it would stay steady for a while. Marzi came out of her office and said she was headed home. Taru checked her chron and saw how late it was and wondered why she had stayed so late. Taru's shift was half over already.

It was just her luck that twenty minutes later she ended up with a new table that was trouble. It was four men who looked sort of like traders, but there was something not quite right.

"Hey baby," one of them greeted her, "are all the girls here so smoking?"

She tried to ignore his comment, but he persisted. "What time do you get off work?"

"After you leave," she snapped. Aren and Burz heard her and looked in her direction. If it had been something she couldn't handle, she could have used one of the signals Marzi had taught them.

"Hey, girl," one of the other men said, "you are here to serve us."

"Food and drink yes. What you are asking can cost you your manhood." She made a quick calculation in her head and decided that this had gotten to the point when even Marzi might lose her cool.

"I don't take kindly to such threats," the second man said. He tried to grab her wrist but missed.

"That's it, get out!" Her volume caught everyone's attention in the entire bar. "I don't need to hear any more out of you, just go."

"We'll go when we are good and ready. We want food and drink."

"You'll have to get it somewhere else. You aren't getting served here."

"Where's your manager?"

"Right now, that's me. Out!"

She felt someone come up behind her and thought it was Aren and Burz, but the look at the men's faces made her glance. It was a human trader and a Ka'rhe'eran. She'd seen them sitting nearby in Aren's section. They were staring intently at the men.

"You heard the lady," the human trader said.

The Ka'rhe'eran growled for effect, but didn't say anything. The effect suited Taru. The men got up and left. She didn't really breathe until they were gone.

"Some people have no respect," the Ka'rhe'eran said in a warm voice that would have ruined the mood a moment ago. Now it seemed to release the tension.

"I'll go make sure they've really left," the man said.

Aren and Burz came over.

"What was up with those guys?" Aren asked.

"I suspect they were pirates, not traders," The Ka'reh'eran said. "Kon will make sure they are gone and then we will alert the port and Customs."

The Ka'rhe'eran's voice was calming, but the events of the evening were mounting up and Taru wasn't sure she could hold it together. What a first day back.

The man the Ka'rhe'eran had called Kon, came back in and said, "They've gone. I watched them get on a transport."

"I think they were pirates," the Ka'rhe'eran said.

"They were. Hey, Yhir, you don't expect me to call them in."

"It would be the proper thing to do."

"Damn! I knew you were going to say that. Where's the comm?" he asked Aren. She took him back to the office.

"Thank you, Yhir," Taru said.

"It is Su-Yhir. Kon tends to shorten everyone's name. We are bridge crew on a commercial freighter that just landed. I can't speak for Kon, but I will stay around for a while and make sure they don't come back."

Taru looked up at Su-Yhir as he was speaking and couldn't help laughing. The two Ka'rhe'eran earlier hadn't said much, and had concentrated on their food. Resembling a humanoid canine, watching them eat was rather frightening, but watching Su-Yhir talk and hearing him sound so educated and normal compared to the sharp teeth revealed whenever his mouth opened just seemed comical. It was better to laugh than cry.

The laughter had snapped her out of her downward spiral and she smiled for the first time in a long time. "You two have just earned yourselves a free evening. Whatever you want is on me."

Burz's eyes grew wide and she quietly went back to her tables. Kon and Su-Yhir were in Aren's section.

"That is not necessary," Su-Yhir said.

"No, but it is a thank you for what you've done."

Kon and Aren came back and Kon reported that the port authorities didn't seem to care, but Customs had been very interested. Taru pulled Aren aside and told her she wanted to pay for their meal and Aren shook her head. "This is what comping it is for. I agree with you and I could see to it, but why don't you finish taking care of them."

Kon and Su-Yihr were almost finished with their meal but they decided to stick around for some drinks. Kon shrugged it off since their ship had arrived fully loaded and was delivering their entire cargo here, they had plenty of time. "We really didn't have any plans," he assured her. "About the extent of our plans involves saving up and getting a ship of our own."

"Have you been here before?"

"We've been to this planet a few times, but this is the first time we've had leave. We weren't sure where to go and this was the first place we found."

"It usually is. We're in a good location. What sort of ship you are after?"

"Whatever we can afford. Something small that the two of us can run. I'm a pretty good pilot and Yhir is an excellent engineer. Between us we should be able to operate something along the lines of surplus Customs grade courier."

Taru could picture the type of ship he was talking about. She'd lived by the port her whole life. Couriers were small and had powerful engines and minimal cargo or passenger accommodations, but enough room that a pair of industrious traders like Kon and Su-Yihr could eke out a living.

The hour started getting late and Kon and Su-Yihr eventually excused themselves. Taru was on shift until Surhi showed up. She was their reliable overnight person. Her husband was a retired Customs guard and he joined her as defacto security until Marzi and Halzon showed up in the morning. Aren's shift ended and she headed home. Burz normally got off early, but with Taru out and Gargi not being the most reliable, she had been staying late. Tonight it would just be the two of them.

It started getting quiet and Taru was starting to count down the final hour when they had a late night wave of customers. She and Burz split them, but Taru ended up with a problem table.

It was a group of four humans, two men and two women. They had been somewhere else already and were pretty drunk to start with. She tried to cut them off from talk of another drink and get them to eat something, but their goal was clear and she could not budge them. Marzi was always willing to give anyone one drink, but passed that, she told her staff it was at their discretion.

Taru served them the one round and warned them that unless they wanted to order food that would be all. They seemed to agree and Taru left them to take care of her other tables.

Ten minutes later they were even rowdier and were insisting on another round.

"I told you when I served you the last round, that was it."

"We want more," one of the men said. "You are in business to sell and we can pay so you have to serve us."

"You wouldn't be the first party I've kicked out of here tonight. This is not a good day to mess with me. I'll serve you food if you are hungry, but if you aren't going to order food, it's time to go."

"Where is your manager?" one of the women demanded.

"I'm the last word."

"There are laws." The other woman added.

Taru laughed. "The law says that if I think you've had too much, I can cut you off."

The first man opened his mouth to speak and Taru cut him off. "No more complaints. Out!" When they didn't move, she added, "Now!"

None of the four were quite steady on their feet and Taru didn't do a thing to help them, she just followed them and made sure they left.

The first woman called back as Taru stood in the door and said, "Everyone is going to hear about this."

"Try it and you'll get sued. We have you on the security vid."

Sometimes she wished she could lock the door behind some customers. Being open all hours made that impossible.

When she turned around to get back to work, Surhi and her husband were standing there.

"Bravo, Taru," Surhi said. "Naro couldn't have done it better."

"Yes, very forceful, without any force," Naro said. "I probably would have thrown them out physically."

"Is my shift over already?" Taru asked.

"Not quite. We are early. Marzi was worried about you."

"I've told her several times today that I'm fine."

"Of course, dear," Surhi said with an expression that said she didn't believe it for a moment.

She only had one table after Surhi got there. It was an old man who lived nearby and came in at all hours. He tended to be very slow deciding what he wanted and took his time eating. He always ordered from the old menu, even when Halzon was in.

This night he was no faster and with her shift nearly over, Taru found herself less tolerant of his agonizingly slow process.

"Now, Miss, I can't remember if it was the Red House Sandwich or the Blue Garden Sandwich that has those pickled fishes that I don't like."

"It was the Red House Sandwich," she told him, trying to keep from snapping at him to hurry up.

"Were you the one who helped me last time? You suggested that soup that was so divine."

She was about to reply when Surhi came up behind her and whispered, "I'll take over. If we quickly switch places, he won't notice."

Taru waited a moment until he looked at the menu pad and then quickly swapped places with Surhi. "Now Mister Madvich, you know that when you come in at this time it's because you wanted something light. I know just the thing if you'll trust me." Surhi handled him perfectly. He'd been coming here longer than she'd worked here, which was almost as long as Nova Trango had been open.

Taru slipped into the back and changed. She put the dirty uniform in the cleaner. It would analyze it and clean it if it wasn't too bad and replace it completely if it was. In either case, there would be a fresh one waiting for her in about half an hour.

Once ready to go, Taru just stood there. She hated that empty house and didn't want to go there. She realized she was hungry and went out to the front to get a bite to eat before she left. She served herself from the replicator and had a seat in the unused section and ate quietly while Surhi and Burz worked. There weren't ever many customers at this hour so the work was light. Burz would get off in an hour. Since Marzi had called Taru in, she had not worked a full shift. Normally this shift came in an hour before Burz and left an hour earlier. Even this short shift had been a bit much. While she wanted to get back to work, there were too many reminders of her mother around here. She'd worked here for a long time and just being here made her feel sad. She'd see what the investments came out to and see what she could do with it.

When she had finished eating, she cleared her table and cleaned it off. She said a quick goodbye to Burz, Surhi, and Naro and saw herself out the back.

The house was dark when she got home. It always was these days and it really didn't feel like home anymore. As she tried not to break down all she could think of was how she had said she was fine all evening and she really was anything but. She was a mess and likely would be for a while. She just needed to get back to work.

She wasn't sleepy so she put the data chit in her reading pad and went over what it had. She had grandparents and an uncle she had never even heard of before. She looked them up and they would be easy to contact. Her grandparents hadn't moved in a long time.

It was the idea of finding her father at last that fueled what she came up with for her next course of action. She would go see her grandparents and then find her father. Although she now had a name, finding him was not going to be easy. Sevam Pondelur hadn't put out any music for over a decade and no one seemed to know where he was. He'd made plenty to retire to any corner of the galaxy he wanted to and remain safely anonymous.

Somewhere as she looked at the information, she decided that she would find her grandparents and make sure they knew that their daughter was dead and see if Sevam Pondelur had ever contacted them. Then she'd try to find him. She didn't really stop to think right then of how it might impact Marzi or if it was even a good idea. Something about the idea seemed so right. She didn't think she would still have the nerve in the morning but she did as much planning as she could before she started dozing off and decided she might as well go to bed.

Her night had not been not quite what she'd expected. Her mother had to have known what revealing this information would lead to. That was probably why she'd put it off until she was gone. Taru couldn't just sit here in this empty house and wonder, She needed to find these people and see if having a blood connection made them family.

As she drifted off to sleep, she knew that when she woke much of this excitement would have worn off and she'd go back to work and spend another day doing the same thing. But this would eat at her and sooner or later she would find a way to act on it. Her day had been challenging and full of stresses, but this had given her a distraction and something to plan for the future. She had made it through her first day back.

Seeking Justice
4614 GCE

Wally got off the liner at Quetle Station and passed through the station's check-in without problems. His false ID had let him live again. As Parlismon Jervung, he could arrive and be just another green skinned Zeccan traveler. The humans didn't recognize him as Wallivo Haroong or have any idea he was wanted on every Zeccan world.

Visiting his brother wasn't quite as easy as getting on the station. Manny still used his real name and had become successful partly because of their family's standing. He was outcast from the upper end of society, but in the lower levels, being associated with a member of the old royal family, even an outcast like Manny, was a big deal. It would explain why Nilondur kept his secrets. She worked for Manny and had recognized Wally instantly, but had never said a word.

Wally made his way to Manny's shop and found a human he had never met manning the store. She was rather short and her hair in braids that were artfully wrapped around her head. He'd seen the same style on Leywan and guessed it was the latest trend.

"May I help you?" she asked him.

"Yes, I'm looking for Manny."

"Mr. Haroong doesn't like to be called Manny. If you must use his first name, you should use the full form, Mannislon."

Wally smiled at her lack of knowledge of who he was. He couldn't blame her, she had no idea Manny's criminal brother would show up. "Is Mr. Haroong in?"

"I can try him on the comm and see if he is available. Who should I say is here?"

"Parlismon."

She went to the back for a moment and then came out with a very embarrassed look on her face. "I'm so sorry for the delay. He said to send you back immediately from now on."

Wally just smiled and he headed to the back room. His brother greeted him warmly and escorted him to the office.

"Another new girl?" Wally joked.

"Yes. Nilondur is the manager now. She is very good. Sara just started a few weeks ago. She is very good for a beginner."

"Manager? She's hardly worked for you any time at all. Are you...?" Wally left it hanging, but it didn't take genius to see the brewing romance.

Manny didn't answer right away. He looked like he was trying to read Wally's expression but wasn't having any luck. Wally smiled to give him something to go on. Working for a trader who dabbled in smuggling was giving Wally some interesting skills, especially if he could stump his own brother.

"You saw yourself that she is attractive," Manny reminded him. "And she is good company."

"Are you going to go through the formalities?"

"I don't know yet. I've been trying to find out where she stands on that. It would be hard with our family. You are not the only one our parents don't speak to."

Wally shook his head. Their parents still lived in a dream world where the ancient Zeccan monarchy still thrived. They still had a place in social circles, but they had no political clout. From his memory, Wally didn't think that Nilondur was from a society family so skipping the formalities might go unnoticed. He'd have to help Manny out. For now he decided to change the subject.

"Like I told you in my message, I'm off for six months. Were you able to arrange anything?"

Manny's thin shoulders sagged. "I have too many shipments coming in to get away. I'm sorry."

"You can't get away anytime during the next six months?"

"Maybe after these big shipments come in. That will be at least six weeks"

"I can keep busy until then."

"Just be careful, Wally. There are a number of Zeccans who come through here who would recognize you on sight. That would not be good for you or for me."

Wally knew better than to argue with him. If there was any chance of a trip in six weeks, they would have to wait until closer to that time before any plans could be made. That left catching up. It was something they both enjoyed and once they got started they tended to talk forever.

It was apparent from the conversation that Manny was intent on making Nilondur his wife, and when she joined them two hours later, any pretext that she was not Wally's future sister-in-law vanished. Wally could plainly see that she was as intent on the relationship as Manny was. Since they were alone, she gave up the pretext that she didn't know who he was and called him Wally. It was too soon for him to ask for a more familiar nickname to him to use with her so he politely continued to use her full name, but he started treating her as his sister from that night on.

They stayed up until the early hours of the morning. Nilondur gave up long before either of the brothers showed any sign of flagging. When Wally got up the next morning he was still groggy, but mentally refreshed. He wandered over to Alderin Balerio's office to see if he had any work for a pilot.

Balerio and his captain were good friends and Wally was ushered into his office minutes after he got there.

"Why are you looking for work?" he asked Wally.

"My captain decided he needs a vacation and has given us six months off."

"What is he going to do?"

"He didn't say. The ship is laid up having an AI installed, but that is only supposed to take three or four months. I think he just needs some time off."

"Well, it just so happens that I am in need of a pilot. You would be on one of my small courier ships making some small deliveries to some of the nearby systems. Will that work? I know your brother is here and I don't want to occupy too much of your time."

"That should be just fine."

Wally loved the compact feel of the small courier ships. They were nimble and fast and he could maneuver with them in ways that the freighter he normally flew was not physically capable of. It was a pleasure to fly on his own again. He had not touched the controls of another ship since he had abandoned his stolen one on Sachis Lunan.

The delivery runs were easy and not very time consuming, but there were a lot of them. After two weeks, he thought he'd hit every inhabited system within several parsecs of Quetle Station. While in some ways the runs were very dull, the flying was amazing and he hoped his vacation was full of this sort of fun.

He checked with Manny every time he was back on the station. Manny was truly busy, but Wally didn't dare help out. If anyone found out Manny had seen him and not reported it, Manny's career would be over. He just laid low unless they were alone.

Nilondur began treating him like a brother. He had no reason to fear that his secret was not safe with her. She indicated to him privately that she hoped she and Manny would get married but that she didn't expect the full formalities. She was from a trading family and all she had wanted was a well off trader so she could give her children what she'd had growing up. Wally had kept his composure or he would have snorted in amusement. He had looked her up and her mother was one of the most powerful traders in the outer Zeccan territories. She expected a lot of a defunct prince from an out of power royal family. They had a huge trading empire, but with Wally accused of a crime and Manny publicly defending him, both were outcast in their own way. Manny at least had contact with their family and they had set him up here on Quetle Station so he would stay out of their way.

Wally and Manny hoped to turn things around and really get into the trading end of the business. They had goals and every time they got together their plans became grander. Nilondur would be a valuable asset to Manny. But Wally knew his brother and Manny would never think of such things. He was too honest, at least in relationships. Wally had never seen him in action bartering for a better deal on goods. If he had half their father's skill, he would be formidable and from the success of his business on Quetle Station, that was entirely likely.

With his skill piloting and Manny's skill in the business of trading they could build up a good company and be much more than just store owners or ship captains. He could envision a large company with several ships. The one drawback was his status. While he was wanted by the Zeccan authorities, it would be impossible to openly be a part of Manny's business ventures.

His current position was providing a safe haven, but that could not last forever. With an AI, there would not really be any need for the captain to keep the pilots or navigators for much longer. He would soon have to find a way to clear his name.

This might be the right time to do something about it. He had the time right now and taking action before he was no longer needed would give he and Manny time to get things going.

He knew Manny wouldn't like the decision he had come to so he decided not to share it. He would act alone and take the risks himself. Manny had his own life and had found someone to build a life with. He would be successful even without him. Not that Wally intended to let himself get caught before he could prove his innocence.

There was only one person who could really help him with this. Balerio had resources and a far reach. He could help Wally get back into Zeccan space and help him connect with the few people who had believed in his innocence. He knew where to go and who he could rely on, but he would not be able to reach them without help. That was the main reason he hadn't tried before now.

Plus, given that seven years had passed, he hoped that it would be easier now. He didn't look the same as he had. He'd been young and whiskerless but now the creamy white whiskers graced each side of his mouth and he looked like an adult. He'd put on some weight as well and was no longer a scrawny kid.

The next time he was back on the station, he talked to Balerio about his idea. He expected him to be totally against it, but he was strangely receptive.

"I think you need to take care of this," Balerio told him. "If you have plans with your brother, you need to take care of this. If you are linked to Manny, his career is over and he'll have to move and rebuild elsewhere and your opportunity will be gone. You are being paid for your time, take advantage of it. I can get you to Zecca if you can get to the people you think will help you."

"You'll help me?"

"I know your captain considers you a valued crew member and you have already shown how valuable you can be to me with those runs you've done. That takes some piloting skill to carry that off as fast as you do. You deserve the help and I will do what I can. It also works as cover for Manny. If you are working for me and have to be away for a while, he can't suspect that what you are up to. But I don't think he would be as against this as you think."

"He might not, but it is better if he doesn't know. I've got to do this on my own."

"It will take me a while to arrange so why don't you go spend a couple of weeks with Manny, see if you can get him off the station, and I'll make the arrangements and let you know when I'm ready."

Wally was leery of Balerio's willingness to help. It didn't fit his image as a shrewd business man. When Wally challenged him, Balerio burst out laughing.

When his laughter died down, he said, "I hope what I want is simple enough. I want you and Manny to base your business here on Quetle Station."

Wally saw no reason not to agree and didn't think that Manny would object so he said, "I think we can agree to that. How many years do you want us to commit to?"

"I think ten would be good. I understand that a good business can grow and need to expand to new territory, but even after the ten years I would like you to have a presence here as long as I am around."

"I think I can get Manny to agree to leaving his store in place indefinitely. And you are right about needing time to grow."

"Then we have a deal. I'll do my best for you because this venture is in all our best interests."

Wally left Balerio's office feeling elated. He was being given a chance to redeem his name and he was going to take it.

He went and spoke to Nilondur first. He knew that if he convinced her, that she could get Manny to go away for a vacation for a couple weeks. He wasn't naive enough to believe that his upcoming adventure wasn't without serious risks that could land him in prison for a long time, or worse. He wanted to spend time with his brother and have an adventure like they used to. He had a destination in mind that would be relatively free of Zeccans and any danger of being recognized.

Nilondur listened to Wally and then took it from there. She revealed that she had been trying to get Manny to take a vacation for a long time, but he would not let things be and insisted that he had to be there to manage things. She knew he didn't really, but was worried about his employees. They were trustworthy and she could keep them in line.

It took two days for her and Wally to convince him. In the end, Wally still had to drag him to the passenger liner under protest, but when the hatch closed and the ship pulled out of the dock, Manny was aboard.

Wally was refreshed. Several weeks of vacation with Manny, cut off from his work, and the two brothers once again felt in sync like they had before life had taken them in different directions. Even after they got back to Quetle Station, Manny did not dive back into work in the same way. Instead he was truly courting Nilondur and making a sincere effort to make their relationship official.

Wally had spent enough time around humans to become somewhat accustomed to their mating rituals. They were very informal for the most part. They had several stages from romantic friendship, to engagement, to actually married, but then they would end those marriages as well. Zeccans tended to move slower but more deliberately and steadily toward marriage, and while they did have a process for dissolving a marriage, it was only for cases where one party in the marriage abrogated the marriage contract. The reasons that could happen were pretty standard. Zeccan marriage did not tolerate physical or mental abuse. They did not tolerate it in any family situation. Humans seemed to end a marriage for a host of reasons, rarely for any sort of abuse, and they rarely used anything approaching a marriage contract.

Nilondur's family was from a prominent, but lower class, trading family. She did not expect much past the contract itself, but Manny was having to earn the honor of asking her. The end was a forgone conclusion at this point, but it would be reached through a serious of negotiations, both in the relationship and in the contract.

Fortunately it would still take a few months before they reached the point where they would have a ceremony. That left Wally free to clear his name on Zecca. Balerio had made all the arrangements and Wally was finalizing his end of the preparations. He was just waiting for word that it was time to go.

He was with Manny and Nilondur in Manny's back office having lunch when he got the call from Balerio. He was keeping the mission from Manny so he wouldn't worry. He might be okay with the concept of him clearing his name, but if he knew it was happening now, he might blow things with Nilondur and that was more important. As far as Manny was concerned, he was on a mission for Balerio, same as he had been on since he arrived more than two months ago.

"Balerio has the cargo ready and wants me to leave in about an hour," Wally said.

"We're good here. I'll see you when you get back. You said this run would be longer?"

"It's a series of runs. One of his suppliers can't get his cargo delivered in time, so I'm to pick it up directly from them and run the deliveries from there."

"Be safe and we'll see you when you get back."

Wally nodded to both and left. He hated being deceptive, but it was so good seeing Manny so happy.

Balerio had arranged for Wally to fly into the Amer sector under his normal alias. Once there, he would have to make the last stages under medical suspension in a crate. Not the most fun way to travel, but it beat getting caught.

"Are you sure you are ready for this, Wally?" Balerio asked him. "This isn't something to do lightly."

"I'm sure. I've put it off for over seven years."

"That's good to hear. I have you traveling with the one employee of my company I completely trust. Me."

"I can't let you do this yourself, it's too dangerous."

"I'm only going as far as the Amer sector. I have business there myself and I want to make sure you get started to where you are supposed to be. Besides, it means you get to travel in style. Can you really pass up a private suite?"

Wally could not, but he still felt guilty. Balerio did indeed know how to travel. He had chartered a ship for his business and they were pretty much alone except for the crew. It was a luxury yacht, and while not quite in keeping with those of his own family, it far exceeded what he had seen since leaving Zecca. During the brief trip, his every comfort was seen to. He and Balerio talked and Wally realized how important it was to him to have reliable people on the station. He was only a part owner as the current head of the Alderin family, but anything that was in the best interests of the station was in his best interests. Wally committed again to the time frame they had talked about and hinted that certain aspects of the Haroong family presence on Quetle Station might be permanent.

To avoid anyone knowing that the crate being shipped to Zecca contained a person, Balerio had arranged for the yacht's doctor to put Wally under. He would pass through the Sprigard port without anyone knowing he'd been there, not even himself. He submitted to the doctor after confirming he was qualified to put a Zeccan into hibernation. Each species was different and Zeccan's had some oddities. The doctor was ready and before he could again thank Balerio, he was out.

Wally had been in hibernation before, but not often enough to get used to it. His body was technically awake before his mind was able to exert any control or consciously realize it.

His first conscious thought to was to take a deep breath of the familiar Zeccan air. Most planets had a unique combination of gasses that comprised the atmosphere. Add to that all the natural particles and smells that ship life support usually filtered out, and the uniquely Zeccan air brought a smile to his face.

As he took in his environment, he saw the person who had woken him up. He tried to say something, but he couldn't form words.

The Zeccan smiled and said, "Your voice will return. You need some hydration." He handed Wally a large drink bottle. "I'm Gamisvir Romirlung. Balerio said you needed to safe place to start out. I can give you that. I always thought that you were accused unjustly. Bad timing if you ask me."

Wally let him talk as he drank down the cool sweet beverage. It hit the spot perfectly, but he could feel he would need more than just a drink. He needed a swim to get his whole body hydrated. "Do you have a pool?" he finally managed to croak out.

"Of course. From the look of you, you could use it. Follow me if you have your balance."

Gamisvir led him to an adjoining room half filled with a clear pool. Wally quickly stripped and thought about diving in, but wasn't sure he was ready so he more sedately climbed in. Once in the water, his caution ended. He launched to the far end and swam as fast as he could. He swam back and forth and round and round until he felt his skin loosen up. When he felt like himself again, he swam toward the edge and flew up out of the water and landed beside the pool.

"Showing off a bit?" Gamisvir asked.

"No. That has always been my problem. I do what I'm good at and what I love and people accuse me of showing off. I only do what I do for myself. My current employer appreciates it."

"So does Balerio. He told me to take good care of you and help you as much as I can."

"I'm going to need to make some contacts. Is there a secure comm station I can use somewhere?"

"Not here, I'm afraid. There is too much risk of being found. You are going to have to find one to use. In preparation for your arrival, Balerio sent some cover identification." He handed a small bundle to Wally

He took it and examined the contents. The alias wasn't very creative, but it would do for what he might need. The goal was to clear his name so he could move about freely. He probably would have to leave in secret as well, but he had hopes he might be able to leave openly.

"So, what help are you here for?" Wally asked him.

"A way in, a place to stay, and a way out. My resources are limited, but you can be assured I support you."

"I know, or Balerio would not have risked this. I guess I need to go out and use a comm unit."

Gamisvir provided Wally with a change in clothes and Wally stepped out into the Zeccan sun for the first time in over seven years.

Since his mission was to access a comm terminal, he wasn't trying too hard at a disguise. He was relying mostly on the seven years of maturity to obscure the memory of the boy he had been. He took a transport several stops away to hide his location and then found a decent comm terminal with some privacy.

He'd carefully examined everyone he'd known in school and compared notes with Manny and had some good ideas who he could trust and who might be responsible. Manny thought that it was a large number of people who had turned against him, but Wally was sure that it was just a few who had started it and just one, though which one remained a mystery, had committed the offense. He'd checked and everyone he wanted to talk to was here on Zecca.

The first objective was to gather any allies he might have. First on his list was Aliharon Furzilom, a good friend who'd never been bothered by either his family or his skills. He'd stood by Wally through the initial accusation and Manny said he'd never swayed.

"Hello," Aliharon said as the comm connected.

"Hello, old friend," Wally said.

"Wallivo?" Aliharon said, the disbelief plain on his face. He too had matured. He looked like a respectable adult with his side whiskers.

"Yes, it's me. I need your help. I think it is time to clear my name."

"Wally, it's too dangerous. I have a family now and I don't know what I can do to help that won't endanger them."

"You never were much for adventures. Don't worry, I don't need that kind of help. I need to figure out who did steal and crash that ship and I need proof. Manny wasn't in any of our circles and he's the only one I could safely contact all these years."

"Whoever really did it, they never would have let me find out. I would have found a way to tell you."

"I know. But someone does know and it's time to find out."

In the end the only help Aliharon could give was his list of suspects and allies. One important name on that list was Palanur Mariloong, a girl he vaguely remembered, but who Aliharon claimed had had a crush on him.

After the length of that call and with the information he'd gotten, he went back to Gamisvir's to reformulate a plan.

A week of covertly making inquiries and sneaking around to meet with people had gotten Wally one step closer to the answer he was looking for. Those he had risked contacting had helped him narrow in on one small group from his school who had been particularly jealous of his flying skill. Everything pointed to one of them stealing the ship and crashing it and he was close to having the name.

That was only half the battle. Once he knew who it was, he had to find a way to prove it. The ship had been totally destroyed and the most they had been able to determine is that no one had been in the wreckage. He had been charged because he had the motive, no alibi, and the skill. His lack of alibi still bothered him. When he was in school, it was rare that he couldn't account for where he was or what he was doing. He had no idea how they had managed to pick the one day when he had no record of his activities. He remembered that day clearly and he knew where he'd been every moment, but unlike most days where he was in a public place or working on a terminal, or checked into the simulator, he had been studying flight patterns of wild birds for one of his classes. He hadn't had to do it on that particular day, but it had put him alone in an unverifiable location during the exact time. To this day he could not remember telling anyone what he had been planning. He could only guess that they had someone keeping an eye on him and had sprung their scheme when they knew they could get him.

Unlike the other students in the class, Wally had understood why studying wild birds was important. They were one with every control surface. They could feel every change around them and adapt instantly. Their fight became instinct more than conscious thought. Wally had learned a lot and had always hated that because of the charges against him he had not been able to complete that class. He'd never gotten a chance to hear the instructor's thoughts on natural flight. What he had gleaned from his studies had forced him to learn how to feel the large metal ships that the sentient species of the galaxy created for flying through air, space, and hyperspace.

He still remembered the first time he had to put that into practice. The ship he was currently serving on had gravitic thrusters and was very sensitive. Flying it for the first time had been an experience, but that feel he had learned to find had helped him to instantly adapt. Of course the hundreds of previous craft he'd used in school and on vacations had helped hone his abilities.

He hoped the AI being installed would not change how she flew. He really enjoyed flying that ship more than any other and had considered purchasing one like it if he and Manny got their business off the ground.

That was all dependent on finding the guilty party and proving it. The few people who might have known and not defended him seemed to be elsewhere. Wally hoped it was a guilty conscience, but it was more likely that they had just moved on and did not give it a second thought. Far too many people had held his background against him and believed that was how he excelled, not his natural skill. If only they had known that most of his instructors had been tougher on him because of his family. The old royalty was often looked down on in modern society.

His ruminations led him back to his flight science instructor. The very one who had sent him out to look at wild birds. He had seemed so nice, but was the one person responsible for Wally being out watching the birds that day. He'd been critical of Wally's previous observations and told him he'd missed something. Wally had gone out that day to find out what he had missed and had found it. The instructor had been hard on him, but Wally had believed it had been to make him learn. What if he'd been wrong and he was in on it. Everyone in the flight school had to make the same observations, but that was the one day he went out alone when someone else might have known.

He checked on that instructor and found he still held the same position. He would pay him a visit and gauge his reactions.

He spent the rest of the day preparing. The instructor lived near the school so he would need to be very careful. From his memory, the best time to make his visit would be first thing in the morning, before many people were moving around. There were three possible outcomes and he wanted to be ready for each.

He slept early. Seven years as a trader, visiting planets where the day/night schedule varied widely, had taught him how to sleep at nearly any time. He awoke in the early hours and made his way to the instructor's home.

It had been a common youthful prank to break into an instructor's home for some sort of mischief. Wally had never participated, but he had learned how to break in just in case. He slipped in easily and took a position to wait.

He'd timed it right. He only had to wait fifteen minutes before he heard the instructor's alarm and heard him moving around. Wally waited as the instructor went through his morning routine of getting breakfast.

As soon as he sat down to start eating, Wally greeted him in a loud voice, "Good morning Instructor Moniloszur."

The instructor visibly jumped. "What are you doing here?" he said in reflex before he had good look at Wally. When he finally placed the face and voice, he simply said, "You."

"Yes, me. I've been putting pieces together and I have noticed that you seem to have a part in my fate."

"Yes, I'm going to contact the authorities right now."

"You would need your comm for that. I think you left that in the other room."

"What do you want, Haroong?"

"The truth. I've gone over every minute of that day. I've gone over every possibility and I realized that the perpetrator of the crime knew I was without an alibi. And that is your doing. Intentional or not, you are the reason I don't have an alibi."

"Because you did it. We all know it. You constantly flaunted your family in front of us, showing off."

"That's the thing, I was not showing off, I was trying to do my best. At the time I did not think you were the type to be swayed by my family background."

"I wasn't."

"But you were. You are showing it right now. You were swayed to dislike me and make it tough on me. Then when some of my classmates wanted to pull a prank on me, you nicely told them that I was out working on your little bird project. You were just about the only one besides my brother who knew where I'd be."

"I didn't send you."

"No, but you found fault with my work and you were very aware of what I would do immediately after class."

Moniloszur remained silent.

"I know that you hold my family against me. You knew that after our conversation that I'd immediately go try to fix it. If just one person who had it in for me found out..." Wally let the implication hang.

"You are relying on a lot of supposition. Have you become that desperate living the life of a criminal?"

Wally let out a low laugh before he said, "I used to respect you and I thought that was mutual. I want to know who you told."

"I didn't have to tell anyone. We weren't alone when I talked to you. I'd just talked to Dormusong and he was still in the room. He waited around and left right after you did."

Wally searched his memory and could not recall seeing anyone. But Dormusong was one of Buiaro Zerholnom's cronies. That led right to the group Wally suspected. Zerholnom had hated him and had always been a distant second in their flight competitions. "I'm guessing that you scheduled us in that order on purpose. Did you tell Dormusong I was going to be next?"

"I can't recall what I may have said to him other than his work was below standard. Your name may have come up, maybe it didn't. I can't say for sure."

Wally knew him better than that. He could quote from conversations five minutes after they'd happened. He'd told detailed stories from various flight logs, exactly quoting the dialog without need for any notes. Wally had noted that and compared his rendition to the recordings and he'd even gotten the pacing down perfect. There was no way he would not remember what had been said seven years ago. "I think you know, but don't want to say. That is fine. You gave me what I came for."

"It won't do you any good. You have been tried and found guilty. You will never be able to undo that."

"I think I can. Not everyone took such a dislike to me. You hid it well."

"I never disliked you for your flying skill, unlike some. You are of royal blood and I wanted you to honestly earn everything you got. I made sure it did not come easy. But you were too good, Haroong. Jealousy is a horrible thing. I knew others hated you and didn't mind helping them out to make it harder on you. I didn't think this would turn you into a hardened criminal."

"I'm far from it."

"What do you call breaking into my home and interrogating me like this?"

"I call it seeking the hidden truth. I will find out who set me up and I will make sure they are found out and pay the time for it."

Moniloszur nodded. "I see many of my lessons stuck. Did you learn that last one?"

"I think so."

Moniloszur smiled, that same smile he'd used on Wally when he was a student. Wally finally understood that this man had been pushing him hard and the events of that day had spiraled out of his control. When Moniloszur spoke, Wally again saw the kind instructor he remembered. "Then you deserve to fly. Don't get caught and keep flying. Your family has been highly embarrassed by this and even if you manage to clear your name, they still will not have you back."

"I have my own plans that have nothing to do with them."

Moniloszur nodded again. When he spoke again, his tone had changed, "Now go. I will not tell anyone you were here, but if they press me I will have to admit it."

It was Wally's turn to nod. He quickly rose and left.

Having narrowed in on Buiaro as the likely culprit, Wally now had to figure out how to prove it. That would not be easy. His time was running out.

He started with the assumption that someone who would go to the effort to frame him would end up doing other equally criminal or unwarranted things that would make other enemies. If he could round up enough of Buiaro's enemies, he could find at least one who would help him gather the evidence he needed.

As he started to compile a list of those who might carry a grudge against Buiaro, it started to grow. He started to just make it a list of people he might be able to trust and who might be effective. That shortened it to just eleven. He made some subtle inquiries and found that three of them might be willing to help him. One was a classmate, but he didn't know her very well.

He decided to pay a visit to each of the three to gauge their reactions. He would not reveal who he was unless they were willing. As he thought about it, he wasn't sure that was even necessary.

The first person was one of Buiaro's current co-workers. He was a senior graduate of the academy and was as jealous of Buiaro's rise in the company that had hired them both as Buiaro had been of Wally. That coupled with Buiaro's abrasive nature toward those under him made him an excellent prospect. Wally found a way to meet him at a local hangout after work.

Buiaro had risen from a pilot for the second largest trade company on Zecca to be the pilot coordinator for the company. That meant he didn't actually fly anymore, but assigned other pilots. Hysmaur Gilarvor had gone to the business branch of the academy and reportedly had to fix Buiaro's mistakes on a daily basis

Hysmaur had a group of friends at the hangout so it proved difficult at first for Wally to speak to him, but his friends only stayed a couple hours and Hysmaur remained afterward and ordered a stronger intoxicating beverage.

Wally saw his chance and joined him.

"What do you want?" Hysmaur growled. Wally could tell he had already had quite a bit. He didn't think anything of it for a moment, but then remembered that while that was very human, it was unusual for Zeccan culture. His drinks must have been stronger than most people drank when with friends.

"We have a mutual enemy, Buiaro Zerholnom."

"Don't ruin my evening with talk of that puddle of bilka slime."

"I want to bring him down."

Hysmaur focused on Wally seriously for a moment. "You mean that, don't you? There is no way. I've tried."

"There is one way. He committed a crime and someone else got blamed. If we could prove he did it..." Wally let the idea trail off so Hysmaur's imagination could take over.

"Then maybe I would get his job. A nice idea, but how do we prove it?"

"Does he still keep trophies of his victories?"

"Does he ever? Last month he orchestrated a debacle for our competitor, you know them, the old royal family, and he has the news article posted on a special screen on his desk."

"Did he do anything illegal?"

"Who can say, but everyone knows he is responsible."

Wally could barely contain his elation. If it was something the public didn't like, then when the facts of the theft and accident came out it would be better received.

He would need to talk to Hysmaur when he was sober so for the rest of the night Wally kept him company and paid for all his drinks. If Hysmaur remembered this conversation, he had a strong contender.

The next day he found his classmate, Zurien Vasloron. She worked for Buiaro as a pilot. He knew of her in the academy but had never actually met her. He'd heard that she defended him on at least one occasion. Arranging to meet her had proven a challenge, but he happened to catch her in port and when he mentioned a project against Buiaro, she agreed to the meeting.

When he saw her, he wondered how he had never noticed or met her. She had to be the most beautiful woman he had ever seen. She was dressed as a pilot, but that did nothing to hide her flawless glowing green skin or alluring golden eyes. He was mesmerized as she joined him along the lunch bar.

"When I saw the name," she started, "I almost didn't answer, but your subject intrigued me. I did not imagine I would find the star of our class himself." She leaned in and whispered, "Wallivo Haroong."

Her presence was electric and he was still so in shock from her beauty that he almost didn't register that she'd recognized him. "And still you met me?"

"I wondered how long it would take for you to return to clear your name. I can tell you that you found the right person. I knew he did it at the time, but I can't prove anything. It was the one time he didn't keep a trophy of his victory."

They chatted for several minutes and selected their lunches. Zurien suggested they go someplace more private to talk and suggested her apartment.

"I thought this would work better than wherever you are staying. I don't want to blow your hiding place," She said when she gestured to the low table.

They sat on the floor at the low table and ate. Wally was finally getting accustomed to being with this vision of Zeccan beauty, though he found she even ate in an attractive manner. She finished first and waited for him before she said anything.

"How do you plan on clearing your name?" she asked.

"I need to prove he was guilty and quietly leave. If I am found here, even after that, I think it will be bad. People will think I planned this in revenge and I'll be in the same position I am now. I've talked to Hysmaur Gilarvor and I think he can help. I'm sure he kept a trophy of what he did to me like he does of everything. If we could find that it might tell us something."

"We'd need to break into his home for that. I don't think he'd have it at work."

"I'm not so sure," Wally said. "I'd like to check both places."

"I can get you into the office after hours, but his home is something I wouldn't dare have any part in."

"Don't worry, I will take that risk on my own. I just need someone inside to make sure he isn't headed home."

"I'm sure that Hysmaur and I can handle that."

"What I really need is a vid of him admitting to doing it that the court would accept."

"That will be harder, but I'm sure something can be arranged."

They discussed several ideas but no better idea of how to do that materialized. They were talking about when they should meet again when Zurien suddenly exclaimed, "I've got it. He always makes someone else do things for him so it would be easy to have someone contact a security company to have a video surveillance system installed in his home and office. Then we can catch him looking at it. But how do we get him to do that?"

"We need him to show it to someone. We'll have to think about it, but first, I want to find it, then we install the security system. That should give us some time to find out how to get him to do what we want."

They ended their day with a solid plan. Wally wasn't going to waste any time and planned on looking around Buiaro's home the next day. Zurien would signal him once she verified that he was in the office and would keep an eye on him to make sure he didn't leave. She had plenty of reports to file so her being in the office would not arouse any suspicion.

Wally returned to Gamisvir's to prepare. On the way he gathered a few items he might need. He had a nagging worry that Zurien could easily betray him, but if that had been her plan, she would not have let him know she knew who he was. He was sure he was being paranoid, a natural result of being on the run for so long, but he took precautions just in case.

The next morning, he was in position when he got Zurien's signal. He put his plan into motion.

He used his scanner first and found that the home was already protected by a security system. He and Zurien hadn't spoken of that, but he was prepared. It was inferior to the system his parents had when he was growing up and that had been easy enough to bypass. But he didn't want to just bypass it, he wanted to tap into it and record it. That was a little harder.

The scanner showed him where the security system connected to the power relay. It also showed that Buiaro didn't seem interested in trespassers, the security system only covered the interior and the power relay.

He used his comm, set to a unique frequency, to jam the security comm and casually walked up to the relay. He attached the signal duplicator he'd picked up the day before and attached it to the back of the security box. If he tried to crack the box, it would alert the security company, even through the jam, but all he was doing was making it so he could copy and even access the security settings without raising an alarm. The things he'd learned as a kid hadn't been his fault, Manny had a fascination for this sort of thing and had shared everything he knew with Wally. Manny could have done this job with much more skill. Wally considered himself an amateur in comparison.

It helped that Buiaro had a low end system. Wally moved away from the security panel and activated the connection to his data pad. It was an encoded signal. No big surprise and it took Wally about fifteen minutes to find the right decoder to reveal the signal. The system had about ten cameras. He used the scanner to pinpoint all of them in the building and what direction they faced and then overrode the home controls and deactivated the system making all the cameras go dark. He was inside moments later.

Buiaro had a nice place. It was a lot of room for a bachelor. He went from room to room checking the placement of the cameras and what they covered. If he had any trophy from that night, Wally was sure it was here and would be covered by the security system. He found one very odd room. It probably had been designed as a child's bedroom, but Buiaro was using it for something else. It was covered by three cameras. On instinct Wally did a more detailed scan of this room and found that a crate sitting by one wall, incidentally covered by all three cameras, had a separate security system. He carefully scanned the crate to get the details of the security system.

It was easy to deactivate and Wally proceeded. He opened the crate and inside he found a ship data recorder. It showed some signs of damage, but the data ports were intact. He knew he had found what he'd been looking for. The data recorder from the crashed ship had never been recovered. How Buiaro could have gotten his hands on it, Wally couldn't guess. He tried to connect to it to download the contents, but all he got was the ID screen. He knew that number. It was the very same data recorder. That changed his plans. He sealed up the crate and reactivated the security system and then left the building and reactivated that security system when he was a safe distance away. He jammed the signal again briefly to make anyone reviewing it think it had cut out for the last hour due to interference.

He caught the transport and headed for a seedy area near the port. It took him more than an hour of looking before he found the right sort of data pad that could read a flight recorder and copy the data without doing an official download or leaving a log. It cost way too much, but he was in a hurry.

He returned to Buiaro's and quickly deactivated the security system and went back to the crate. He carefully deactivated it and then activated the data pad. It connected to the data recorder and signaled that it was copying. It took longer than he felt comfortable with, but it finished without any errors. He sealed everything back up and left. Other than the system override, everything was just as it should be.

He signaled Zurien that he was done and went back to Gamisvir's to review what he had found.

The data for small ships was usually limited to the last Zeccan day. In this case it was much less. Everything was recorded from the position of every control to the audio and visuals of the cockpit. It revealed what Wally had guessed already. Buiaro was at the controls. The date and time confirmed that it was the flight that crashed and had gotten Wally in trouble.

As he watched, he detected the mistake that had caused the ship to crash. Not an error he would have made, and not one that normally would have caused a crash, but with the way Buiaro was flying, it was inevitable. He didn't waste a moment. He copied the data into a file packet on his comm and linked to Gamisvir's hypercomm and transmitted it to Balerio for him to get to Manny. He wasn't going to risk the data being erased or lost. But the only way to prove his innocence was to get that data recorder to the correct authorities.

He would be able to trick the security system into recording when it shouldn't, so it was all a matter of getting Buiaro to reveal his possession of the data recorder to the camera. Once it was officially recorded, it was a simple matter to force the security company to forward that to the authorities. They had to report any illegal activities.

A solution was slow to come to his mind. It wasn't until he was on the transport to meet Zurien that one piece of it came to him. Some ships were programmed to send the same data recorded on the data recorder to a remote location. He could use the data he'd downloaded to fake such a remote recording and make Buiaro think someone had found out about his deception. It was a start but they still needed someone to witness it. Preferably someone Buiaro thought he could trust but was on their side.

Zurien was excited to see the vid from the cockpit. She also caught his error on the first viewing.

"You know, this vid is almost enough."

"No, I want it solid so he finds it as impossible to get out of as I did."

"I think Hysmaur might be our man. You said he doesn't like Buiaro, but in the office, that isn't so widely known and I'm sure that Buiaro has no idea or he wouldn't be his assistant."

Zurien had a good point and Wally started thinking about how that might work. It would take some planning but it was doable.

"I think we have the makings of a plan," he told her. "I may just get my life back."

Wally was frustrated. There was no way to guarantee that Buiaro would go check his treasure, much less take anyone with him to do it. Zurien had not been able to come up with a way either. That one piece stood in their way.

Other than that, they had his every move under surveillance. That had been easy to accomplish as the official documents that showed Buiaro ordering the security monitoring himself. He used a personal transport, not public, so they included that. They could watch him at work, home and on the move, all of it going to a security company for constant review. They had even managed to get the security feed from his home installation copied to the second company as well. If he said or did anything they would have it on record.

They wasted valuable time wracking their brains for a good idea. Zurien even consulted a criminal expert and came back with nothing useable.

In the meantime, Wally found himself spending a lot of time with Zurien. He was scared it was his imagination that she was starting to have feelings for him. When she had to get on the rotation and was gone for several days, he waited impatiently, but when he knew she was arriving, he forced himself to wait to see if she would contact him. He was about to lose his resolve when his comm beeped with her signal.

Any thoughts of romance vanished when she went directly to their project by telling him she had thought of a way. It would take some careful setup but they could do it. Hysmaur was the key. There was a conference that several people in the company should attend. They would get Buiaro and Hysmaur to attend together. Buiaro would insist that they travel there in his personal transport. They would send him the message at the end of the day just when they were getting in the transport to leave. Buiaro should drag Hysmaur with him when he went to check the secured crate.

When she shared the idea, Wally was sure it would work. They set about making the arrangements. The conference was in just over a week.

As they got into the details, it looked like the plan might fail. They needed another person at the conference to signal them. Wally didn't like idea of getting the key to his escape route involved in this, but there was no one else he could trust besides Gamisvir. Fortunately he was willing to do it.

He and Zurien spent hours going over the plan. They kept Hysmaur and Gamisvir separate. Wally didn't want Hysmaur knowing about the other half of the plan. Wally worked on the vid. He ran it through some distortion filters so it looked transmitted and degraded. He had to play with it so it was noticeable, but not overdone. The shock factor should hide anything else out of place.

On the first day of the conference everything worked perfectly to start with. Buiaro took Hysmaur in his private transport. The conference proceeded normally, as far as they could tell as outsiders. Gamisvir was positioned to wait for them to come out. But the time they were supposed to come out passed with no signal. Wally was getting worried.

"Don't worry," Zurien said. "It's a three-day conference. We have two more chances if today doesn't work."

"The plan was for today."

"You need to get used to failing sometimes."

The signal from Gamisvir came when they had just about given up, almost an hour after they had expected it. Wally quickly sent the pre-made message and they waited. The message had an auto reply for when it was read, but they didn't need that. They could tell the moment Buiaro got in his personal transport that he had seen it.

They watched the security feed as the transport carried Buiaro and Hysmaur. Hysmaur tried to find out what was troubling Buiaro, who, from the conversation, had been pretty jovial before he got the message.

"How bad can it be?" Hysmaur asked him.

"Pretty bad."

"Is it something with work?"

"No. It's something from my past. Do you mind if we stop by my place first? I need to check on something."

"No, I had nothing planned. I thought maybe we'd find a party after the conference."

"That's usually on the last night. Anything going on tonight or tomorrow is probably an evening business meeting. I'm glad I didn't have any of those today."

Hysmaur tried to keep him talking, but Buiaro gave him a nasty look so he stopped. When they stopped at Buiaro's home, Hysmaur got out, too.

"What are you doing?" Buiaro asked.

"You want me to stay here?"

Buiaro considered it a moment and shrugged. "I guess it doesn't matter."

They went inside and moments after Buiaro deactivated the security system, Wally reactivated the cameras. He double checked that the feed was going to both security companies.

At every step Buiaro tried to get rid of Hysmaur, but he seemed to make sticking close to Buiaro seem innocent and Buiaro eventually let him.

They went to the room with the secured crate. They watched as Buiaro deactivated the security system and opened the crate. He used his data pad to link to the data recorder and called up the ID and log. Since Wally had used the correct type of data pad, it had left no log entry and it only showed when he had last accessed it, which looked like two years ago.

"What is that?" Hysmaur asked.

"It's a souvenir. My uncle gave it to me. I keep it to remind me that anyone can fall."

"That's a weird thing. Why do you keep it locked up?"

"I value it. You are asking too many questions."

"I must have had one too many of those drinks they were giving away. They were good weren't they?"

"Yeah. Now that I checked on this, it's time you headed home. I'll just send you in my transport."

Hysmaur left and almost as soon as the transport was out of sight, Buiaro used his comm to make a call.

"We have a problem, Uncle. Watch this."

There was a moment of silence that about equaled the length of the vid before the uncle said, "That isn't possible."

"I checked the recorder and no one has accessed it but me. The ship must have been sending a signal somewhere."

"That's not possible, Buiaro. I checked it over myself. I was with my men when they found it. None of them has ever said a word."

"Someone knows, Uncle. You'd better find out who."

Wally was flying high. They had him. All of this was exactly what he needed. Now they just had to file the report. Wally checked with the security company he'd arranged for and they had seen the vid. Wally told them to check the serial number that had appeared when Buiaro had checked the recorder. It was linked to a criminal investigation into a crash. The security person checked for a clear frame, isolated the serial number, and looked it up. Seconds later he was on another communications line reporting the criminal activity. Wally quickly disconnected the comm. He and Zurien left the apartment he had rented close to Buiaro's home. He dropped the comm unit in a disposal unit and made sure it cycled.

They met Gamisvir at a small shop where they got a bite to eat before going their separate ways for the night. Wally would contact Zurien later to see what, if anything, resulted from their efforts.

Zurien hadn't wanted to tell him anything over the comm so Wally met her at the small dining shop where they'd been meeting during the day. He didn't even have to ask her before she started talking.

"Buiaro was fuming this morning. Some investigators went to his home and took something. He wouldn't say what it was, but what else could it be."

"We should check the security recording," Wally suggested.

"Is that safe? If they are investigating, they may be monitoring the systems."

"Not likely. They would have gotten the security recordings from the company and then reviewed them. It's taken four days for them to do anything."

"They are moving slow, maybe we should hurry them along?"

"What do you mean?"

"We have the two recordings, the one off the data recorder and the one from the security camera. They both clearly show that Buiaro did it and has been hiding it. If we sent it to the right people, they will have to act."

"You really don't like him, do you," Wally said, stating the obvious.

"No, I don't. But I do like you. It's sad that as soon as your plan works you will have to leave."

"My brother Manny has a shop on Quetle Station. He usually knows how to find me. It would be nice to hear from you. It would be even nicer to see you."

They were both quiet for a moment. Zurien broke the impasse by saying, "You are right, we should check the security camera. Want me to do it?"

"I'll take care of it. And you are right, we should send the vids to someone. Did you have someone in mind?"

"I have family connections to the crash investigation manager. Unfortunately he wasn't in that position back when it would have done the most good."

"Oddly enough, Zurien, looking back I wouldn't change a thing. I've gotten to serve on a fantastic ship and now I've gotten to meet you. If we can undo what Buiaro did, I've got a good future ahead."

They agreed to meet up again after Zurien was finished at the office. She'd talk to Hysmaur to see what he'd heard. Wally headed off to check the security recordings. He hadn't wanted to check until he'd heard something had happened.

It was all there. The investigators arrived and Buiaro acted very indignant, then they took his secured crate and he nearly flipped out. They weren't in his home for more than ten minutes, but he was freaking out for the rest of the night. He captured it all and he was glad he had. Buiaro had contacted his uncle, Wally assumed the same uncle who had given him the data recorder, and tried to get him to do something. Evidently from the content of what the security company had sent to the authorities, they had started an investigation of him as well and he bluntly told Buiaro that he couldn't do anything.

Wally compiled all the vids; the original crash, Buiaro opening the crate, the investigators taking the crate, and his call to his uncle, and made a data chit to give to Zurien. While he was at it, he copied it into a data packet and sent the whole thing to Balerio.

He decided that this evening with Zurien needed to be special. He wanted to make his intentions clear, especially since any night could be his last on Zecca. He made some fancier arrangements and sent a message to Zurien to meet him at the location he'd picked.

When the time rolled around, he went to the restaurant and found that he was very early. He didn't mind waiting. When she was late, he started to worry. For a while he thought she wasn't coming and he was almost ready to give up when she finally arrived. She had evidently decided this venue required nicer clothes.

He didn't need to say a word. Zurien knew what the location meant. He dealt with the business of handing over the data chit right off. She didn't wait and immediately got out her comm and sent the data to her relative. She wouldn't say who it was, but Wally gathered it was someone close to her.

"I just don't want to risk Buiaro having some connection that will let him get out of this. I've already talked to my relative and they are going to monitor the investigation to make sure it is done right."

"I appreciate it."

"I do have my own selfish motives."

"I'm glad you are being selfish."

"Before I forget, Hysmaur had quite a story when I talked to him. Buiaro called him into his office and blamed him for this. Good thing we never told him what he was looking at. He was able to deny the whole thing. If they need him to, he is willing to verify the security recording. I think we have everything covered."

Wally and Zurien enjoyed the evening and said goodnight. Wally had barely gotten back to Gamisvir's place when Zurien sent him a message that Buiaro was to be arrested and it was time for him to leave. Wally replied that he was ready but he hoped to see her on Quetle Station.

"Looks like I did it," he told Gamisvir. "I need to leave tonight."

"I can't get you out tonight, but the next cargo flight I can get you on is about a day away. If I put you in hibernation now, I can get you to the port and on the ship in plenty of time."

Wally nodded and said, "Let's do it."

Wally stepped off the freighter onto Quetle Station with a sense of relief. Buiaro had been arrested and charged. Now he and Manny could push forward on their business idea. He might be jumping the gun a bit, but he was sure that his name would be cleared, at least officially if not publically, very soon. The damage had been done years ago and he had moved on. Now he could openly move on.

He wasn't confident enough yet to use his true identity. It was still as Parlismon that he officially entered the station, but this time he had less to fear of someone linking him and his brother.

He went straight to Manny's store and found Nilondur and Sara working, almost the same as last time. Nilondur waived him back and he found Manny at his desk, completely absorbed by work.

"I did it," he announced.

"I've heard, but he has not been convicted yet."

"I don't think there is much doubt, is there?"

"You know how news commentators are. They twist everything to fit their view. It seems that all the news outlets firmly believe you did it, even when the original vids were released."

"At least public opinion doesn't affect the courts."

"Don't be too sure of that, big brother. Until it is finished and your name is cleared, don't act like anything has changed, because it hasn't."

"What a way to put a damper on my good news."

"Wally, I'm your brother. I know you. Someone needs to bring you down to reality before you do something stupid."

Wally sighed. "You are so right."

"On the bright side, even if things don't go well, we have copies of all the vids that show who really is at fault and with that in hand the chances of them coming looking for you have dropped dramatically. Balerio forwarded me your messages."

"So you agree we have something to celebrate."

"I just don't want you getting out of control."

They had a private celebration in Manny's apartment. Nilondur knew how to make a traditional meal and had been able to get a fresh temnaroon fish from Zecca. Manny and Wally had never learned how to prepare fresh food and welcomed the change from replicated food. Manny had a carafe of potent Zeccan yarmo wine to go with it.

After the initial celebration, things fell back to what they'd been before Wally had left. He went to Balerio, who congratulated him on his success, to see if he had some runs to cover these last few weeks before it was time to head back to work.

Balerio had a short set of runs but most of what he had available were longer and required a full ship. Wally jumped at what he was offering and was back in the pilot's seat of a courier again.

The first run was flawless and he just had time for dinner with Manny and Nilondur and a good night's sleep before the next one. He did three runs the next day and then the last two the day after that.

He'd just gotten his pay from Balerio and was headed to meet Manny when he saw a very familiar Zeccan on the Quetle Station's main plaza. She was walking in the general direction of Manny's shop so Wally took a back way to try to beat her there.

He went in the back of the shop and surprised Manny. He went up behind the door, but did not open it. He could hear Nilondur greeting someone.

"Yes I'm looking for Wallivo Haroong."

"I'm sorry, I've never met him. His brother owns this shop, would you like to talk to him."

"I think we both know that his situation has changed. I actually came to deliver some good news in person."

Wally couldn't resist any longer, he opened the door and went out. "What good news, Zurien?"

He and Nilondur both caught her flush and the smile that found every corner of her face. She was too surprised to speak for a moment, but she slid a chit across the counter. It bore the official seal of the Zeccan Commonwealth.

It was Wally's turn to be surprised. He pulled out his data pad and slid the chit into the reader. It was not a vid or audio message but an official text document. He read it over and wanted to shout.

"Like I said, good news," Zurien said.

He called to Manny and they heard him grumble but he came through the door after a short delay. He was taken aback when he saw Zurien. Wally covered for his distraction by handing him the data pad. As Manny read it, his eyes grew wide. He didn't hold back and shouted.

"You are completely exonerated!"

"Not just that," Zurien said, "He has now officially graduated from the Academy and is cleared to resume his duties with the family company, politics, or anything else he would like to do."

Wally quickly introduced Zurien to them and it was all too obvious to them that there was more going on than just delivering a message. Manny shooed them away so they could be alone.

Wally took her to a place on the plaza he'd always wanted to try and they had an early dinner. A few other Zeccans were out and stared at him. He was sure they recognized him but it no longer mattered.

"Why did they give you the message to deliver?" Wally asked her.

"I wanted to see you so I asked. It doesn't hurt that my father was the one who issued it. I'm acting as a special courier and officially we have just met."

"Love at first sight," Wally said before he realized it.

"That it is," she agreed.

Wally felt that in many ways he did not know her so he asked a bunch of questions as they ate.

He found out that her father had launched a deep investigation into Buiaro's action and his uncle's as well. Both had been arrested, tried, and convicted. The verdict had not been popular, but as soon as the trial was over he had released the vids to the public and had made an announcement. He said that the bad feelings toward the old royal family were no reason to allow an individual to be falsely charged with a crime and to have that crime covered up. If any member of the former royal family was to be charged with anything, it had to be valid. The overwhelming evidence and the attempt to hide that evidence and let public opinion sway the courts was unjust. Zurien had a recording of it if Wally wanted to see it, but he liked the way she told it better.

"Remind me to thank him," Wally said.

"You can do it when you go through the formalities."

Wally was taken aback by how clear she was being. "Won't that hurt your father's career?"

"He already knows. I told him before you had even left Zecca. He knew why I wanted to deliver his message."

"I'm not sure that my family will have anything to do with me?"

"Wally, as you said many times when we were talking, Manny is your family. Regardless of what your other blood relatives do, my father will work with Manny on the family details."

"I have a job to get back to."

"Are you trying to slip away from me?"

"No, I just don't want you to leave."

"I won't go anywhere, Wally. You are stuck with me."

"That's the nicest thing you've ever said."

"So I'm going to need a new job. Got any recommendations?"

"But you have a good job?"

"Hysmaur got Buiaro's job and he thinks he is interested in me. I want to leave and make it clear I'm not interested."

"Alderin Balerio always has small jobs he can use a good pilot on. I could talk to him."

"Who is that?"

"He's the owner of the largest trade company on this station. He pretty much runs things."

"Oh. Sounds like my kind of job."

"Only until Manny and I get our company going and need a pilot."

"Yes, that is even better. Would I have to call you captain?"

"That depends on when we finish the formalities."

Wally was glad that he didn't have any other flights before he needed to head back. He had time to spend with Zurien. She easily found a position with Balerio and was soon preparing for her first flight. It has seemed like barely any time at all had passed, but it had been a couple weeks on Quetle Station and a couple months before that on Zecca. She'd been there long enough that he'd gotten his new ID with his real name.

News of Buiaro's conviction and Wally's name being cleared had circulated the Zeccan community along with the unknown woman he was associating with. Wally was disgusted. They had pointedly ignored he and Manny all these years as they had lived as outcasts and now that they were back in good graces, everyone wanted to know their business again. Fortunately Balerio didn't tolerate too much of that sort of thing on Quetle Station so it did not intrude on Wally's daily life.

It looked to be on the verge of endangering Manny's marriage to Nilondur and Wally had to step in and make things clear that he and Manny had been abandoned by the family when they had needed support and they were not taking the family back now that it was no longer impolitic to associate with them. He and Zurien had to sit down with a couple of the longtime Zeccan residents to make that point perfectly clear so that it filtered through to everyone who was coming to Quetle Station to gawk.

Zurien joked one evening that she didn't know if she could take being associated with the nephew of the uncrowned king and Wally just about lost it.

"I'm sorry, Wally," Zurien said. "I didn't know you took it so personally."

"I don't mean to take it out on you. It's my background and how people treat me because of it. It has been so nice these last few years being anonymous."

"You still would be if someone hadn't plastered your pic all over the news articles. They all talk about how you have been exonerated and are making a big deal about it."

"If I ever found out who did that... But what's the use. I think I just need to get back to work."

"I think if you do that, things will die down after a while. You said your captain stops here a lot."

"He does. It is one of the best places in the sector to find work I'm sure he'll stop here in a month or so. If he doesn't, I'll ask."

"You really don't need to make a special effort."

"Yes I do. I'm going to make sure I get here as often as possible. I just need to make sure it doesn't affect my captain's business or he'll think I'm a pain."

Zurien smiled at him. "My dear Wally, I don't think you could make a pain of yourself, even if you tried. Now, I have to go. Balerio said I'd be gone a week. You leave on time. Or maybe you should leave early and go somewhere without any of our people for a day or two before you rejoin your ship."

"Excellent idea."

The next day just hours after Zurien left, Wally snuck out of the station and Parlismon was back on the move.

A Captain At War
4626 GCE

Through the blackness raced the small tradeship *Mirka Ve'sura*. Her Hilven captain, Laren d'Borchas stood behind his ace pilot, J'sevi.

"That's all she's got, captain," J'sevi said.

"How long before we can jump to hyperspace?" Laren asked his Stavian navigator.

"Ten minutes," Ladna informed him.

"And how long before they catch us?"

"Six minutes."

Laren shook his head and picked up the comm mic. He set the channel and activated the message. "Captain, I think they might have us. We're trying to outrun them but the bastards already got in a lucky shot. We could use your help. If you don't hear from us, it means we've been captured or destroyed." Laren cut off the comm and verified the message had been sent. "Do your best. The Captain can't help us unless we get away."

Ven was enjoying a drink in the open air patio in Siffaro, Brazonas' main port city. It was a nice quiet day. He had just delivered a large cargo of much needed medical supplies and wasn't scheduled to leave for another forty-eight hours. His quiet solitude was interrupted by his comm silently buzzing at his waist. He ignored it at first because he really didn't want to be disturbed. But it buzzed in the pattern that indicated his ship was calling.

"What's up, Nova?" he said after he keyed the comm on.

"I just received a distress call from *Mirka Ve'sura*. They are in trouble and need help."

Ven cursed under his breath. It was bad enough that the big trade corporations had started an openly violent conflict with independent traders, but now the Customs Major for this sector had decided to get involved. He knew without Nova having to tell him that they'd been attacked by a Customs ship. "Have you found Berglund?" he finally asked.

"He was easier to track down than you were for a change. I had to hack through three different systems before I found your comm."

"I can't hide from you even if I try. As soon as Berglund gets onboard, power up and get clearance to leave. I'll be there in just a few minutes."

"Of course."

Ven looked at his drink. At least he'd finished half of it. He'd have to leave the rest. He'd just have to come back this way again and have another.

Since he was just outside the port, it only took him ten minutes to get back to the ship. Berglund was already there and Nova had the ship ready for departure. They still had five minutes before they were cleared to leave.

Ven sat at the pilots console on the port side of the cockpit and monitored as Nova lifted off and accelerated out of the atmosphere once they had clearance. Nova far exceeded what most pilots could do. The AI had been taught by some excellent teachers. He'd gathered a good crew back then and their skills and spirit lived on in Nova. But this wasn't the time to re-live old memories, he had to find and rescue two members of his former crew.

Nova flew to the hyperspace beacon and initiated the jump. Ven had long since ceased worrying about where the ship was going. Nova always got him to where he needed to be.

"Our ETA is fifty-four minutes, Captain," Nova informed him. "We should come out of hyperspace within scanning range of their last position."

"I couldn't ask for more. Just get us there."

"Why haven't they closed yet?" Laren asked of nobody in particular. The Customs cutter had caught up to them but had matched speed at a distance of 500 meters. At that distance they could fire at will. All Laren could do is push his ship to the max of what it had left.

"I'm not the best engineer around," Chup said from the hatch, "But I could have a look and see if I can do anything."

"Thanks, Chup. Normally I wouldn't accept help from a passenger, but any student of Berglund's is more than welcome."

"Samber and I will see what we can do."

Samber was already checking the systems over by the time Chup caught up to her. "That shot knocked the primary feed out of alignment," she told him.

"I could tell that just from the feel. Is there anything we can do about it?"

"The mechanism is jammed so unless we want to EVA under the gunsights of that cutter, we'll have to find another way. Damn thing would only take five minutes to fix if we could go out. I'm checking to see if there are any rerouting possibilities."

"Can we supplement with the backup feed?"

"Normally no. It's supposed to be for emergencies only and only operates at seventy-five percent."

"What about this?" Chup said as he keyed a work around.

Momentarily the power readouts dropped and then jumped up to one hundred percent.

"Show off," Samber grumbled. She keyed the comm to the cockpit. "You should have more power now, Laren."

On the bridge J'sevi had already seen the power increase and channeled it all into acceleration. Momentarily they sprang ahead of the cutter.

"We'll never outrun them." Laren thought through his options in the seconds as his ship enlarged the distance from their pursuer. "We only have one option. J'sevi, prepare to cancel acceleration. When you do, initiate a controlled tumble and bring them into a good firing position."

"I got it."

The customs cutter accelerated to close the distance again. While they were still closing the distance, J'sevi cut the engines and they sputtered and died throwing the ship into a seemingly uncontrolled tumble. The cutter had to veer off to avoid a collision. As the tumble brought the bow to bear on the cutter, J'sevi opened fire, dealing the cutter a critical blow. The cutter tried to maneuver to return fire but a secondary explosion left them dead in space. J'sevi didn't wait around and took off leaving the cutter drifting.

"Good shot, J'sevi."

"Um, Laren," Chup's voice crackled over the comm from engineering, "They've also knocked out the hyperengine and life-support. I don't think we can fix them. Looks like several key components blew."

"You win some and you lose some," Laren muttered.

Nova dropped out of hyperspace nearly on top of where the distress signal had come from. She paused as she scanned the area. "Ven, it looks like they headed off toward the nebula. I'm picking up one ship adrift at extreme range."

"Is it them?"

"No, it doesn't match the *Mirka Ve'sura's* configuration. I think it's the customs ship that was after them. I'm also picking up a faint radiation trail consistent with the damaged engines Laren reported."

"Let's see where it leads."

They approached the drifting ship cautiously. When Nova reported that their life support was functioning, Ven elected to avoid them completely and stick to the radiation trail.

"Ven, I'm showing that the trail ends."

"Can you guess their destination from what we found?"

"I can follow the course, but there isn't anything on the charts along this course. I think they were trying to flee into the nebula."

"Let's follow the course and see what we find. Maybe we can catch up to them."

"Captain," Ladna said, "I'm detecting a ship following us."

"How close is it?" Laren asked.

"It will catch up to us in twenty-five minutes."

"More importantly, what is it?"

"I don't know, Captain, but it's big."

"Is it..."

"I think it is."

"We have a serious problem." Laren keyed the comm. "Chup, we have new company. Can you work a miracle and squeeze some more power out of this old girl?"

"I think she's got more to give. I'll see what I can do."

"Ven, I'm picking up a ship ahead that wasn't there before." Nova said.

"I take it that it's not *Mirka Ve'sura*."

"No, it's something bigger. I suspect it's a larger customs ship. The cutter must have sent a signal."

"How do we compare?"

"The weapons I carry are likely a match for them. If we can catch them, we should be able to disable them. Catching them is the problem. We aren't gaining on them but they are probably gaining on their prey."

Ven keyed the comm. "Berglund, I need everything you can bleed out of Nova's engines. We have to catch them before they are captured."

"You know what she can do, Ven and I'll get it for you."

Moments later Ven could feel the engines go past the factory safety mark. It was a dangerous game to ignore the safeties, but Ven trusted Berglund to get the performance without damaging the ship.

"You've got it," Laren told Chup. "You've gained us some time."

"I don't think it will be enough."

Chup was right, the repairs gained them several minutes, but the Customs corvette closed the distance. When Laren refused to acknowledge their hails, the corvette let loose with their forward weapons. J'sevi deftly maneuvered the ship and avoided any serious effects. After a few such maneuvers the corvette's crew anticipated and their next volley ripped into the trade ship.

The engines were spared, but the ship shuddered and J'sevi couldn't get out of the way of the next volley. A direct hit took out the port engines and the ship tumbled out of control. Another shot hit, rocking the ship as something exploded and cut the power, leaving the ship dead in space and the crew and passengers floating in a gravity-less hulk.

"They've stopped," Nova informed Ven. "We will intercept them in two minutes."

Ven and Nova were silent as the last klicks passed by. Nova put the scanner image on the screen as soon as the details resolved. It showed the smaller ship tumbling out of control and the larger ship attempting to close, match rotations, and lock on with little success. The image increasingly resolved as the scanners then the cameras picked up more and more details.

"Remember, Nova, don't give away your maneuverability too soon."

"Of course."
"Ready weapons."

"There's nothing. All systems are out. The main buss is dead," J'sevi reported.
"Are you sure it's the main buss?" Laren asked.
"There is no power to anything. Even life support is out."
"We'd better prepare to be boarded."
"With the way we're tumbling, they are going to have trouble linking up."
"At least there's some good news."

"They've seen us," Nova told Ven.
"Open fire as soon as we are in range. Target power systems."
The corvette turned from the disabled trader and accelerated to meet them. The distance diminished quickly.
"Target coming into range," Nova stated. "Preparing to fire."
Ven felt the rumble as the weapons discharged. Nova's aim was true and the bolts of glowing energy struck the corvette. Moments later it returned fire, but their aim was not as true and the shots narrowly missed. Nova fired again, including a tiny missile with a little surprise. The second shot was as true as the first. Ven saw the corvette fire before the missile exploded in an obscuring cloud of white gas.

Nova preformed a deft maneuver that put her in a superior firing position. She fired twice in quick succession. Before the shots could strike, the corvette changed course to intercept, but the cloud had given Nova a temporary advantage and she took it by firing two more times. The previous shots impacted the corvette, but not where Nova had intended. The follow up shots were targeted to where Nova knew the corvette would have to be in order to catch her. The sensors showed they impacted on target.

The corvette began to tumble and drift, but not before their weapons could be trained on *Nova Trango*. One powerful beam caught the lower port engine. The explosion pushed the ship into a spin.

"Berglund, can you get handle on the damage. Shut the engine down so we can get things stabilized."
"She's gushing plasma, Ven. It's going to take a while. Have Nova go with the flow. The power only dropped twenty percent so we aren't in any immediate danger."

"Okay. Got that Nova?"

"I don't like spinning. It makes the calculations much harder which translates to a higher error rate in tracking that corvette."

"We don't have much choice."

Berglund shook his head at the damage. He'd already been in an environment suit. Ven and Nova weren't known for having perfect records in combat. Case in point the vacuum he now found himself in.

The diagnostics didn't tell as much as the eyes. The engine casing was cracked and bent by the explosion, but it hadn't failed. Structurally the engine housing was intact so the ship was going to be fine. The engine itself was probably pulverized. The shut offs were jammed by the explosion. The trick now was to shut down the engine without shutting the power down.

He rerouted the power to the hyperspace engine to act as a capacitor. It took a while for the power level to build to where he needed it. He reconnected the power to the hyperspace engine to do a slow draw to power the needed systems and then jumped across the room. He shut down the engines and the fuel system. According to his chron. he had about ten minutes to disconnect the engine from the fuel system and restart the other five engines before the power drained out of the hyperspace engine.

He took one look at the connections and started swearing in every language and dialect he could think of. It was a mangled mass of metal. He hated the thought, but the only option was to cut the fuel line and seal it. He activated the fuel flush system and then started cutting. He had the operation done and tested the newly sealed end with just over a minute left. He brought the other five engines online slowly and transferred power with six seconds of time remaining.

"She's all yours again, Ven."

"I knew you'd work a miracle. Just don't tell me what it's going to cost me. Not yet anyway." Ven checked the scan displays to decide the next move. The combat had taken them further from the damaged trade ship. Nova was closing the gap to put them in place to launch a rescue, but just how to do that without causing any further injury was perplexing.

"Nova, can we match their spin and dock up that way?"

"I wouldn't recommend it. I can do it, but it is very dangerous for both ships."

"How about using a tie down cable to snare them and pull them out of the spin?"

"With what is available to us, that is the best option."

"Have you scanned it?"

"Yes. There are several life signs. The ship itself is dead. The power relays have been severed and the engines are dead. It is doubtful that it would be repairable."

Ven pondered for a moment before sharing his plan with Nova.

"I want you to fly in a tight circle so that we are constantly near the tail. We'll try to implant a tie down spike in the dead engine and then gradually tug them until they stop spinning."

Nova proceeded to fly in close and at an increasing speed to match the major spin. It would be difficult since the damaged ship was spinning in multiple axis. After several rotations, Nova finally matched the correct motion and the ventral scanner showed the nearly motionless engine below them.

Ven fired the mid-port tie down. It narrowly missed. He waited for a moment and then fired the mid-starboard tie down. It impacted the engine sending out a cloud of debris. When Ven tried of take in the slack, the tie down spike pulled free.

"I don't think that engine has enough structure to hold anything," Ven stated. "Let's try the through the side of the engine housing instead."

Ven reeled in the two cables and readied them to fire again while Nova readjusted her course. He timed it carefully and fired the mid-starboard tie down. The spike struck the hull and embedded itself almost completely. Ven carefully took in the slack and the line tightened. "It's up to you now, Nova."

Nova took time to gently pull the crippled ship from its wild tumble. In just under two minutes Nova had corrected the tumble enough to properly dock with the ship with some degree of safety. The docking corrected the last of the tumble and Ven and Berglund prepared to transfer to the other ship armed with tools and first aid kits.

Berglund was shocked at the total lifelessness of the damaged ship. Even with the engines out there was supposed to be some reserve power to operate the emergency systems. He had to use a remote power module to open the airlock. They used their hand lights to see into the absolute blackness inside the ship. Ven realized that all the airtight doors were sealed and couldn't be opened without a power source.

Berglund swore to himself as he tried to open an access panel. He shook his head when Ven looked at him questioningly, then disappeared back to *Nova Trango*. He reappeared a moment later dragging a cable with him. He attached it to the power relay outside the airlock and flicked a switch. Some of the ships lights came on and the door panel controls were activated.

"To the bridge first," Ven said. They hurried down the long central corridor to the bridge and he keyed in the lock override code that he and all the captains under him had chosen. When the doors opened, the bridge was empty. Ven quickly checked to see if the panels had any power. Except for the emergency comm system, everything was dead. He flicked the comm on and set the band. "Nova, do you copy?"

"You are coming through."

"Monitor for any signals from this ship."

"I'll let you know immediately if I hear anything."

Ven left the dead bridge and proceeded to check the doors into the quarters while Berglund tried to get a status on the ship.

The first set of doors on either side of the bridge were empty. The next set were likewise empty. Ven was concerned and quite surprised to find the last empty as well. He didn't remember Laren having any hiding places that would fit the crew. He checked each room with greater care as he headed back to the bridge and again came up empty.

"Berglund, are there any places to hide on this ship that I wouldn't know about."

He turned and gave Ven an odd stare. "I don't think you've ever actually been on a ship of this model, have you?"

"No."

"There aren't really hiding places. There are several access panels that would let someone get to the service areas in the hull. Nova wouldn't be able to do a scan because Laren made sure everything was properly shielded."

"Is there any way to get more power to get the gravity and internal systems running?"

"No. Whatever took out their main bus seems to have shorted virtually every system on board."

Ven pondered for a moment. There were seven people on board and no sign of them. Laren would have left a clue that Ven could understand, but the question was where. He left the bridge and returned to Laren's cabin. He entered and closed the door behind him. In a corner that virtually everyone would miss if they weren't actually looking for it, Ven found a cryptic code. He smiled when he saw what it meant. He opened the door again and went across the corridor. It looked like it was the guest suite where Chup and Samber had been quartered. He found the access panel and popped it open. It looked harmless enough until he reached around and triggered the mechanism. The innocuous components slid up revealing a tight crawl-way.

Ven raised his voice and called, "You can come out now. Help has arrived."

"You don't have to shout quite so much, Captain," Laren called back.

It took a few minutes for the five of them to get out of the tight space. "Where are Chup and Samber?" Ven asked.

Laren's face usually wasn't very expressive, but Ven could instantly tell that the news wasn't good.

"They were down in engineering. We wouldn't have made it this far without their help. That boy of yours is quite an engineer among his many other skills. Last we heard from them was just before that blast cut the power."

"And we already saw what shape it's in from the outside."

Nova's report on the condition of the hull was not encouraging. Berglund and Ven donned EVA suits to examine the damage first hand when they discovered that access to engineering had been severed along with the main bus.

"This is bad, Ven," Berglund said when he'd looked into the jagged maw. "This ship is never going to fly again. It's lucky it didn't break apart when Nova pulled it out of the spin."

"That corvette is pretty heavily armed. I'm glad Nova didn't take a worse shot than she did."

"I'm sure Nova will learn a lesson from her skirmish."

They floated into the hole using their lamps to look for something recognizable. There had evidently been a secondary explosion. Berglund soon began to understand what had happened and what the twisted pieces of metal had been.

"Look over here. That shot must have superheated the primary fuel and ruptured the tank, then spilled into the power-bus and exploded. No wonder this hole is so big."

"But where is, or was, engineering."

"It should be intact over there behind that piece of tank."

The piece of tank that Berglund referred to was almost three meters long and over a meter wide and still attached to part of the ship. Berglund tried to pull it away from the hatch with limited success. Ven joined him and they moved it half a meter. Ven tried the hatch, but it wouldn't move.

"Ven, we're going to have to cut our way in. We should do it from the other side. There's no telling just how mangled this bulkhead is. And on that side, Nova can dock with the hull so we won't need an airlock."

"Nova..."

"I've been monitoring your conversation. Please exit and climb onto the docking connector."

Nova saved them several minutes by taking them to a point Berglund suggested and docking with the smooth hull. Berglund used his best torch connected directly to Nova's power system and began cutting. It took a painfully long time to cut through. Ven and Berglund remained suited in case the engineering compartment had lost pressure or had any harmful gasses.

When Berglund broke through, there was a small hiss of air as the pressure equalized, but without a doubt there was air inside. Ven took a quick reading of the air to find it within tolerable limits. He entered the hole first with Berglund not far behind.

They found Samber first. She was bleeding into a fist-sized bubble of blood clinging to her head. She was unconscious, but alive. The limited medical training Ven had was sufficient to tell him she was in no immediate danger.

Berglund found Chup near the controls. He'd been thrown into the remaining good engine and some debris had shredded his left leg. He had lost a lot of blood and his pulse was weak.

"We need to treat him here or we could lose him," Berglund warned.

"He's going to need more than first aid. We need to get him to a medical facility now."

"He's your son, Ven."

Ven's comm crackled. "Ven," Nova called. "I've been monitoring that corvette. It's regained attitude control and is moving in our direction."

"I think that decides it."

Ven used the hibernation prep mask on Chup and used a the first aid suction to capture the pooled blood. The instrument showed him going into proper hibernation so that he could be safely moved.

Berglund expanded a stretcher and they moved Chup onto in before he went back for Samber. Berglund stopped only long enough to suction up the blood and wrap her injury before grabbing her and pulling her to the newly cut docking hole.

Ven gave Nova a short set of orders to complete while he settled Chup and Samber into the small medbay. He put Chup into the hibernation chamber and did a scan of Samber's injuries. She had a minor concussion and the cut to her head, but was otherwise okay. He put a blanket over her to help with shock.

"We are docked again, just as you asked," Nova told him.

"Good. Prepare to detach as soon as we're all aboard."

Ven rushed onto Laren's ship and found the crew where he'd left them. "We need to go now. That corvette has recovered and is headed this way. She may not have speed at the moment, but she's got firepower over us."

"What about my ship?" Laren asked.

"I'm afraid she's a loss and if you don't want to be lost with her, you'd better gather anything you might have left and get moving."

Laren hurried to his cabin and in under two minutes had gathered his things. He waited until his four crewmen were headed to Ven's ship before he would let Ven lead him out the airlock.

"The corvette is approaching firing range," Nova told Ven as he entered her airlock.

"Detach and keep Laren's ship between us and the corvette. Don't take your weapons off them for a moment."

Berglund settled three of the crewmen in the guest cabin while Ladna waited in the cockpit. He had served as Ven's first navigator before Nova's AI had been installed. He'd taught Nova the fine art of navigation as only a Stavian could.

"It's good to see you again, Laren," Nova said as he and Ven entered the cockpit. "It's been too long. I'm sorry for the circumstances."

"Nothing we can do about that now, Nova, but thanks."

"No time for chatting, we have a corvette to avoid," Ven reminded them

Nova was backing away from Laren's ship. She was easily outpacing the corvette. Twice the corvette tried to change course to see beyond the damaged hulk in the way and Nova carefully moved to keep it between them.

After a short five minutes, the corvette started to come around the ruined trade ship. Nova fired a volley of missiles. The corvette moved to easily avoid the missiles and they impacted Laren's ship in a precise pattern. Laren's ship disintegrated. Chunks of debris hit the corvette and sent it careening out of control clearing the way for Nova to escape.

"Sorry about that, Laren. There really wasn't any other option," Nova said in a soft voice.

"That's all right, Nova," Laren replied. "This is a war and some sacrifices have to be made."

"Don't worry, we'll get you a new one," Ven told him. "It might take a bit, but we won't leave you stranded."

Ven was waiting when Samber woke up a couple hours later as they sped through hyperspace to a medical facility that could properly care for Chup.

"I knew you'd get to us in time," she said weakly. "Where's Chup?"

"We had to put him into hibernation. We're headed to I'ab. They have the best facility within easy reach and they won't ask any questions."

"Is it very serious?"

"I didn't have a chance to scan him properly. I think there are some internal injuries and his leg is pretty bad. He needs first class attention."

"You're the one person I trust to get Chup what he needs."

When Nova announced a medical emergency to the port control, she was given clearance to land directly at the medical center. Chup was rushed to the emergency facility and Ven and Samber were left to wait.

It seemed like hours before a doctor came out to talk to them. "It's a good thing you had a hibernation chest on your ship. It saved his life. The surgeon is working on him now. So far things are looking good."

"How long before you'll know something more certain?" Samber asked him.

"It shouldn't be too long."

An hour later a different doctor came out.

"He's in the clear. He should be awake in just a few minutes."

Chup recovered quickly. The accelerated healing had his leg strong enough to support his weight after a day and he was fully mobile after two and was released. The doctor said he would need to take it easy for a week or two and may notice some lasting effects for a few months.

Ven delivered Chup and Samber back to their own ship. Outside of being attacked on the way home, their mission had been a success.

He invited Laren and his crew to stay aboard until they could make proper arrangements for a new ship. It would hamper their efforts to defend their fellow independent traders and Ven set his sights on getting Laren onto a new ship as soon as possible. They were at war and needed every available ship, especially in this sector where they not only had to deal with the corporate thugs like the rest of the galaxy, but also with the sector's Customs forces and their overzealous Major.

Index

A general guide to pronunciation: While the body of this work is in North American English, the names of people and places are, for the most part, rendered using international pronunciation rules.

People

Akbret - crewman on Harmilon's Haven circa 4607 GCE
Alluren Beldaras - Owner/Captain of Lehra Aur circa 4614
Aren - Server at Nova Trango circa 4614
Balerio - Alderin Balerio, CEO of Alderin Trade Corporation on Quetle Station circa 4609-4614 GCE
Berevazik - trader captain circa 4312 GCE
Berglund - Ven's engineer circa 4597 GCE
Bezzed - crew member on Karnock's ship circa 4585 GCE
Brenker - Hazdon Brenker, Owner/Captain of Sword of Lashus circa 4312 GCE
Buiaro - Buiaro Zerholnom, Zeccan, Wally's old rival 4614 GCE
Burz - Server at Nova Trango circa 4614
Carrella - Nelmon's wife
Chansor - Command Sergeant circa 4607 GCE
Chimra - Chimra Veldagol, Brenker's client circa 4312 GCE
Chup - Chupardeth Zaran, Kotula and Ven's son
Dakka - Gadul Dakka, gangster circa 4312 GCE
Dan'ernar - Captain of Auberken's private yacht circa 4607 GCE
Dani - Danoray Murask, server at Nova Trango circa 4594 GCE
Dazloth - informant on Ekom-dorun circa 4312 GCE

Durkol - crew member on Karnock's ship circa 4594 GCE
Errubo - Mazzan Errubo, gangster and Tramp's cousin
Gamisvir - Zeccan who helps smuggle Wally circa 4614 GCE
Gargi - Server at Nova Trango circa 4614
Gelsulan - Hotharg Gelsulan, Brenker's Snagtharian cargo master circa 4312 GCE
Halzon - cook at Nova Trango circa 4614
Hanzin, Colonel - Member of Stormy's review council circa 4607 GCE
Hapshekish, Senior Colonel - Head of Stormy's review council circa 4607 GCE
Hie - Kewdar Hie, pilot on Lehra Aur circa 4614
Hilum - Herkon Hilum, First mate and lead Pilot on Lehra Aur circa 4614
hra'Sivana - Paimes hra'Sivana, Brenker's Stavian second pilot circa 4312 GCE
Hysmaur - Hysmaur Gilarvor, Zeccan, Buiaro's unwilling assistant 4614 GCE
Jaf Darres - Ven's friend on Tursk's ship who introduced him to Tint circa 4585 GCE
Jasoph d'Harrel Auberken - retired owner of a large AI manufacturer circa 4607 GCE
Jehnshan, Major - Member of Stormy's review council circa 4607 GCE
Jekky - Stormy's pilot/weapons officer circa 4607 GCE
Jemlon - Stormy's scanning officer circa 4607 GCE
Jeshmar - first mate on Karnock's ship 4594 GCE
Jessik, Colonel - Member of Stormy's review council circa 4607 GCE
Jessila - Melina's twin and Soriya's sister circa 4609 GCE
Jester - Bard Sudel, first mate/pilot on Thief of Hearts circa 3625 GCE
Jim - Jimmed Albanis, Customs Corps intelligence circa 4609 GCE
Jissik Vattila - Captain/owner of Harmilon's Haven circa 4607 GCE
Jo - Jo'ikyum Youveh, owner of Nova Trango Bar circa 4595
J'sevi - Laren's pilot circa 4626 GCE
Karnock - Ven's captain 4585-4597 GCE
Keffel - Stormy's old commander on Nejak-Felhak circa 4607 GCE
Kenzulat - Aimasta Kenzulat, Brenker's lead pilot circa 4312 GCE
Kirch'kal - Stormy's engineering officer circa 4607 GCE

Kon - trader pilot/Nova Trango patron circa 4614 GCE
Kotula - Kotula Gaskonya Zaran, Ven's wife & Chup's mother
Ladna - Ladna Vor'Ches, Laren's Stavian navigator circa 4626 GCE
Laren - Laren d'Borchas, Hilven trader captain circa 4626 GCE
Loris - Morva Loris, Lead Navigator on Lehra Aur circa 4614 GCE
Manny - Mannislon Haroong, Zeccan, Wally's brother and shop owner circa 4614 GCE
Marzi - Marzitah Youveh, owner of Nova Trango Bar circa 4614 GCE
Mauri Frenit - traveler in distress and vid star circa 3625 GCE
Melina - Jessila's twin and Soirya's sister circa 4609 GCE
Mezolik - crew member on Karnock's ship 4594 GCE
Moniloszur - Yamaris Moniloszur, Zeccan flight instructor 4614 GCE
Monsara - Alderin Monsara, Balerio's cousin's daughter circa 4609 GCE
Mutt - Dergo Fesh, navigator on Thief of Hearts circa 3625 GCE
Naro - Surhi's husband circa 4614 GCE
Nelmon - Captain of Star of Argent circa 4609 GCE
Niffy - Jekky's friend circa 4607 GCE
Nilondur - Zeccan, Manager of Manny's shop on Quetle Station circa 4614 GCE
Nova - AI on Nova Trango circa 4626 GCE
Papa Riz - Nova Trango patron circa 4614 GCE
Raxan - Raxan Jennel, gangster on Shimoxra circa 4609 GCE
Rezav - Larshon Rezav, Brenker's Ka'rhe'eran first mate/engineer circa 4312 GCE
Samber - Samber Drunin Zaran, Chup's wife
Sara - Sara Hollens, works in Manny's shop on Quetle Station circa 4614 GCE
Savvir - Major G. L. Savvir with Azot-Siomar Police circa 3625 GCE
Sevam Pondelur - Taru's father, semi famous musician
Soriya - Jessila & Melina's sister, Jim's romantic interest circa 4609 GCE
Stormy - Stormus Rolfel, Customs Corps patrol commander circa 4607-9 GCE
Surhi - Server at Nova Trango circa 4614 GCE
Su-Yhir - Ka'rhe'eran trader engineer/Nova Trango patron circa 4614 GCE

Taru - Taruba Murask, Dani's daughter circa 4594, server at Nova Trango circa 4614 GCE
Tramp - Len Darvon, Owner/Captain of Thief of Hearts circa 3625 GCE
Tursk - Ven's first captain circa 4585 GCE
Ullan - Stormy's defense systems officer circa 4607 GCE
Urazid - Sumra Urazid, navigator on Lehra Aur circa 4614 GCE
Uvik Tumal - Nova Trango patron circa 4614 GCE
Ven - Vendarka Zaran, trader and smuggler circa 4585-4626 GCE
Wally - Wallivo Haroong (aka Parlismon Jervung), Zeccan trader pilot circa 4614 GCE
Welkaire, Major - Member of Stormy's review council circa 4607 GCE
Wyas Dek - Danoray's estate attorney circa 4614 GCE
Yaskis Meliaska - forty-something command sergeant circa 4607 GCE
Zurien - Zurien Vasloron, Zeccan, Wally & Buiaro's classmate and Buiaro's employee circa 4614 GCE

Ships

Clarion Spectre - Karnock's ship circa 4585-4597 GCE
Lehra Aur - Beldarus' ship circa 4614 GCE
Mirka Ve'Sura - Laren's ship circa 4626 GCE
Nova Trango - Ven's ship circa 4626 GCE
Star of Argent - Ven's first ship circa 4597 GCE, later owned by Nelmon circa 4609 GCE
Sword of Lashus - Brenker's ship circa 4612 GCE
Thief of Hearts - Tramp's ship circa 3625 GCE

Species

Halarivans - short stature, always staring and being nice and polite
Hilven - olive green, scaly skinned, very reserved
Human - most prolific species in the galaxy
Ka'rhe'eran - tall with canine appearance, generally have light colored fur
Neathmodin - tall and willowy with nearly pitch black skin

Snagtharian - tall, stocky, greyish toned skin
Stavian - thin, long lived repilian, generally with green to yellow green skin
Zeccan - dark green skinned amphibian

Planets

Arseris
Azot-Siomar
Dezera Junction
Eknamatil
Ekom-dorun
Hafestbur Nuris
Hissus Prime
Iosep-Ebris
Irbenrab
Jedorfa
Leywan
Menansel
Neskellior - Stormy's home port
Pargila Vekris Station
Petadaltora
Prixnar IV
Quetle Station
Shimoxra
Tennarsus III
Urasha-menda
Valerapon
Vedder
Xinar Lamgun
Zecca

About the Author

Scott Seldon lives in Colorado with his wife and family in a house brimming with old and new computers. He is a student of technology, history, anthropology, languages, and cosmology. Each separate direction of study has enriched his imagination, but he credits the creative output of George Lucas and Isaac Asimov for the direction it has taken. He turned his creativity to science fiction in his teens and has never looked back.

In his writing, Scott strives to create rich worlds and characters. Although his stories take place in the future, he often looks to the past to give his stories a solid background. He's is more likely to watch Captain Blood than Star Wars to find inspiration on the feel of a story. He reads the latest titles by Jack McDevitt followed by C. L. Moore's stories of Northwest Smith written decades ago with Les Miserables and the Princess of Mars next on his reading list.

Connect with Scott
Facebook
www.facebook.com/srseldon
website
sites.google.com/site/scottrseldon/
email
srseldon@gmail.com

Manufactured by Amazon.ca
Bolton, ON